# Tight Squeeze

## Debbie DiGiovanni

HOWARD
Fiction

OUR PURPOSE AT HOWARD PUBLISHING IS TO:
- *Increase faith* in the hearts of growing Christians
- *Inspire holiness* in the lives of believers
- *Instill hope* in the hearts of struggling people everywhere
BECAUSE HE'S COMING AGAIN!

*Tight Squeeze* © 2005 by Debbie DiGiovanni
All rights reserved. Printed in the United States of America
Published by Howard Publishing Co., Inc.
3117 North 7th Street, West Monroe, Louisiana 71291-2227
www.howardpublishing.com

Published in association with the literary agency of Janet Kobobel Grant.

05  06  07  08  09  10  11  12  13  14      10  9  8  7  6  5  4  3  2  1

Edited by Ramona Cramer Tucker
Interior design by John Mark Luke Designs
Cover design by Nikki Dugan

Library of Congress Cataloging-in-Publication Data
DiGiovanni, Debbie, 1960–
   Tight squeeze / Debbie DiGiovanni.
     p. cm.
   ISBN: 1-58229-425-9
     1. Mothers—Fiction. 2. Housewives—Fiction. 3. Married women—Fiction. 4. Female
friendship—Fiction. I. Title.

PS3604.I35T54 2005
813'.6—dc22

                                                                          2004060709

for Jessica and Steve,
who have such bright and promising futures

# Acknowledgments

I want to acknowledge my large family. We make many choices in our lives, but family is the one choice God makes for us.

Michael, for everything you are. Chandra, Jeff, and Keelia, who are living in Seattle. Sometimes it seems too far away, but I know God has you there. Gianna, you make being a mother a most satisfying job.

Mom and Dad, thank you for allowing me to observe the constancy of your faith.

Judi, you are a great big sister. David, I think of you as wise. Mary, I admire you for your ability to live in the moment. Becky, you have the sweetest spirit. Dan, you have a wonderful sense of humor. Tim, I respect you for making a difference. Tom, you are not forgotten. Mark, congrats on your latest beauty.

A hug to all the spouses! We chose well, didn't we?

And though our ninth, Jim, is gone from us, he is not gone from our hearts. Every day I think of him . . . and will continue to do so as long as I dwell on this earth.

Hello, nephews and nieces—too many to count. Jennifer, you were the first and are a good friend. Solomon, you have been a supporter in my writing, and I thank you. Joey, I'm proud of you. All the rest of you are thought of as well, but I must mention Jesse specifically for his service to our country.

I wish to greet the DiGiovanni clan in California—each and every one, but in particular Mike and Gina and their beautiful families. You are all special to me in your own way.

# Chapter

# One

I am in hot water up to my neck—literally. It is the only place I can find solitude. I'd have taken a walk, but I'd never make it to the sidewalk without being accosted by one of my children. They'd want to know what I'm fixing for dinner or where they left their science project crawling around. I don't know the answer to either of those questions. I'm fortunate to know my name right now. It's Rebecca Joy, by the way. No middle initial. But most people call me Becca.

If any or all of my four children knew I was soaking in the tub, they'd be banging on the door. *Four children is nothing*, I keep telling myself. My mother had ten. Judy, my neighbor, has six.

*Judy. Judy. Judy.* Judy Anderson is so perfect. Her hair, her teeth, her figure . . . her husband, kids, and house. Even her dog is groomed and obedient.

I don't know how she does it. Take our houses, for example. They are identical from far away. (We live in a matching neighborhood.) But close up the difference is painfully apparent. The Andersons' hose is neatly wrapped on their well-manicured lawn like a sleeping snake; ours roams free on the overgrown grass. Their picket fence gets painted once a year; ours gets painted when the kids get punished. Next to Judy's award-winning garden, mine is "strictly loser" (my daughter's term).

I'm normally not such a whiner, but this has been an extremely difficult day, week . . . month even. As the emperor would say, I've lost my groove. If you've seen it, give me a call. If the line is busy, try again. I have teenagers.

I don't hear any noise out there, and I've been submerged for so long I'm at the prune stage. I think it's too late to fix dinner. I'll call Doug and tell him to pick up Pizza Hut. He knows the stress is getting to me. I suppose I did overreact to the note from the elementary-school cafeteria lady last night when I cried, "Why is she doing this to me?"

"You miscalculated by a quarter; it's okay, Becca," Doug had assured me. "It doesn't mean you're a bad mother."

The phone is ringing. Probably Doug.

I dry off my hands and grab the cordless phone I brought with me to the tub.

"Becca?"

It's Allie Ray. We've been best friends since the second grade, when I took her sack lunch by mistake and liked it better than mine. We were inseparable until she moved five years ago from Denver to Atlanta.

"Where are you? You sound like you're in an echo chamber."

"I'm in the bathtub, trying not to be discovered."

"Are you okay?"

"What answer do you want: the right answer or the honest answer?"

"The honest answer, of course."

I readjust my body, being careful not to drop the phone in the tub. I dropped a phone in the toilet once. Needless to say, it was unsalvageable.

"I guess you'd know if I wasn't being honest," I say. "You know all there is to know about me. Even the sins of my youth."

"I only know of one: the incident in the gym with the plaster."

"Okay, let's not go over it again."

"So what's up? Why are you taking a bath in the afternoon?"

"Because the book said to."

"What book?"

"*Mommy Stress.* It also suggested a hike in the Himalayas or a spa in Palm Springs, but my private plane is being serviced."

"Palm Springs sounds good to me." Allie sighs. "Why are you stressed? Your kids are great."

"I know they're great, but my life is a tight squeeze at the moment. Someone better move over, because I need some breathing room. By the time I do everything I need to do for everyone else, I'm exhausted."

"I guess that would be hard."

"I've got dirty laundry piled to the ceiling and no dinner planned." I step out of the bathtub but leave the drain intact so I won't have to shout, or I might be heard.

"Do you want to know what I think?"

"Yes." I'm dripping all over the floor. (The bath rug is in the dirty laundry pile.)

"I think Auntie Allie should come to visit and help Mommy out."

"Really? Can you take the time off?"

"I quit my job, and I'm going to open up my own counseling practice. So, yes, I have the time."

"That's great! You've been talking about doing that forever," I say while drying off.

"We'll talk more about that later. Right now I'm too excited about seeing you."

"Me too."

"Ahhhhh!" the cries come down the hall and land outside the door. "Mom!" *Bang. Bang.* "Mom, Logan took the Nintendo controller while I was playing!"

"Ben, please let me finish my bath!" I yell.

3

The cry travels back down the hall.

"So when are you coming, Allie?"

"Next Thursday. I'm staying for ten days, if that's all right."

"Next Thursday; that's great!"

More disturbance on the other side of door. Squawking, shoving. "Mom! Mom!"

"I better let you go."

"I'll call you back tomorrow, Allie—unless the mechanic fixes my private plane and I take off for Palm Springs."

"Okay. I'll talk to you then!" I hear the click of Allie disconnecting. Then I turn off the phone, lay it on the hamper, and put on a robe.

"Mom! Mom!"

The kids won't stop shouting. I guess they know I'm not going anywhere. I open the door to two distressed male faces and smile pleasantly. "Yes?"

Ben starts in again about Logan, and Logan starts in about Carly. Carly walks in and complains that she didn't do anything.

I stand there, nodding in agreement to everything.

Tawny walks in the room and yells, "Who's on the phone? I have to use the Internet right now!" Sometimes I wonder what happened to the once-sweet kid who now inhabits this pushy teen's body.

"I'm just off the phone," I say as Ben tugs on my robe, trying to catch my attention, which is everywhere and nowhere.

Tawny leaves, and Doug, my loving husband, crowds in. "What are we all doing back here?"

"Mommy was taking a bubble bath," Carly announces.

Doug shakes his head. "Why are you taking a bubble bath at four o'clock in the afternoon? What about dinner?"

"It wasn't a bubble bath; it was just a bath. As for dinner, I have nothing planned. Not a thing."

"So we are supposed to . . ."

"Starve or order in pizza," I say, void of expression.

"Pepperoni," Carly says.

"Meat Lover's," Logan insists.

"Cheese," Ben begs.

"Order the 4forAll, Doug. Tawny will want Hawaiian."

# Chapter

# Two

"You look exhausted," Doug says a week later as I throw another relic on the throwaway pile.

"Keen observation." I give the growing pile a glance. "I was cleaning out a drawer for Allie's visit and found a size 6X dress in Carly's drawer. The next thing I know, I have a truckload for Goodwill."

"You mean Carly's not that size anymore?"

"She's size eight, the same as her age." I examine a worn flowered blouse. "I wouldn't dare look in the boys' drawers."

"Or Tawny's." Doug sits on Carly's unmade bed.

"We're not welcome in Tawny's room. Didn't you see the sign?"

"I'll get her to take it down."

"Don't do that, Doug. She's a drama queen these days. Typical fourteen-year-old behavior."

"She's been awfully thin-skinned." Doug picks up Carly's tattered teddy bear and pulls the shredded ribbons through his fingers. "Soon Carly will outgrow this pink, girly bedroom."

I close a drawer and nod. "And Ben likes a girl a head taller than him." I laugh.

"Logan and I were looking at college brochures last night."

Doug pauses. "You blink and they're out of the house," he says, looking downhearted.

"I know that, and I want to enjoy this time." I touch the material of Carly's old Easter dress to my cheek, thinking of the quilt I had always wanted to make with patches from my children's clothes. "But to tell you the truth, sometimes I feel like I'm treading water. What if they leave and I'm still trying to stay afloat?"

"You expect too much of yourself."

"Judy Anderson makes her grocery-shopping checklist out by aisle. She keeps a file on each of her children with their sizes, medical histories, and favorite colors."

"And you carry a file of your children in your heart." He stands and holds my chin with his accountant fingers.

I smile and then resume my one-sided competition. "Yesterday Judy brought me over a bar of homemade soap. She said her next project is making hurricane candles."

"When was the last hurricane we had in Denver?"

I grimace. "The point is, she's ridiculously efficient."

"What's your obsession with Judy? This comparison game you're playing is not like you, or healthy."

"Don't men compare themselves?"

"Our biceps maybe." Doug flexes his muscle.

"You're right."

"You need a break. Why don't you and Allie go out to eat after you pick her up at the airport? Take your time. I'll handle the kids."

"Really?"

"Yes, really."

"Oh thank you! You're wonderful!" I kiss him repeatedly.

"I'm wild about you, baby," he says with this penetrating gaze that lets me know he means it.

And suddenly I feel shy, like I'm in first grade again.

In the airport bathroom, I apply pink lipstick, because it's the clos-
est thing to fun I can find, and I haven't had fun all day. I daydream
as I walk past Cinnabon's delicious aromas and then rush to baggage claim to meet Allie.

When I spot her, she looks much the same. She's wearing the
same hairstyle she's worn since childhood—long and straight. I notice she's hippier in her dark blue corporate suit, but even one
pound would show on her willowy frame.

We hug. She smells like Cinnabon. She says it's essential oil of
cinnamon and that men are supposed to love it. I start to say that
it might remind them of their mother's baking but don't.

"You look great," I say.

"You lie," she says.

We watch the suitcases glide by on the conveyer belt. I try to locate hers, though I don't know what hers looks like.

Allie tugs on a Louis Vuitton bag in the mass of luggage and
then looks at me for instructions.

"Let's go out to eat," I suggest enthusiastically.

"Sure. But I'm on a diet. I have to lose ten pounds before our class
reunion. Too much Christmas is getting harder to take off every year."

"Our class reunion is over two years away."

"I know, but I want to look great."

"Twenty years. Do you think there could be some kind of calendar misprint, Allie?"

"I don't think so." She matches my stride through the busy airport. "I can't wait to see your family."

"You'll get your fill of them, trust me. They'll have you playing
Monopoly, Nintendo, watching *American Idol* . . . you'll need a vacation to get over this vacation."

"How's your salad?" I ask Allie at The Cheesecake Factory, my favorite place to dine.

"Low-calorie." She sniffs my side of the table.

"This Chicken Madeira is delicious. Want some?" I pass the temptation under her nose.

She shakes her head. "I've been doing really good on my diet so far."

"How long have you been faithful?"

"Four hours." She laughs. "I managed the willpower to abstain from the pretzels on the plane."

"Strong resolve."

"Actually, I'm very happy with my salad. I love these crunchy things." She picks one up and examines it.

"Have you tried the Mandarin Chicken Salad at Wendy's?"

"You eat at Wendy's?"

"Every other day. After Ben's soccer games, Logan's basketball games, Carly's music recitals, and Tawny's cheerleading events."

"Here you are with time away, and you're talking about your kids."

"They're adorable; there's no denying it."

We talk for a while about the most trivial things, like how women blink twice as much as men. Then the waiter asks if we'd like some dessert.

"No, thank you." Allie stares down at her bare salad plate.

"Yes," I say and then order a slice of White Chocolate Chunk Macadamia Nut Cheesecake.

Allie sighs, long and hard, as the waiter speeds away.

"I'm sorry. I love you, Allie, but the cheesecake here is too divine."

"I know about the cheesecake. We have The Cheesecake Factory in Atlanta."

"Then you're familiar with the creamy, velvety texture—"

She interrupts. "Are you going to torture me the whole time I'm here?"

"Sorry. It's just that you have so few character flaws. You're so . . ."

"I'm so *what?* Go ahead and say it."

"Okay, I was going to say you're so perfect. But I'm giving up the comparison game. Doug says it's not healthy."

"It's not. The only thing you should be comparing is prices."

"It all started with my perfect sister, Valerie," I interject.

"No one is perfect, Becca. Remember Adam and Eve and the Fall?"

"You're a counselor. Give me some psychobabble explanation about my quirk of comparing myself to anything that moves."

"We compare in order to have an accurate view of ourselves."

"Hmm." I think on that. When my cheesecake arrives, I offer Allie a bite. "It's very yummy."

She shakes her head several times.

I take a massive bite and roll my eyes in delight.

By the time the waiter returns to replenish my coffee and Allie's water, I feel like a bloated whale.

We grab our purses and pay. When we reach the exit, an older woman smiles at me and exhales.

I smile back, wondering if I know her.

"When is your baby due?" she asks.

"My baby?" I reply, baffled.

"Now dear, don't let anybody tell you that you're too old. I had my son at forty, and he turned out fine. He's a doctor here in Denver."

"Really?"

"Charlie is a podiatrist."

"That's very nice," I say as Allie searches in her purse for nothing.

"When I was pregnant, I had foot problems," the gray-haired lady continues, oblivious to my horror. She pats my tummy. "But not everybody does. Good luck, dear."

I smile dimly at the woman. We walk outside into pure April sunshine, but I feel dark clouds hovering above.

"My dignity has been injured." I stare down at my middle. "That sweet old lady thought I was pregnant."

I'm utterly depressed as we walk down the street—me and my whale of a body.

"You just ate a huge meal," Allie offers as an excuse.

"I haven't been on a scale in ages."

Allie pats my shoulder.

"Tell me the truth. Am I getting . . . pudgy?"

"Define *pudgy*," she hedges.

"Chunky. Plump. Am I getting fat?"

"Of course not . . . maybe a little fleshy," she says timidly.

"I gave up the gym months ago. I was walking, but I haven't even been doing that lately. I'm so out of shape; I didn't even ski this year."

"Seven pounds would do it," she remarks warily.

"I feel bad for giving you such a hard time." I drop my head, slump, and watch the sidewalk passing under my feet.

"I have an idea. Let's make it a fun competition," Allie suggests. "Whoever loses five pounds first . . ."

We stop in the middle of the sidewalk.

"Gets treated to dinner by the loser," I finish.

"Something better."

"Gets an all-expense-paid vacation to Palm Springs?" I try.

"Not *that* much better."

We both think a minute.

"How about the winner gets five hundred dollars to pamper herself into oblivion?" Allie offers.

I like her proposition. "Okay. I have a stash in my lingerie drawer. I've been scrimping and saving, but I wasn't exactly sure what I wanted to do with it."

"The rules are, we eat the same thing."

"Matching meals. Cute," I say.

"And we eat healthy."

"Deal," we say together, and shake on it.

A gust of wind sweeps through the street, blowing dust and debris everywhere. We race each other to the car—Allie in heels, me in Keds.

# Chapter

# Three

My house is pandemonium, and Allie finds it amusing. All my children love Aunt Allie. She's going to have a tea party with Carly, draw with Ben, take Tawny shopping, and she just told Logan that his idea of going to college in Hawaii so he can surf shark-infested waters is a good one.

"Who was that at the door?" I ask Allie as I recover from the fourth run over Carly's third-grade spelling list.

"Judy. She said not to bother you. She dropped off some candles and asked if I liked homemade apple butter."

"Oh really." I quench my jealousy with a sip of Diet Pepsi.

"I told her it wouldn't fit in my suitcase, so she's knitting me a sweater with wool she hand spun on her loom."

"That woman is—"

"I'm joking, Becca. I'm joking."

I grin, sheepishly.

"Mom, you promised to help me with my homework." Ben sits next to me at the breakfast nook.

"I know, Ben."

He opens the book and displays the meaningless numbers in front of me.

I grunt. "Pre-algebra in the sixth grade? Why do you have to be so smart?"

He grins, because math is his strongest subject.

I notice five-foot-eleven Logan swinging on the kitchen cabinets. "Logan. Stop swinging on those cabinets. You're going to break them."

"I'm starving, Mom. There's nothing good in this house. It's all healthy food."

"I'll fix dinner in a minute."

"What are we having?"

"Stir-fry."

"Again?" he asks with a disapproving expression.

"Yes, again."

"Can I eat at the Andersons'? They're having steak. Brett invited me."

"He invited you, or you begged?"

He doesn't answer the question—merely pulls up his baggy jeans.

"Go ahead."

"Mom." Ben tugs on my sleeve.

"Just a minute, Ben," I tell him, because Tawny is now in the room, suffocating us with bad perfume.

"I'm going over to the Andersons' for dinner too," Tawny announces.

I frown. "That needs to be in the form of a question, not a statement."

Tawny tries again. "May I? I was invited."

"All right." *Anything to breathe again,* I tell myself.

"And can I borrow your red shirt, Mom?"

"The one you stained the last time you borrowed it?"

"Oh." She tosses her long dark hair from side to side.

As she walks away, I'm thinking, *Her jeans look awfully tight. We need to have a talk. Again.*

"Can I go too?" Ben asks.

"Have you been invited?"

He looks down. "No."

"Then you're stuck with me, kid."

"Carly is over there playing with Amanda," he rationalizes.

"You have homework anyway." I examine his textbook. "Ugh."

Suddenly the room is quiet. It's strange how that happens—like when Mile High Stadium clears after a Broncos' game.

Allie rescues me. "I'll help you, Ben."

"Good," I exclaim. "I'll start dinner."

Before I finish chopping the vegetables, Ben is thanking Allie and asking me if he can go outside to play.

"Go ahead." For a moment I just stand there.

"You okay?" Allie asks.

"I feel like a washer on spin cycle." For another minute I just stand there.

"You have a good life, Becca," Allie says in her calm counselor voice.

"Wanna borrow it for a while?" I ask, 99 percent joking.

"Naw. I'm happy with mine." She pulls up a stool and shares an afterthought. "I wouldn't mind a husband, though."

"Maybe if I simplified my life it would be—"

"Boring," Allie concludes.

"Ever notice we're always finishing each other's sentences?"

"Yes, I do. We need to stop that," Allie says.

"Boring? Are you sure?"

"Yes, I'm sure. I love your house; it's so busy and—"

"Chaotic?"

"Child focused."

"Hmm." I grin. "I think I like that term."

Allie makes a neat pile of the school notices strewn all over the counter.

"Well, I better get back to work. The sole breadwinner should

14

be here any minute." I feel a smirk form on my face. "When he finds out what we're having for dinner, he'll want to go over to Judy's too."

&⁂&

"I need to be brave." I try to convince my feet to stand on the scale. "You're sure you lost two pounds? It's only been five days."

"I've been running every day," Allie says.

I moan.

She draws a breath in through her nose. "You checked it three times. Do you want to get a weight specialist from the scale manufacturer out to verify the numbers?"

"No. I want to take a spaceship to the moon."

"I thought you were feeling better about earth today."

"I want to weigh twenty pounds. That's what I'd weigh on the moon. On Jupiter I'd weigh over three hundred pounds. I read that in Ben's science book." I plant my feet and close my eyes.

"Do you want me to check it?" Allie asks.

"Okay."

Silence. Then, "You've gained two pounds."

I open my eyes. "No possible way. Did you rig this thing?"

"Let's call off this silly competition." Allie tries to smile.

I sink my plump body into a beanbag and watch my pink toe-nails wiggle. "I don't get it. We ate identical tofu."

"Maybe it hasn't taken effect yet." Allie gives a hesitant grin.

"I'm going to have to get a fatter best friend to make myself feel better," I wail.

"What are you talking about? I have more weight to lose than you," Allie says.

"Maybe I should join the circus as the fat lady."

"Is that how you want Tawny to think of herself? Or Carly? Or do you want to be able to look them in the eyes and tell them it's their spirit that matters?"

"You're right," I agree. "I'm just upset, that's all. I've been trying so hard."

"You'll lose next week." Allie helps me up off the beanbag.

"Do you want to go to Baskin Robbins and blow it with a double cone? German Chocolate? Or better yet, Jamoca Almond Fudge?" I ask hopefully.

"I would rather not," Allie says.

"You're right. Why should you blow it just because my metabolism is faulty?"

"Becca, you have to take a test."

"What kind of test?" I look at Allie with suspicion.

"A test that could show why you're gaining weight instead of losing."

It hits me like a huge brick. What an unbearable thought. "Is it the kind of test that means I'm going to lose this dieting bet? Like I'll-be-perpetually-fat-for-nine-months-at-the-age-of-thirty-six kind of test?"

"You know it, don't you?"

"I guess I do. I didn't think it was possible."

"I'm not going to ask you why. But I think we should do it now, before the kids get home. I've got it here."

She takes a purple and white box out of a paper bag. I visit a distant memory.

"Do you know what Doug and I did the day Carly was out of diapers? We had a party. We wore cone hats and blew on kazoos."

"Think of it as a new adventure."

"Doug and I always talk about how we're going to buy a motor home and travel America when the last kid leaves. I thought we'd still be young."

"You will still be young."

"It couldn't be. I couldn't be."

"Snap out of it, Becca. Some women can't have children at all, and besides, we really don't know anything for sure yet."

*I do. I know.*

"Give it time."

I lay on the couch and notice the ceiling fan needs a good dusting. *I can't keep up with my housework now. And with a baby . . .*

"You're feeling a little hormonal, that's all."

"When I was pregnant with Logan, I ate nothing but chocolate. With Tawny it was Chinese. With Ben it was anything pickled. And with Carly I used to drive thirty miles for baklava. I can't stand baklava now."

"Take the test. And if the news is good, I'll eat a cone with you. Double scoop."

"Chocolate brownie?" I ask, feeling teary.

"Anything. Anything for you, Becca."

# Chapter Four

By 2:45 we have read the instructions on the test box a dozen times and followed them precisely. Now we are waiting for the pink line to appear, or not.

This is the longest five minutes of my life—longer than waiting to see the principal in the fourth grade after defacing school property (drawing a happy face on my math book), longer even than waiting for my mother-in-law to exit the plane after Doug and I married a week before the elaborate wedding she planned for us.

"Well . . . is it turning colors?" I ask, closing my eyes like I do when I don't want something to be true.

"It's starting to look pink. Think about the ice-cream cone. It's getting very pink."

*This is some kind of chemical reaction, I'm sure. I've been drinking this terrible-tasting tea for my blood circulation, and that's why the false positive. Cabbage. I had cabbage last night. Maybe there's something in the antioxidants that could be causing this.* I'm thinking all this, but I know it isn't true.

Allie shows me the results.

I look at my moment of truth and then close my eyes again.

"The scale didn't lie. This test isn't lying either. You are pregnant, girl!" Allie's brown eyes are shining.

Allie hugs me, and I open my eyes slowly, as though they are glued shut. Her smile is a mile wide. I try to smile on her account, but suddenly I feel tired, like I could go to bed for a year.

"What time is it?" I ask, even though the clock is right in front of me.

"2:50."

"Doug. What is Doug going to say?"

"You and Doug take some time together," Allie suggests. "I'll take the kids to some fast-food place I can't stand. That way I won't be tempted to blow my diet."

If I were very spiritual, I would not be thinking about how ugly maternity clothes are or how my feet are going to swell like balloons and my bladder will shrink to the size of a quarter. I wouldn't be considering stretch marks, spider veins, raging hormones, leg cramps, heartburn, skin pigmentation, and sleep deprivation.

I would be glowing like expectant mothers are supposed to glow.

One consolation: as soon as I have some cravings, I'm giving into them. I'll have an excuse to eat anything I want. I don't get morning sickness—and this, all my friends assure me, is a huge blessing.

On the way to Doug's office, I drive my practical brown van up to the Java Junkie espresso stand. (My dream vehicle is a yellow Hummer, fully loaded—and I don't mean with candy wrappers and crunched homework.) I order a twelve-ounce caramel fudge latte, and emphasize the word *single* twice, because I suspect the owner instructs the employees to *accidentally on purpose* make a double so he can make a couple of extra quarters.

I give the bored after-school teenager my money and then my

coffee card to punch. It's the wrong one. Five cards and a thousand eyeball rolls later, I find the right card and hand it to the girl, dying to ask if her eye muscles are sore.

I drive to a corner of the parking lot and take a sip of the whipped-cream delight. One sip, that's all.

They say a moderate amount of caffeine is permitted during pregnancy, but when I was pregnant with Logan, my mother-in-law said caffeine was linked to birth defects. Studies have shown it isn't true, but I'd never get past the guilt—the same way I have to make my bed before breakfast and have to brush my teeth for two full minutes, because the hygienist said to.

"Good-bye," I say to my caffeine buddy as I place it in the cupholder to throw away later. (Decaf is useless, in my opinion.)

For a while I stare at the weeds in the adjoining field, hoping for a good cry that never comes. A good cry would be therapeutic. But if I started crying, I wouldn't be able to stop. My eyes would be red and puffy, and the people at Doug's office would ask what is wrong. I need to be mature about this. *Be strong for Doug*, I tell myself. I tell myself this continually for the ten-minute drive to Doug's office.

I walk nonchalantly into the office of Adams, Brown, Gibbs, and Associates. The first things I notice are the parenting magazines on the coffee table in the waiting area. I never noticed them before. What are baby magazines doing in a CPA's office? Tax deduction, I surmise. Now there are two good things: no morning sickness and another tax deduction. Oh, and the dependent-care exemption (I think that's what it's called).

I feel terrible that I'm thinking in terms of tax benefits. I can't yet see this life inside me as a tiny soul, and that's hard to admit. I'm a visual person. When I see the baby on the ultrasound screen, I'll weep like I did with all my other children. I know I will.

Marge at the front desk nods as she talks to five people at the same time. I walk down the halls. The number crunchers are busy, for which I am grateful. The fewer questions the better.

I walk past Ursula Andrews's office. Ursula wears these cat-eye glasses that have been out of style for fifty years (which is probably how long she's been with the firm). Al Samson doesn't notice me either. He's one of those stereotypical accountants who wears polyester blue suits and has zero social skills.

You can imagine how exciting the Christmas office party is.

Randall Peterson is hunched over his desk but manages to spot me through peripheral vision. He waves with his left pinkie. Mr. Nerd, I call him affectionately. He really is a nice man. He gives to charity and takes in stray cats he's allergic to.

And then there's my Doug, fifth office on the window side of the building. His office is the only one with the blinds open, allowing the sunlight to stream in. Doug is not your typical accountant. He is dynamic and interesting. He skis, bikes, plays on the church basketball team, and has even been known to dare a few ramps at the skateboard park with Logan every now and then.

"Becca! What are you doing here?" He stands up (looking very dapper in his black suit, I might add).

"Visiting you."

"That's very nice." He kisses my cheek.

His desk is neatly cluttered.

I look at the piles. "Unless you're busy."

"Of course I'm busy; it's tax season. But never too busy for you, honey." He gives me a warm and lingering hug.

"Allie offered to take care of the kids, and I thought it would be nice to spend some time together."

"Actually, I haven't had a break all day," he says, his red eyes showing it.

"Are you hungry?"

"Yes."

"How about Chili's?"

"Great."

I follow Doug out to his maroon PT Cruiser (which is a wild car for a left-brained guy). He opens the door for me. I sit down. When he is situated on the driver's seat, he squeezes my hand.

"Do you want my latte?" I ask.

"Don't you want it?"

"No."

He helps himself.

I watch Doug sip my latte. His bone structure is superb, his skin an olive brown. His eyes are brown. But I can always see the sky in his eyes; it's the most amazing thing.

We make good babies together. All four of our children are gorgeous, and I can hardly imagine the one on the way.

"Why are you staring at me?"

"Because you're beautiful," I say.

"You too."

"I should have ordered the baby-back ribs," Doug says.

*Is that what I ordered? Oh yeah, baby-back ribs and iced tea with extra lemon.* But I couldn't tell you if the waitress is blond or brunette or redheaded, if she walks fast or slow, or wears glasses. I keep crossing the line over to la-la land and back again.

"Let's switch meals," I suggest.

"If you're sure."

"Yes, I'm sure." Doug looks happy.

*Baby* back ribs, I think. It occurs to me my subconscious is working overtime.

I'm tempted to blurt out, "We're going to have a baby!" Instead I drop a hint. "I wish they had *baby* lima beans."

"My dad was in the navy before he was a reporter. We ate lots of lima beans growing up," Doug says. His cell phone rings. "No, Hannah, there are no special tax breaks for students."

I'm thinking of my options. I could write, "We're having a baby" on the bathroom mirror, or I could fill the living room with pink and blue balloons. I could serve baby food for dinner—that's a popular one.

Our food arrives. I'm nervous and don't feel like eating. Still I bite into Doug's Grilled Caribbean Salad. He's sinking his teeth into my baby-back ribs with extra sauce.

"That *bib* is so cute, Doug."

"Messy meal, isn't it?"

"Yes, it is. Look at that *baby* over there with the sauce all over his face."

"I think he classifies as a toddler, Becca. Cute kid, though."

By the time we are halfway through our meal I have brought up the word *baby* several times in one form or another. I brought up tax deductions. I brought up the fact that Maggie from church quit her law practice to be a stay-at-home mom with her *baby*.

Now, Doug is a very smart man with a great deal of logic. He knows about Ancient Mesopotamia and numerical theories as they relate to the stock market. But, to be blunt, he lacks intuitiveness. So I decide I need to be more obvious.

"What was the name we had picked out for Carly in case she was a boy?" I ask, not remembering myself.

Doug plants his elbows on the table. A rush of recognition lights up his face. "Okay, I know you're getting at something."

"You do?"

"Ben talked you into it, didn't he?"

"He did?"

"And I think it's a terrific idea!

"You do?"

"I do." He tugs on his conservative tie.

I don't remember Ben mentioning that he wanted a baby brother or sister. I remember him suggesting we give Carly up for adoption and send Logan to the military academy. Besides, what does Ben have to do with it?

"If Carly were a boy, she was going to be named after your

father, and you know it," Doug says, opening a towelette and wiping his fingers.

*I do know that. What's wrong with me?*

"Jake is a good puppy name, isn't it?" he goes on.

"I guess." Now I'm stumped.

"In fact, it ranks fourth—after Sam, Max, and Buddy." He is smiling as wide as Allie was a couple of hours ago.

"You keep track of puppy names?" I ask, incredulous.

"Ben does. He bought *All about Dogs* with his allowance, and that's all he's been talking about."

"Oh yeah." A weak smile forms on my lips.

"It's a puppy you want, right?"

I shrug, wondering how we got so many pages apart.

"You didn't have to take me out to eat, honey. Ben convinced me last night." He laughs. "That kid will make a good attorney."

"Ben wants to be an artist." I toy with a piece of lettuce.

# Chapter Five

There couldn't have been a more opportune moment to deliver the baby news, but just then Al Samson shows up in his blue polyester suit, looking friendless.

We invite Al to join us, though I secretly hope he'll decline our generous offer. He squeezes in on Doug's side of the booth and starts in with tax talk.

I'm literally falling asleep by the time they are halfway into a conversation on standards of professional conduct. I want Al to leave, but he's so busy talking, he hasn't even touched his ribs.

Suddenly Al looks at his watch and gasps. He devours his dinner, making a bigger mess than the toddler. (I'm tempted to wet my napkins and wipe off his face.) Then he explains he has to get back to the office. "See you all later." Al grabs his check and briefcase.

As I'm summoning my courage and rehearsing in my mind the words to tell Doug about the baby, the waitress comes by. "Are you sure there's nothing else I can get you?" she asks in a tone denoting finality.

"Nothing I can think of," Doug replies.

Since I was a waitress once, I take the hint right away and move on to plan B.

"How about a drive?" I ask.

"Sure."

"I'll drive," I offer, because I'm afraid he might run us off the road when I share the shocking news.

$\approx \mathcal{X} \approx$

"Remember how we used to do this *BC*, 'before children'?" I ask as we head down the interstate.

I hear negligible agreement, silence, and a minute later, contented snoring.

Doug wakes up thirty minutes later, a block from home, wide-awake and smiling. "I'm afraid I wasn't much company," he apologizes.

"You've been putting in a lot of hours. Besides, it's getting late, and the kids probably need us."

Allie is on the lawn, waiting with an anticipatory expression. She looks thoroughly disappointed when I shake my head and mouth the words, *Didn't tell him.*

Doug misreads the situation again. "Yes, Allie. Ben is getting his puppy. You ladies think you're so clever."

And then he proceeds to the shower.

Allie gives me one of her wild sideways glances.

$\approx \mathcal{X} \approx$

The kids take up the next twenty minutes filling me in about their day and asking for money for this and permission for that. I call Mrs. Round, because Carly forgot her important homework assignment in her desk and then Ben's soccer coach to apologize for not enclosing the check with his registration form.

Later Doug squishes in between me and a kid or three on the couch. I ask Allie to put on an episode of *I Love Lucy*. The couch clears rather quickly because I am what some people might refer to as an *I Love Lucy* fanatic, and my children do not share my fanaticism. I own the entire video collection (which, by the way, was released on DVD three minutes after I made my final payment).

It is no coincidence that the episode Allie *happens* to put in the VCR is the one where Lucy is *enceinte*. Just as Lucy is sitting on Ricky's lap, ready to share the news of the blessed event, Doug yells for the kids to come back in the family room—now.

I hear "Not another family meeting," mumbled in disgruntled tones, and for one hallucinatory moment, I think he has figured out all the pieces of the puzzle I've been waving in front of his face.

Doug stands up. I offer him my glass of water, because his mouth seems dry. He lifts the glass, takes a big swallow, and announces, "We're getting a puppy!"

Ben gives a look of triumph, and then the kids begin shouting the names of the breed of dog they feel would be the best addition to our family.

"Golden retriever!"

"Beagle!"

"Labrador!"

I had almost forgotten about the puppy. Or maybe I was just trying to forget about the puppy. Either way I try to hide the grief on my face.

Allie whispers in my ear, "We have to accept life as it comes."

Though I'm sure she means it as a comfort, Allie's unsolicited advice sounds so counselor to me.

At that exact moment, Ricky Ricardo bursts into a chorus of "She's Having a Baby" on the TV screen. I start in with hysterical, nervous laughter and cannot stop for anything.

Allie dashes out of the room. Frankly, I'm sort of mad she's leaving me in such a state. I'm still laughing uncontrollably. Tears are streaming down my face.

"You amaze me, honey," Doug says. "How you can watch these episodes a hundred times and still think they're hilarious."

Ten minutes later I am still laughing. My left eye starts

twitching like it tends to do when I am delirious.

Doug starts theorizing, as accountants tend to do. "Maybe there were sulfites in the salad, and you're allergic to them. Does it feel like your throat is tightening? Do you have a migraine? Do you feel lightheaded or like you need to throw up?"

I assure him I'm fine and turn off the TV. Eventually I calm down, and Doug and the children are convinced I'm not going into anaphylactic shock. And then it really is all very funny.

I am about to tell my family about the baby when sweet Allie, who did not abandon me after all, but made an emergency trip to the Baskin Robbins around the corner, comes out of the kitchen with a heaping bowl of Chocolate Brownie ice cream for me. Logan and Doug wander into the kitchen to dish out their own equally heaping bowls of ice cream, and I share mine with Carly and Ben (my only children who think it's still okay to share Mommy germs).

For the next twenty minutes, Ben reads to us out of his book, *All About Dogs*. I learn about dog breeds I didn't even know existed. The Alopekis, which is close to a fox; the Basenji, whose remains have been found in Egyptian tombs; and the Puli, which sounds like a brand name of designer shoes.

All I can think of is that I'm going to get stuck with the dirty work after the initial puppy enthusiasm wears off.

Here I am in bed after a long, hard day. Doug is snoring like he does when he's utterly exhausted. And I'm wondering why I didn't just say, "We're having a baby!" If men were the ones having babies, they'd say it right out. Something like, "The kid's coming in nine months. We need a crib."

*I have to get some sleep! I have to get some sleep! I have to get some sleep!*

No matter how many times I repeat the phrase, it does not put me to sleep. My prayers, though comforting, do not put me to sleep.

Every time I look at the clock I start to panic. If I don't get my sleep, I'll be a wreck.

At 4:00 a.m. I've had enough. The thought of not getting my sleep is more agonizing than not getting the sleep.

I go to the kitchen and turn on a small light. I sit at the kitchen table with my Bible open to Psalms, but I'm so bleary eyed, I can't read. I'm staring nowhere.

After a while I set out a few candles, light them, and turn off the kitchen light. I watch the flames dance and imagine what it would be like to feel that free. After I'm bored with that, I make some tea, because, for some reason, it's a comforting beverage.

I'm startled when I see a figure emerge from the dark hallway. "Doug?"

"Up for company?" he asks, fully awake. He turns on the light.

"Sure, honey."

I take a deep breath. I take another deep breath. I blow out the candles, and the scented air smells like apple pie.

Doug sits down.

"Do you want some tea?" I ask.

"No. But I am wondering why you're up at 4:45. Is something bothering you?"

The plain fact of the matter is that I need to tell Doug—now. "I'm going to have a baby." There. I said it.

"A baby?" he sputters.

I cup my hand on his. "Yeah. Like in baby-back ribs and baby lima beans."

There is a long pause. I clear my throat.

"That's wonderful," he says softly.

"So you're not upset?"

"No. No." He takes a minute to reflect, and I allow him the time. "You know, I've always wondered if God didn't have something more for us."

*He sounds so spiritual, I can't admit my apprehension now.*

"This is unbelievable, Becca. This is great." And then he stands up and starts yelling, "Whoeeeeee!"

Bedroom doors open like elevator doors. Sleepy children appear in pajamas, rubbing their eyes.

"Your mother is going to have a baby!" Doug announces.

There is a short pause, and then the room explodes in hugs and excitement. There is so much noise I'm worried that we'll wake the Andersons, maybe even the whole neighborhood.

Pure joy descends like sunshine in the night, and the splendor overshadows all doubt—for now.

Allie finally comes out of her room in her robe and purple spectacles, her natural beauty intact.

Logan looks suddenly dazed. His lips turn pale, his eyes dart at rapid speed.

"What is it, Logan?" I ask.

"Where is the kid going to sleep? I'm not giving up my room."

"With me!" yells Carly. "It's going to be a girl, you know. It has to be a girl."

And Logan says, "No, it's going to be a boy. He can sleep with Ben."

"There's school today, and you kids need your sleep," I say like any mother would. "You should go back to bed."

My statement has no effect. Our tiny kingdom is having a royal birth, and the subjects are celebrating imperially.

Apparently I fell asleep at the table around 5:30, and Doug didn't want to disturb me. In that space between dreaming and being awake, I remember Tawny telling us she will be positively humiliated if the baby is named Jake. "Only dogs and heavyweight boxers are named Jake," she said. Then I have a faint memory of Ben yelling that if the dog is not going to be named Jake, could it be named Rover, and Logan saying Rover is a stupid name. The last of my fuzzy memories is Carly saying Persian cats are so pretty and me patting her head and agreeing with her.

Allie shakes my shoulders.

"Not twins! Not twins!" I yell groggily. (Once, in this same state, I gave permission for Tawny to ride on the back of Jonah Tandy's motorcycle—without a helmet.) "Go away," I insist, then realize where I am. The smell of bacon drifts into my nostrils, and I consider yesterday with all its surprising revelations.

"What's wrong? You still don't look happy," Allie says perceptively. "I thought you'd be happy by now."

"Well, I'm not," I state adamantly. I bite into a piece of bacon and realize it is turkey bacon (part of my abandoned diet), which explains why the plate is still full. "Did you make breakfast?"

"Badly," Allie admits.

"Oh." I toss the cardboard back on the plate. Then I moan, whimper, and extend my lip out a couple of inches.

"How do you feel?" Allie asks.

"Indescribable."

I know it's a vague answer, but it's what I'm feeling. I expect Allie to say something profound, but she doesn't. She says she needs a shower and walks away cautiously, the way you would leave a toddler in a room alone with packaging materials.

I open the Bible randomly, hoping wherever my finger lands will apply to my situation and offer me hope. *Practical* hope.

I'd love to tell you that hope was on that page, but it's not true. Not that it doesn't happen that way *some of the time*. But not this time. Not for me.

So I go back to what I know, which is what we all know: my pregnancy is a blessing and part of God's plan for creation. Now if I could only translate that head knowledge into heart knowledge.

At 9:15 Doug calls. He tells me he was still hungry after Allie's breakfast but doesn't want me to tell her. He dropped by McDonald's for a breakfast burrito, and Alda Meyers, who volunteers at our

31

church, just happened to be there picking up Pastor Ramsey's coffee, because the church coffee maker is on the blink.

I'm sure this story is leading somewhere.

"I accidentally shared the news of Joy baby number five," he says, his words rushing together.

"You did?"

"It's a natural thing for an expectant father to do," he reasons.

"No. Really. It's okay, Doug."

"I'm glad you're not upset."

"Why would I be upset?" (I am, by the way—very.)

"It's just that I thought this might be a sensitive time for you."

I don't hop on that train. I let it go by.

# Chapter
# Six

Alda Meyers is the church gossip. No, she doesn't lurk in hallways, hoping a juicy story will be spilled so she can wreck someone's life. Most of the time the stories she repeats are innocent enough. It's simply hard for Alda types to understand that people do not want the world to know their flossing habits or that they are a size fourteen instead of the size twelve everyone thinks they are.

Unfortunately, in my case, Alda determined that the whole church needed to know that Doug and I are expecting—again. (Being a man, Doug neglected to say those four saving words: "Don't tell anybody yet.") And when I say the "whole church," I mean the *whole* church—right down the list, A to Z (or so it seems). The Z being Marguerite Zwicker, age eighty-four, who had to adjust her dentures several times during our conversation, which was mostly about the importance of double-rinsing cloth diapers and the proper technique for clothesline drying.

Besides Marguerite's call, I received twelve others. Granted, three of the phone calls were Doug, asking if he could bring me something: chocolate or baklava (he deserves kudos for remembering). But the rest were well-wishers or, shall I say, advisers.

I may not have graduated magna cum laude from an Ivy League

33

university like Allie, but with four children, I do know the basics. Things haven't changed much since Eleanor Roosevelt gave birth. A baby cries, you feed her; a baby messes her diaper, you change her; a baby is tired, you rock her to sleep. And, of course, you give tons of love and follow a reasonable routine to ensure a sense of security and all that.

In the midst of the aggravating phone calls, I made a huge error in judgment. I told Carol that I had been enjoying having my life back with the kids in school, but that now, with a baby, all that would change again. I was feeling like condensed soup in a can.

I don't know why I felt compelled to share my true heart with her. Carol and I aren't really close.

The first thing Allie says when I hang up the phone is, "Why on earth did you say that?"

"I'm pregnant and have no brain cells," I answer glumly.

"Actually, studies with mice show that the brain cells increase during pregnancy. Particularly the brain cells related to the sense of smell."

"That happens to me."

"It's called heightened sensory awareness." Allie fiddles with her contact lens.

All of a sudden I feel cranky, having had little sleep the night before. "I'm going to take a nap. I have heightened sleepy awareness."

"I think that's a good idea."

I flop on the couch and close my eyes. Mother Allie covers me with a blanket.

The sound of female voices lures me awake. I see three women standing over me, like the wise men bearing gifts. One with a silk flower arrangement and two with baskets filled with functional baby things. They lay their donations near the couch—the couch plagued with Ben's Legos and Carly's Barbies, and probably cracker crumbs and pencils and whatever else has been accumulating since I last cleaned under the cushions.

I force a smile, and they all share this expression. It could be joy . . . or pity. It's hard to tell.

I shed my blanket and thumb through the contents of the baskets, half-awake. "Thank you. That's so sweet."

Manhattan is the first to speak. Her New York accent booms through the room.

"Feeling a little overwhelmed, are we, Bex?"

*What happened to "Congratulations"?*

"I thought we could cheer you up," Carol chimes in, obviously feeling good about herself. "I hope you don't mind that I shared a little about your . . . struggles."

I swallow hard but am at a loss for words.

"So what did the doctor say about our little passenger?" Vanessa asks in a cutesy voice.

"I haven't been to the doctor yet," I say.

"You haven't been to the doctor?" Carol makes it sound criminal.

"No. I just took a home pregnancy test."

"I think it's wise to have the results verified by a medical professional before announcing a pregnancy," Carol declares, annoying me.

"Not nowadays, Carol," Manhattan corrects. "People announce their pregnancies as soon as the dipstick turns colors. You can always give the presents back if something happens to the baby."

*Something happens to the baby*

Carol thinks a minute. "I believe it would be permissible to keep the presents in that situation."

"I agree with Carol," Vanessa says. "I think it would be like a wedding. You would keep the presents as consolation."

"I didn't get to keep *my* wedding presents," Manhattan fires back, heatedly. "I had to sell my wedding presents and my engagement ring to pay for all the debt."

"What is she talking about?" Vanessa asks Carol.

"She was left at the altar," Carol whispers, as if Manhattan doesn't know that.

My three visitors squish together on the love seat across from me, looking like they are planning to stay the afternoon.

*Allie, rescue me, please.*

She must have heard my unspoken plea. "It was nice of you ladies to drop by," Allie says, being as obvious as a Kirby vacuum salesman.

The silence is thick and unbearable. The only sound is our refrigerator humming in the kitchen.

"Can I offer you some refreshments?" I ask to shatter the awkward pause.

The ladies mumble in agreement. I head toward the kitchen and moan when I see the breakfast dishes on the counter. I open the refrigerator and stare at the scant contents, thinking, *I need to buy groceries.*

*Oh yuck! A decomposing vegetable. What is this? A zucchini?*

"Come sit down at the table, and I'll make us some tea," I call reluctantly.

The church ladies gather at the table in the breakfast nook.

"Do you like rice crackers? That's all I have, really," I finally admit. "You see I was on this diet—"

"Diet?" Carol asks, alarmed. "You should never diet when you're pregnant."

"Yes, I know. But I didn't know I was pregnant."

"Ouch! What's this?" Vanessa whines as she holds up a plastic toy she sat on.

"Sorry." I take the action figure from her. I spot a wet towel and grab it off the floor. I take Carly's homework off the table.

While I boil water for tea, I arrange the weightless crackers on a pretty plate and place it in the middle of the table.

They all stare at the pizza-sauce stain on my checkered tablecloth (the one I intended to change). Vanessa says she's not hungry, Carol says she had a huge lunch, and Manhattan comments how cute the crackers are but doesn't touch them.

The doorbell rings.

"I'll get it," Allie says, and a minute later, she comes back with Judy.

Judy is holding a pie. "I baked you a buttermilk pie, but I also made sour-cream raisin, if you'd rather have that."

"Buttermilk is great; that's very nice of you." I take the pie and set it on the counter.

"I heard about the baby," she says.

"How?"

"This morning, from Carly. She's so excited." Judy looks elegant in a casual outfit.

"That sure looks good." Carol stands over Judy's pie, looking hungry, like she didn't a minute ago.

"Everyone, this is my neighbor, Judy."

They smile.

"Judy, this is everyone."

The next thing I know the women are enjoying Judy's pie (except Allie, who is just drooling over it). Mouth full of pie, Carol is suggesting some Shaklee product that can remove the pizza stain from my tablecloth.

They are captivated with Judy. They are amazed that she has six kids and is my age, and that her labors last two hours max. They want to know what vitamins she takes and where she gets her hair done and if she can teach them basket weaving. Manhattan wants to know if she has any single brothers.

I suppose I should be grateful for such good Christian neighbors. When we lived on Lawrence Street, we had horrendous neighbors. One, a hypochondriac, never stopped complaining about her imaginary illnesses. Another, a cantankerous old man, called every hour to say one of my kids had stepped on his lawn. A lady down the street honked when her children didn't come out of the house on demand, and a screaming house of teenagers played the theme from *Austin Powers* a hundred times a day.

It's ridiculous how ungrateful I am. From now on I'm going to be grateful and appreciative. I'm going to feel happy for others when they achieve good things and trod my pangs of jealousy to a pulp. I will suffocate my "that should be me" responses.

"Fully loaded?" I hear Vanessa ask over my self-talk, her fork in midair.

"Yes. A new Hummer H2," Judy replies.

My stomach drops. "What color?" *Please, not yellow. Orange sunset. Black. But not yellow.*

"I wanted orange sunset, but Peter wanted yellow. And it is very beautiful, I have to admit." Judy smiles.

*She stole my dream,* I fume to myself. *Without even trying, she stole my dream.*

# Chapter

# Seven

Due to a cancellation, I find myself in the doctor's office on Thursday morning. Before stepping on the official scale, I unlace my Keds and set them neatly to the side. The nurse insists that Keds weigh *nothing*, and I argue that every ounce makes a difference to me right now.

Three pounds gained, the scale says.

"It's accurate," the nurse says authoritatively, before I have a chance to ask.

After my lab work and examination, I sit in the cold, sterile room in my thin gown and ladybug socks, feeling restless and jittery. Before the verdict is rendered, Dr. Christy receives an emergency phone call.

To pass the time, I examine the cute posters (because all obstetricians' examining rooms are full of them) and thumb through two magazines. I even play with the models of a developing baby and, for the first time, consider whether I want a boy or girl. But I come to no conclusion.

Finally, overtaken by the need for immediate gratification, I pull a lollipop out of my purse (I collect them from the bank for my children). A few licks of cherry, and Dr. Christy, gray hair framing his kindly face, reenters the room.

"That lollipop is bad for your teeth, my dear," he advises.

I present my indulgence. He tosses it in the trash can then shakes his head, playfully. "Becca, when you were little, you used to put three lollipops in your mouth at the same time."

I had forgotten that Dr. Christy had delivered not only all my children, but me as well.

"Modern science has confirmed your pregnancy." He turns a circular piece of cardboard and predicts November eighth as my approximate due date.

I want to tell him how scared I am—that this isn't supposed to happen to me now.

"You have to be aware that you're not twenty-nine anymore," he warns.

*Nevermind.*

He reviews the basics. He shares the importance of folic acid and taking my prenatal vitamins. Exercise is fine in moderation, he says.

It's nothing I haven't heard four times before.

"Any complaints?" he asks.

*Physical? Mental? Spiritual?* "Just one," I answer.

His bushy brows furrow.

"These gowns." I examine the thin cotton.

"What about them?"

"I'd like to see them in brighter colors. Maybe in butterflies or hearts, and a thicker material. Flannel would be good."

"Oh, Becca," he says condescendingly. "And I suppose padded slippers and a massage therapist would be nice too." He pats my shoulder. "Why don't you let my receptionist bring you some chamomile tea? You'd like that, wouldn't you?"

Allie and I are in the parking lot, searching for my van. The air has a strange feeling, and the leaves on the trees are shaking, as though they fear a weather change.

We find the van, and the doctor parking his Lexus next to us eyes us accusingly.

"Allie, I parked in the *doctors'* parking space," I whisper. "I've been in this parking lot a dozen times before. I don't even remember parking the van."

"It's fine. Don't worry about it."

But I'm still embarrassed by the parking mistake as I settle into my cluttered vehicle. When my muddy windshield grows muddier with swollen raindrops, I determine that the weatherman I heard earlier on the radio was right.

"It's raining," I moan.

"So?" Allie says.

"It's depressing!"

"Only for moles." She checks her flawless face in the mirror.

"So what now?"

"The gym."

"The gym? Oh, Allie, you're on vacation. You don't need a gym."

"I do need a gym. I haven't worked out in a week. I feel better when I exercise, and it's helping me lose weight."

"Okay, but after Chinese food."

"Chinese food? I just ate five rice crackers while I waited for you in the doctor's office. I had to look at two baby brag books and humor a toddler who kept licking my purse."

"If we go to the gym afterward? Pleeeease?" I beg.

"You do realize you are obsessed with food."

"You do realize I am pregnant and have a right to be obsessed with food."

"Well, all right."

She gives up way too easily.

I follow my instinct down South Broadway, the windshield growing clearer in the downpour, the heater blasting through the chill.

"I need to wash my van more often," I observe. "I can actually see out the glass." I glance at Allie. "I'll bet you wash your car at least once a week."

"Twice," she says.

"Uh-huh."

"Hey, Becca, why aren't you like other pregnant women who are disgusted with food and throw up all the time?"

"I don't know. My mother never got sick either."

"Maybe that's why she had ten kids." Allie puts on Tawny's down jacket (the one Tawny is supposed to be wearing to school).

I don't respond. I'm thinking lemon chicken and sesame prawns and getting very excited at the prospect.

Allie consults her watch. "It's only ten forty. Chinese restaurants don't open this early."

"This one opens at eleven o'clock."

We get to my restaurant of choice and peer through the glass door. I try to look hungry, but the suited waiter ignores us. Battling desperation, I press my nose against the glass.

The waiter points to the sign that clearly indicates they are closed and walks away, shaking his head.

"Let's go back to the van," Allie pleads. "I'm getting rained on. We'll be the first to be seated when they open. I promise."

She leads me by the elbow to the driver's seat and shuts me in. My soggy tennis shoes drench the floorboard, but I don't care (one advantage of owning a kid van).

"Dungeness crab with scallions and ginger," I say absently.

"Crab?" Allie asks as she shuts her door.

"Yeah. Doug and I had it last summer when we ate here for our anniversary."

"You can have your crab. Just don't forget the gym."

"We'll get you your endorphin fix after my crab fix, Allie Oop." I pat her knee, still thinking of the tender delicacy, then I look at the time. "Five more minutes to rapturous joy. And look . . . the rain has stopped and the sun is coming out. Do you know that Denver has sunshine three hundred days of the year?"

"Atlanta was humid when I left."

"Keep talking. It will keep my mind off food."

"Like what?"

"Tell me some *Farmer's Almanac* secrets. Any one of those useless facts you collect in your head for fun."

"Okay." Allie pauses a moment, recalling tucked-away information. "Singapore banned chewing gum in 1992."

"That's interesting."

"Every citizen in Kentucky is required to take a bath once a year."

"Keep going, Allie. Four more minutes."

"Oh, and it's against the law to whale hunt in Oklahoma. Think about that one."

"That's good. A couple more."

"There's a town called Nothing in Arizona and a place called Chicken, Alaska. And how would you like to live in a town called Dead Horse?"

"Keep going, Allie. Soon we can be blown away with flavor."

"A rat can last longer without water than a camel . . ."

After a few more of Allie's useless facts, I yell, "It's ten fifty-eight. Let's go!"

Allie takes off Tawny's jacket. "Hold on." She flips the mirror. "Ugh. Look what the sprinkles did to my hair."

"Who cares? No one will notice you," I plead. "Hurry. He's unlocking the door. People will be flocking here any moment."

Allie ignores me. She searches in her purse for a brush, but I stop her.

"I have to have it now!" I say with the ferocity of a spoiled child.

"Hold on." Allie gathers her long, wet hair in a ponytail. "Besides, nobody in their right mind eats Chinese food at eleven o'clock in the morning."

43

"Hurry," I say again, not at all concerned about my own bad hair. "Analyze me later, counselor. Right now, feed me."

⚜

"I'm so glad we were able to beat the crowd," Allie chides as we walk into the empty restaurant.

I feel rather foolish and dysfunctional, but I almost don't care, because we're here.

Chang's Bamboo Garden is a little dark, but that serves to our advantage right now. I wouldn't dare tell Allie that she looks half porcupine, half raccoon. I'm sure I look as bad.

This is a multigenerational family business. Grandma, in the corner, is adding on the abacus in the old Chinese way, and the cook in the kitchen keeps yelling at two young men scurrying about, who are obviously intimidated by his boisterous manner. I would guess he would be their uncle.

The waitress, whose nametag says Su Ye, has a sweet manner. "You ladies want something to drink?"

"We're ready to order." I don't even have to look at the menu. "I want the Dungeness crab."

"Dangerous crab." She repeats what I didn't say.

"Not dangerous. *Dungeness.*"

"Hold a minute, please." She walks over and speaks with the well-groomed lady, then returns with a big smile. "We are new owners. We don't serve crab, just shrimp."

"No crab!" I say with the intensity befitting the announcement of terminal illness.

"I'm sorry." She nods for Allie to order.

"What is the soup of the day?" Allie asks.

"Bamboo noodle or bird's-nest soup today."

"The bamboo noodle is made with . . . ?"

"Bamboo and noodle."

"And the bird's-nest soup is made with . . . ?"

44

"Bird's nest."

"You can't mean twigs and straw?" Allie asks, dismayed.

"No. From saliva," Su Ye says.

"Saliva?" we chime.

"I don't think you like it. It sort of chewy, rubbery. And very expensive."

Allie and I look at each other, amazed.

"What about eggdrop soup?" Allie asks, blinking her right eye to position her wayward contact lens that has been giving her trouble all week.

"Sorry. Not today."

"Could you ask?" Allie blinks like she's doing Morse code.

"Just a minute." Su Ye steps away and yells something in Chinese. The cook's dark head appears, and he yells back in angry Chinese. Su Ye steps up to the table. "No eggdrop soup today."

"Do you have broth?" Allie asks.

"Broth? What you mean broth?"

"Like in a can," Allie explains.

"Oh, can." Sue Ye yells to the cook again, this time from where she is standing.

"What did he say?" Allie tries.

"He say you can go to grocery store for can broth. He an artist, not stock boy."

"Bamboo noodle, please," Allie says, deflated.

Su Ye writes it down and then looks at me.

"Are you sure you don't have crab?" I ask, like a broken record.

"Want me to ask cook?"

"No," I reply quickly. "I'll take the sweet-and-sour pork. No soup." Resigned, I give Su Ye my menu.

Allie is still messing with her contact lens. "This thing won't stay," she exclaims, frustrated.

A few minutes later, a waiter dressed in black and white sets Allie's steaming soup in front of her.

"Can you say the prayer, Becca? I'm still fooling with this maddening contact."

*Plop.*

"Was that your contact lens?"

"Yes!" Allie fishes frantically through bamboo and noodle. "Oh no!"

I sigh on her behalf.

She comes up with a warped piece of plastic. "Great." She laughs and pushes her bowl away. "Forget the eggdrop soup. This is contact-lens drop soup."

"Sorry, Mr. Magoo," I say.

"Oh well. I have glasses at your house."

"I'll say. You collect glasses like seashells."

She pulls a tissue out of her purse and folds her ruined contact in it.

"I like the way you look in glasses, Allie. Intelligent."

"That is exactly why I started wearing these stupid contacts. I'm so tired of people telling me how smart I look. When I get back to Atlanta, I'm making arrangements for laser surgery."

Allie insists she doesn't want more soup, that she wasn't hungry in the first place.

Su Ye arrives with my meal. I take two bites, and I am dizzy with flavor.

"I just thought of something." Allie says, concerned.

"What?" I try not to chew and talk at the same time.

"That could have MSG. Some Chinese restaurants douse their meals in MSG."

I chew fast and swallow. I catch the waitress whirling by with her cart. "Excuse me, Su Ye. You don't use MSG, right?"

"In Chinese restaurant MSG go on most everything."

She refills our water glasses and leaves.

"This one time won't hurt," Allie rationalizes.

"I can't enjoy my meal, not knowing for sure whether it will hurt the baby."

"Just eat half of it."

Despondent, I push the plate away. "It wasn't meant to be."

Allie sips on her water.

"You know that saying about Chinese food leaving you hungry an hour after you eat it?" I ask.

"I know the saying."

"That only applies when you actually swallow it."

Allie tries to lighten the moment. "What a team we are. Blind and starving."

"You know what? I had forgotten that Chinese food was my craving with Tawny. Back then we didn't care about MSG. This kid deserves her own craving," I say excitedly.

"Her own craving?"

"Sweet, salty, or spicy?" I entertain the choices. "It wasn't Chinese I wanted anyway. It's something yet to be discovered."

"Sorry to interrupt your food fantasy, Becca, but you have a promise to make good on."

"Promise?"

"The gym," Allie insists.

"Rats. I did promise you the gym, didn't I?"

# Chapter

# Eight

Leaving the house for the gym, I'm wishing I hadn't made any promises.

"I can't! I can't go. I'm so out of shape." I hold on to our maple tree, half joking, half not.

"The purpose of going to the gym is to *get in shape*. Get it?" Allie pries my fingers off the trunk as the new red leaves shake. Then she tugs me by my arm toward the van.

"Okay. Okay." I open the van door and gasp. "My heightened sensory awareness is kicking in. There's something rotting in here."

"I don't smell it," Allie says.

"I do. Check under the seats."

"I smell it now." Allie adjusts her daring red glasses.

A minute later I locate the culprit. Extracting a crinkled brown paper bag from under a backseat, I hold the offender out of sniffing range.

"What's in there?"

"I can bet you it's Ben's bologna sandwich." I blow my bangs, annoyed. "He's the only one of my children who insists on taking his lunch to school. Yet every time I make him something besides peanut butter and jelly, he does this. He says he wants peanut butter every day."

"So?"

"Peanut butter and jelly is so boring."

Allie scratches her ear and laughs. "You used to dump your tuna and Spam sandwiches in the trash and beg my meals."

Slowly it comes to me. "Your mom made such good lunches, Allie, and killer fried green tomatoes."

"She sure did."

I toss the refuse in the overflowing garbage can for pickup. I glance at Judy's trash can and am amazed, once again, at how it's never full, despite her large family.

Allie squats to tie her shoe, an act of diversion. I know her all too well.

"I'm sorry your mother's gone. She was a wonderful woman."

"She was my best friend besides you, Becca. And she never told me she was sick until the very last. She died in her garden, nurturing her tomatoes, the way she nurtured everything and everyone."

The neighborhood is quiet, almost too quiet.

"Do your son a favor," Allie whispers in a voice so weak I can barely hear her. "What?" I tighten my arms across my Windbreaker.

"Give the kid peanut butter if that's what he wants."

When we arrive at the Feel Fit gym, I feel paralyzed. The last time I was here was months ago. Even hidden under Doug's sweats (my workout outfit was too tight a squeeze), I am unable to ignore my burgeoning figure.

"For women only. This is a good thing," Allie comments. "Men always forget to wipe their sweat off the machines."

"Your membership has expired, darling girl," Susan, the platinum-haired woman at the service desk, informs me when I hand her my membership card.

She reminds me of the librarian who calls me "darling girl" when she admonishes me for my children's lost library books. (We always find them later, in the oddest places.)

"But I'll give you both a freebie today and a coupon for a free carrot juice at the juice bar." Susan waves the coupons in the air as though they're tickets to Tahiti.

Allie and I look at each other sideways.

"Thank you." I take the coupons and stuff them in my pocket.

"Let's take a quick tour of the facilities first and then set you up with an adviser so we can set some personal goals," Susan says, looking fit in a spandex outfit.

As we walk across the shiny floor, my Nikes squeak. (Tawny borrowed them and left them in the rain.) Susan launches into complicated membership-plan options that would confuse an attorney. She tries to sell us T-shirts and nutritional supplements, and we're not even down the hall.

Allie says she lives out of town. I say I'm only doing this for Allie and politely suggest that we don't really need a tour.

A disappointed Susan passes us off to Kiley, who is tall, hard-bodied, and talkative. She says she just moved here from Arizona because her ex-boyfriend was stalking her.

Kiley asks Allie to flex her biceps and tells her she's in good shape. "You know what you're doing." Kiley directs her to a treadmill, and Allie takes off, running.

Kiley inspects me, says nothing, shows me a couple of stretches, and fits me with a bicycle. I start pedaling. My legs fly, and my aspirations soar . . . until she adjusts the tension, and then I can hardly pedal.

"Keep going, Rebecca," she urges.

Kiley asks Allie to stop her marathon for a moment so she can check her pulse. "Excellent." She returns to me. "Stop for a second, Rebecca," she advises as I catch my breath. She takes my pulse and says gingerly, "We better start reeaallly slow."

"I'm pregnant," I explain.

"Oh, well . . . then," she says, like she just discovered I have some terrific disease. "Follow me."

"Next time let's do a wilderness backpack, or I'm staying home," I whisper to Allie as I pass.

I know there are chubby, lumpy women around here some-where, but I only notice the ones with zero body fat—the ones who don't sweat and are unnaturally tanned for Denver in the spring.

"You will be more suited to a low-intensity workout," Kiley ob-serves.

I follow her toned body to an unfamiliar room covered in floor mats.

"Now take it at your pace." She pats me on the head like people tend to do with pregnant women, dogs, and children.

"This class starts in five minutes," the chirpy instructor says as she arranges the mats.

Admittedly, this looks more my speed. In fact, I'm thinking I look pretty good. But then that may not be a fair comparison since most of these women look ready to burst with child at any moment.

"So are you full-time, part-time, or stay-at-home?" a woman asks as I flop my tired body on the mat.

"Stay-at-home." I look up at the high ceiling.

"I am too."

"That's nice."

"So what theme are you going with?" a young woman who could be my daughter asks.

"Theme?" I'm clueless.

"Yeah. I'm going with Winnie the Pooh. Unless you think it's outdated."

"You're asking me? I don't keep up-to-date on nursery themes. I'll be lucky to find the baby a drawer to sleep in."

"Hey, you're funny," the young woman says.

Another woman joins the exchange. "I'm going with Noah's Ark. It never goes out."

*I'd rather be taking a botany class. This is so ridiculously boring.*

Our instructor steps up, looking deliriously happy. She puts on soft music and says she hopes we are having a good afternoon so far. We do arm circles and head circles and tame stretches, and I start to feel relaxed. Then the music goes ballistic, and so do the instructor and her devotees.

All the ponytails and bellies bobbing around almost make me laugh. But more laughable is the terrible shape I'm in.

*And they call this low-intensity?*

Ten minutes into the class, the instructor is trying to kill me.

Just yesterday I was biking thirty miles a day, navigating steep cliffs, and hiking every other mountain. Or was that ten years ago?

My, how time flies when you're having fun.

⋠🕮⋞

"I'm ready for a nap or some other mind-numbing activity," I say once we're back in the van again.

"Oh, come on. Let's have some more fun."

"I don't trust your kind of fun. You think sweating in a room full of mirrors with talkative women followed by a communal shower . . . is *fun?*"

"You used to think it was fun," Allie remembers.

"*Used to* are the key words here."

"Well, what do you want to do, then?" she asks warily.

"Since you asked"—and I grin—"you know the fried green tomatoes you mentioned earlier?"

"*I* mentioned?"

"Fried green tomatoes is a respectable craving, don't you think, Allie?"

"Hush your mouth, girl. This is Denver, not Atlanta. They don't have fried green tomatoes in Denver this time of year."

"They might, somewhere. Or we can make them from scratch like your mama used to make."

"Nobody makes them like my mama used to make," Allie says with attitude.

"You know what I mean."

"Besides that, you don't plan a craving," Allie reasons.

"Why not?"

"You just have one."

"Sorta like a baby?"

We both laugh. I need the laugh. I'm taking life way too seriously today.

I win out as usual. We go all over town, searching for my perfect green tomatoes. We end up behind these maddening drivers who are admiring themselves in the mirror and searching in their glove compartments for who knows what, and then behind a motorcade of cars leaving the senior citizens' center. I step in chewing gum. I almost get run over in the parking lot. I knock over the display of Ritz crackers in Albertsons. I tell the stock boy I'm pregnant, as though that gives me a license to knock over cracker displays.

Finally, at Safeway I spot three slightly green tomatoes in an upper bin of riper tomatoes and proudly take them to checkout.

When I reach checkout, the checker asks if I realize the tomatoes are green.

"Yes, I do." I give her a look that dares her to criticize my prized produce.

She doesn't.

We leave Safeway with my little bag of green tomatoes. Later I realize I was so focused on my craving that I didn't think about buying groceries to feed my family.

This isn't healthy. This is becoming more than a craving. It's becoming a full-blown physical compulsion. Maybe I need to make an appointment with my pastor.

# Chapter

# Nine

I am intent on making the best fried green tomatoes ever. We stop by Judy's house, and the smell of her pot-roast dinner is tempting, but not as tempting as fried green tomatoes. I know Judy will have a recipe.

"Here it is." She locates "fried green tomatoes" in her alphabetical card index. "You have three choices: *Southern Friend Cookbook*, *Recipes Galore*, or the *Whistle Stop Café Cookbook*."

"You know all that from that one card?"

"Sure," Judy says. "These cards correspond to the cookbook collection in the library."

I opt for the *Southern Friend*, because it sounds the most Southern.

"It says here 'green and firm,' and these tomatoes aren't," I complain to Allie as I stare at the tomatoes that have apparently ripened since we left the store.

"You don't have to be exact."

"Yes, I do."

I wash and slice the tomatoes very thin before soaking them in Judy's borrowed buttermilk. Then I prepare the seasoned flour mixture. After the proper length of time has passed for soaking, I dredge the tomato slices one at a time in the flour and shake off the excess. When I place the slices in the sizzling frying pan, I'm careful not to crowd my babies. I turn them with my spatula until they're perfectly brown, then remove them to drain on a plate lined with paper towels.

"Those look delicious." Allie sighs.

"Oh no," I cry.

"What now?" Allie asks.

"Tomato chutney. It says to serve them with tomato chutney."

Allie grabs the cookbook. "It says 'if desired.'"

"Well, I desire."

"I'm not going back to the grocery store."

"Judy will have tomato chutney. She collects chutney. Mango, mint . . ." I name all the chutneys of all the countries of the world as we walk the stretch of sidewalk to Judy's house.

Fifteen minutes later we return to my prize. My *missing* prize. "I know I put the plate on the counter."

"You did. I saw you," Allie confirms.

I spot a backpack in the middle of the floor, a jacket lying near. "Ben!" I yell.

"What, Mom?" he yells back from his bedroom.

I step into my son's messy bedroom. He's sitting on the floor with a plate covered in greasy paper towels—an *empty* plate.

"Thanks, Mom. These are delicious," he says with his mouth full of the last of my beautiful fried green tomatoes.

I literally want to cry.

"You're the best mom *ever*."

Allie starts to speak. I put my arm up like a crossing guard, and she understands what it means.

"I'm glad you liked them, Ben. Only next time, could you ask *first*, before you do something like that?"

He gives me a repentant look. "Sorry, Mom. But I didn't have much of a lunch."

"I fixed you lunch last night." As I say the words, Ben looks down. "Did you throw your lunch away?"

"I ate the potato chips and the cookies."

"Did you eat your sandwich?"

"I gave it to Riley Moore. He'll eat anything. Are you mad?"

I sigh.

He stands up and sinks his greasy fingers in my waist.

"No, I'm not mad."

"Good." His brown eyes stare up at me.

"You like peanut-butter sandwiches, huh?"

"I love them."

"Every day?"

"Yes."

"Wouldn't you get tired of them?" I ask.

"No."

I secure a stubborn strand of his raven hair. "From now on you get peanut-butter sandwiches *every* day, if that's what you want."

"Every day?" He smiles.

Allie tears.

I could care less about fried green tomatoes anymore.

I forget that my jeans are too tight and that Allie is leaving on Sunday as we share tea and sister talk. We sit in the backyard swing in light jackets, and the birds come to visit my bird feeders.

"I love April, Allie. Especially after a rain."

"I wish I had a backyard. It's so peaceful."

But things change quickly in the Joy household, even with only one kid in the house.

Ben yells out the window. "Mom, Hobbit escaped while I was trying to clip his nails."

"Not again," I moan as we walk in the back door that I notice could use some touch-up paint.

"What's a Hobbit, besides being a dominant character of Germanic society and a pattern of human behavior?" Allie asks.

I would laugh if I weren't about to panic. "Ben's science project."

"Explain."

"A sugar glider. He's fuzzy, pouched, the size of a hamster, only with a tail."

"How come I never saw the creature?" Allie asks.

"I thought you would have smelled it."

"No. I didn't."

"The thing is nocturnal, Allie. It's the most boring pet ever, except when it escapes. I think Ben should have named it Houdini."

For the next half hour, we chase the speedy creature around middle earth. He scurries under the couch and climbs up the curtains and glides. When the chase is ended and he disappears from sight, we check every hole and crack that our little bug-eyed Hobbit could possibly find to hide in. We finally find him in the overflowing laundry basket in the living room.

Now I have to wash the laundry all over again—twice—because male sugar gliders have scent glands that emit a musky odor. (Maybe that's why the people gave it to us.)

"Perhaps I've overrated my physical stamina," I tell Allie as I collapse in the La-Z-Boy. "I hope you're not expecting me to go salsa dancing with you tonight."

Allie laughs.

"And the kitchen is such a mess. I need to fix us something to eat."

"I'll clean up and pick up something. But not Chinese," she adds hastily.

"You're such a good friend, Allie," I say, managing a half smile.

As my eyes roam around the bedroom, I realize it is Saturday morning, and the alarm is buzzing. It keeps buzzing and buzzing and buzzing. I can't think how to shut it off, so I unplug it.

I notice the clothes Doug laid out on his clothes tree are missing. His side of the bed is made.

"Anybody home?" I call.

Allie, fully dressed and smiling, peers into the room. "No one but me."

"Where is everybody?"

"They said they were going grocery shopping."

"My poor family. Starving because of my former tomato fetish," I say, feeling depressed.

"They'll live, Becca."

And then Allie looks very happy. "Hey, I have great news. I think, anyway."

"What?"

"I'm staying another week."

"No way!"

"Yep. My office space isn't ready yet, so I thought . . . why not?"

My spirit is elated; it truly is. But my hormones are playing tag with my emotions.

"You don't mind if I go out for a cup of coffee, do you?"

"I should go with you, Allie."

"No, you stay in bed. You have early pregnancy fatigue."

"Okay."

"Besides, there is a one-in-a-million chance that I'll meet the man of my dreams at the next table."

"What's he like?"

"Good-looking. Intelligent. Funny." She laughs. "A lot like Doug, I guess."

"You know, Allie, Doug has flaws too. Like everyone else, we have our moments. Like when he leaves a drink on the furniture and steals pieces of my hidden chocolate. Sometimes he annoys me to no end, the way he's so analytical about everything. But I still wouldn't trade him."

"I know no man will ever meet my dreams. I do marriage counseling."

I smile, heavy eyes calling me dreamward. "Close the door on your way out, please."

A few winks later, I hear the sound of an army coming up the steps. Sergeant Doug Joy is giving strict orders to the children.

"You kids make your beds while I put the groceries away. And do not enter your mother's bedroom under any circumstances. Do not make any noise. Your mother needs her rest."

I want to yell, "You can bother me," because I haven't been giving my family enough attention. But I don't have the energy. My body is sore from yesterday's workout. Wonder Mommy is exhausted. Wonder Mommy cannot stay awake.

Doug opens the door explosively. I chuckle, because he doesn't realize he just told the kids not to disturb me.

"Don't get up!" he shouts as my fingers search for my robe. "Eggs Benedict coming up."

"That's sweet but ambitious, Doug. Cold cereal is fine with me."

"I'm fixing your favorite. Just like Mimi's Café."

The man has never poached an egg before.

I don't remember the last time I slept in. So I deserve it. *I deserve it,* I tell myself a few times. I smile and kiss the air in his direction, but he's already gone.

"Okay. But just for a moment," Doug says out in the hallway.

Four children pile in around my deathbed (that's how it feels, anyway). One by one they kiss me on the cheek and give me a sympathetic smile. They shuffle out of the room by age order as obedient as the von Trapp family: Logan leading, Carly's Barbie slippers leaving last.

"Close the door," Doug calls from the kitchen.

Someone shuts it.

My sleep is peppered with enigmatic dreams I cannot remember. I stir to the sound coming from the door. I watch a piece of paper edge under the door and know it's Ben's picture. Ben is my artist and the most sensitive of all my children.

I pick it up, knowing he's on the other side listening. "It's beautiful!"

"It's Jesus," he says. "Pulling up the net, Mom."

His footsteps echo on our Pergo floor and fade away. I like the sound of my children's footsteps.

I wish I could be as a child. Think as a child. Accept as a child.

With such beautiful thoughts as happy children and a loving husband, I drift off into satisfying sleep.

But only for a few minutes.

Doug brings me milky coffee in my favorite mug. I accept it without comment. I don't say that I've given up caffeine. I don't tell him that he awoke me from splendid sleep—the sleep I so desperately need—or I will be mean and nasty.

As he hums down the hall, I put the mug on the back of the headboard and try to regain my lost dream.

Three minutes later, or so it seems, Doug is back.

"Is this the right pan for poaching eggs?"

"It's a double boiler, if that's what you're asking," I explain, slightly impatient. I close my eyes again.

Bliss. Sweet bliss . . . for a few minutes.

Another interruption.

"Honey, is whisking the same as beating?"

"I think so." I smile at Doug.

He smiles back. He looks cute in an apron. "Okay. I won't bother you anymore, I promise."

This reminds me of an *I Love Lucy* episode.

I close my eyes again, but my mind will not relax. It's natural that I should feel pensive about the baby. I'm sure Sarah in the Bible went through the same thing. After all, it seemed impossible—she was past her childbearing years. And then there was Elizabeth—even with an angelic visit, she had to get used to the idea of having a baby. I won't speculate about Mary.

I notice Doug left the door open, and to a child, that means entrance permitted.

"Mommy." Carly, my only blue-eyed child, stands at my bedside. Maybe the baby will have blue eyes like hers.

"What is tarragon?"

"It's a spice cultivated in France."

"Is eggs Bendadekit French?"

"Maybe. Mimi's Café is French."

"Are we French?" Carly asks.

"Somewhere down the line, I think." My head hits the pillow, and I close my eyes.

"Mom. Hey, Mom."

Ben is shaking me. This is an all-too-familiar scene.

"What can I do for you, Ben? I loved your picture, by the way."

"Thanks." He litters the duvet with his comic books. "In case you want to read."

"Thank you, Ben."

One more try. I have to try. I am so completely exhausted, I want to cry.

*Fall asleep. Fall asleep. Fall asleep.*

Three seconds later. *You're not listening, Rebecca Joy. I told you to fall asleep!*

"Here you go, sweetheart." Doug's gentle voice leads the parade.

I sit up.

A decorative tray is arranged on my lap with breakfast that's intended to be eggs Benedict, and then Carly places a plastic daisy in a vase filled to the top with unnecessary water. Ben takes my mug off the headboard and sets it on the tray. He spills coffee all over. And there are no napkins. Of course they forgot the napkins.

But they are all very proud of themselves.

You know that feeling beyond crying? When you're about to get frantic and then later you have to make a dozen apologies? I'm almost there now. It's lack of sleep, I know. But knowing that doesn't help.

In comes Logan, charging like a bull and asking if he can go skateboarding with Tommy. This reminds me of the time I blew my tire out on the curb. Like slow motion his elbow is coming toward me.

There goes the water vase.

"Go. Go to Tommy's. Please go to Tommy's." I try my best to sound in control, even though I feel like I'm about to lose it.

"Come on, guys. Let's let Mom enjoy her breakfast."

*Oh good. Doug isn't catching on.* I smile big. "Thank you. All of you. I can't tell you how special you have made me feel."

"I think we'll go to the pet shop to check out puppies," Doug suggests.

"Yes!" The enthusiasm is shared among the ranks, and suddenly Logan wants to go there instead of Tommy's. I don't ask where Tawny is.

"Have fun," I say.

"Bye," they all call together.

When I hear the automatic garage door hitting the cement, I let all the air out of my lungs and fill them with new air.

The cold, soggy mess on my plate is inedible. I'm not hungry anyway. I drag my body to the kitchen and dump the contents in the garbage disposal. I run the water and the disposal extra long to be sure all evidence is gone.

The fruit of their labor down the drain. Poor things.

The phone rings, but I let the answering machine pick up.

"Rebecca, we've heard the news, and your father and I are thrilled."

Oops. I forgot to call my parents. You don't think Alda would call them all the way in Florida? . . . Naw.

"Your father wants me to remind you that Jake is a good name. Now get your rest, dear. That's the most important thing."

I nod in agreement.

"You know how testy you get without your sleep."

I nod my head double-speed at that.

"I'll call back tonight."

All the way to the bedroom, I shake my head.

I fluff my pillow and ignore the dampness on the bed from the spills.

I pray for sleep and quote one of my favorite psalms. "I will both lay me down in peace, and sleep: for thou, Lord, only makest me dwell in safety."

# Chapter

# Ten

The distant scream I hear does not belong to a member of my family. It is not an agonizing scream. Come to think of it, it sounds almost happy.

I put on my robe and walk downstairs, bumping into the hall walls in my disoriented state.

Another scream. This time I recognize the culprit as Allie.

"I lost five pounds! I lost five pounds!" she screams again as I reach the bottom step.

She is doing this barefoot dance—wiggling her hips and shimmying her shoulders, jamming in a sharp Liz Claiborne outfit—with a kind of enthusiasm I haven't witnessed since we were on the cheerleading squad together.

"Wow, that's great news, Allie."

"I know. I can't believe it. Five more pounds. I can handle five more pounds," she says, winding down like a spinning top.

"Listen—I'll be right back," I tell her.

I dash up the stairs to my lingerie drawer and retrieve a flowery yellow envelope. I'm not as happy for my best friend as I should be, and privately I'm ashamed of myself. Bounding down the stairs, I say a quick prayer that God will squelch my envy and restore my peace again.

"Here you are, Allie. Well deserved. Pamper yourself into oblivion, girlfriend."

"No. It wasn't a fair bet."

"I insist."

"Well . . . okay," she says, and takes the prize.

*Would I have taken the money?*

Once back in my room, I reach for my journal on the nightstand.

*Dear Journal:*

*It's been a long time since I've written, and this is a good thing. You know I only write when I'm on the brink.*

*My best friend is losing weight, and I am gaining weight. Plus, Allie stole the five hundred dollars I've worked so hard to save . . . Okay, I gave it to her, but the bet was her idea.*

*If you could speak your mind, you would tell me it's my hormones, wouldn't you? And you would tell me to go to God. But God seems far away. Then you would say, "Guess who moved?"*

*Oh, Journal, that is so bumper sticker.*

*I wish there were a button called Acceptance, and I could just push it and everything would be sunshine again.*

*A month ago life was good. But you wouldn't know that, since I only write when I am unhappy.*

*My body is growing against my will. Does that seem fair to you?*

*Okay. Okay. Doug and I had something to do with this. But, Journal, please understand how it feels to want to go back to yesterday where it was safe but you can't. This is all too scary. When I was young, scary was exciting. But I am not young anymore. Yes, you would tell me that too, Journal. Why are you so blatantly honest?*

"Mom."

"Oh, hi, Tawny."

I close my journal and put it on the nightstand with my pen. I fluff my pillows and resituate my blankets.

"I like to write in my journal too. Especially when things get hard."

"Hard?"

"I know you're going through it, Mom. And it's okay."

"You're growing up."

"I'm sorry if I haven't been a good daughter lately."

*And I thought I was failing you as a mother.* "You're a wonderful daughter—always."

"I guess I'm striving for independence. That's what our youth leader says."

"That's not a bad thing." I stroke her cheek. I watch her smile and remember her first smile. I used to dream of Tawny in her prom dress. And now it's coming up too soon.

"I'll help when the baby is born. You and Daddy can go on dates together."

"I know you'll all be great. I'm just a little tired right now. I'll be fine."

"Mom, I like a guy at school. His name is Keegan, and he is so sweet and adorable. And, best of all, he's a strong Christian."

"I'm happy for you, sweetheart. Thank you for sharing that."

"I never forget all the things you tell me. About morals and all that."

"I'm glad."

"I want to be the kind of mother you are one day."

"What kind of mother is that?" I ask, curious for the answer.

"One who is always there but doesn't interfere. Who shows me the way but doesn't push."

My heart is full, so full I cannot speak.

"And I'm sorry for saying Jake was a terrible name. I forgot that Grandpa is named Jake."

"It's fine. Really, sweetheart." In that moment I wish more

than anything else that I could cradle her in my arms. "I guess it's time to get out of bed. To face the world."

"It's what you would tell me to do." She smiles and walks away. I am overcome with emotion.

*Dear Journal:*

*Won't be writing for a long time, I hope. Sunshine once again.*

"I'm going to splurge. I'm going to primp and pamper myself into oblivion." Allie dances in the laundry room as I add the Shaklee detergent Carol sold me in the swishing washer. In addition to removing the pizza stain from our tablecloth, Carol promised it would brighten our laundry. Like bright laundry is my main goal in life.

"I'm going to eat a load of caviar, because it's low-calorie and expensive." Allie continues her annoying victory dance, nearly crushing my toes in her lunacy.

*Allie has gone mad. Oh no, not Allie.*

"And I'm staying in a fancy hotel with silk sheets," she gloats in a singsong voice.

*Now this is getting to me. Sunshine. Sunshine, come back!*

"The kind of hotel that turns your bed down and leaves Belgium chocolates on your pillow."

*Smile. You can do it, Becca. Fake it for the benefit of childhood friendship. Smile.*

"Family meeting!" I hear Doug yell from upstairs. "Family meeting!"

As I run upstairs and into the living room feeling rescued, I am greeted with a united, "We have a surprise for you."

"Did you pick out a puppy?"

"We couldn't agree on one," Doug replies.

*Good.*

Allie bounces in the room. "You're going to pamper yourself into oblivion *with* me, girlfriend!" she announces.

"You're sharing your fortune with me?" I ask, suspicious.

"All of it—with my best friend."

I hit Allie on the arm with a loose fist, because I'm finally *getting it.* "You brat. I thought it was rather out of character of you to flaunt that way."

"It was Doug's idea." She points the finger.

I hit Doug on the arm. "So *you* put her up to it. You bigger brat."

"We're getting an extreme tax refund. Allie changed her plans so she could stay longer, and I'm flying you both to Palm Springs on Tuesday," he announces in a radio voice.

I change my tune. "You doll, you."

I kiss him repeatedly.

"Doug! Doug!" I yell from the laundry room.

*Can't I make it through ten lousy minutes without some catastrophe?*

"What?"

"Help me! The washer is overflowing."

We grab some clean towels from the dryer and sop up what we can.

"Kids!" Doug yells up the stairs. "Get some towels from the dirty laundry."

Ben runs downstairs and drops a load of dirty clothes and runs back up for more. Logan and Carly come to the rescue. Tawny takes her precious time.

Tawny observes the effort. "Yuck—I am not touching dirty towels. Who knows where those have been?" She's back to her teenage self again.

"There are no more clean towels, Tawny. We have no choice," I say, bathed in lather.

"I think that soap is concentrated." Allie holds my dripping bathrobe. "I think you put in too much."

Ben calls from upstairs, arms full of dirty laundry. "Help! I forgot to close the cage when I ran downstairs. Hobbit is missing."

"Let's get this cleaned up first, and then we'll find Hobbit," Doug says patiently.

*I'm not going to make it three more days. I'm not going to make it to the plane.*

# Chapter

# Eleven

Yesterday afternoon after church Doug and the children left myste-riously, and when they returned, they had a puppy in arms. The little angels wanted to surprise me, and I *was* surprised.

I had hoped the puppy idea had been forgotten. I had no basis for this hope. If you have children, you know that they do not, all of a sudden, forget permission for a puppy. They nag you and beg you and draw little pictures and leave them on the refrigerator.

They named him Blessing. Yes, that is the name they gave the beast . . . er, the Dalmatian (all except Ben, who insists the dog's name is Rover).

After Doug dropped Blessing in my arms, he said he had to at-tend a meeting of a church committee he chairs. How convenient for him.

Blessing is enormously cute and cuddly, and I liked Blessing for about five minutes—until he started getting busy learning to be a dog. It started with incessant barking, and then he graduated to making a puddle on the kitchen floor—and you can't blame a puppy for that. But the kitchen was already a disaster since I'd had the brilliant idea of cooking meals and freezing them so my family wouldn't have to lift a finger while Allie and I are in Palm Springs.

It's domestically correct behavior, but it was like a medical procedure (the lasagna in particular).

*Eliminate stress by cooking thirty meals at a time*, the book says. *Yeah, right.*

So I shooed Blessing into the living room, and all the children promised they would watch the puppy like a hawk. Because even I, who have never had a puppy in my life (we had cats), know that it doesn't take much for a puppy to get into trouble.

But there is a strange occurrence that happens in families with more than three children. It goes something like this: "I thought you were going to . . ." "No, I thought you were going to . . ." "Well, you said . . ."

Carly, who had to practice her flute, thought Ben was watching Blessing. Ben, who waited until the last minute to finish his homework, figured Logan was. Logan had no excuse whatsoever but apparently left the puppy unattended anyway. And Tawny. Tawny somehow thinks she is exempt from all responsibility.

Let me recount the damage. Because the bathroom door was left open, Blessing managed to rip the toilet paper off the thingamabob and left evidence of his new bad habit of drinking toilet water all over the floor. Then his sharp teeth ripped through Tawny's Skechers and Logan's Doc Martens, which I am constantly reminding them to put away. (And won't they be surprised?)

I was thinking of calling the vet for an emergency prescription for puppy Prozac.

"Logan, take that dog outside!" I yelled, because I heard him on the phone (ignoring our no-phone-calls-on-Sundays rule). All the children suddenly appeared and started rewarding Blessing with affection for his bad behavior.

"I want all four of you in the backyard with that dog for at least thirty minutes. If you think I'm going to be the one to take care of him, you are dead wrong!"

"Gee, Mom," one or two of them said.

"And make sure the yard is puppy-proof, and give the dog some of your old toys—but not any that have stuffing."

They took the puppy and left. They knew better than to say anything when I was using that tone.

"I knew this would happen, Allie." I blow my bangs in the air.

"Soon we'll be lounging by a pool," she reminded me.

I resumed my cooking operation, and Allie headed to the bathroom to clean up Blessing's mess.

Listening to the playful voices echoing in the yard, I thought about apologizing to the children for overreacting. I remembered how Doug spoke with such affection about his dog, Wilson, who met with some freak accident with farm equipment when Doug was a little boy.

"We'll make this work," I said to the deserted room.

The next thing I knew, fur blurred by the window. Blessing had escaped our yard for greener pastures—specifically, for master gardener Judy Anderson's pasture.

"Who let the dog out of the yard?" I screamed.

"Carly! Who else?" Logan yelled through the half-open window. "She left the fence wide open."

You see, Carly is my absent-minded child. She leaves lids off jars and forgets to screw juice caps on all the way. She is basically responsible for all the refrigerator spills and the bathtub water running over. Stuff like that.

Dalmatians are speedy dogs. Within minutes the whole family had converged on Judy's perfect front yard, and there was Blessing, waving his tail, looking so proud of himself with a newly planted vegetable in his mouth. And Judy's raised vegetable garden? Let's just say it couldn't make soup.

Judy wasn't home at the time. The whole family was off doing some charity work. They didn't get home from the gala until after midnight (I know, because I stayed up, waiting for them to come home) and then I was hoping that, even with a full moon, it would be too dark for them to see the damage.

This morning I headed over to Judy's to apologize. "Our new puppy demolished your garden yesterday, and I am sooooo sorry. We will replant every seedling. My children will wash your cars for the next year. Doug will build you a new brick barbecue. And I will wash and fold your laundry."

"I saw it last night when we got home, and I was very upset," Judy admitted. "But an apology is all I need. You don't have to be so dramatic."

I got up off my knees.

Judy laughed. "Are you sure you're okay?"

"I'm pregnant."

"Yes . . . yes, I know," Judy said. "Come in. Would you like the rest of the eggs Benedict I made? That is, if you like eggs Benedict."

Now, I ask you, how can anyone dislike a woman that charitable?

It's early Tuesday morning, the day of our departure to Palm Springs. Four tired children form a semicircle around me, like the planets.

They are all tired for different reasons. Logan and Tawny for their shifts with the puppy, Ben for his night terror (he watched *Jurassic Park*), and Carly for sleeping with her new, uncomfortable orthodontic appliance that is costing us a fortune.

I too am exhausted, but I haven't stopped long enough to feel it.

"You know we need to be at the airport two hours before take-off," Allie informs me. "All those extra security measures."

I look at my watch. "We better get moving, then."

The phone rings. It's Doug. "Sorry, I can't drive you. I can't get out of this last-minute meeting. Logan is going to have to take you to the airport. Call me tonight to let me know you arrived safely."

"Okay. I love you."

"You too."

"Logan is going to drive us," I tell Allie.

"Way cool!" Logan exclaims. "I'll get the keys."

Driving with a testosterone-ridden teenager to the airport is not my idea of fun.

Suitcase in hand, I remind my children of things mothers remind their children of before they go on trips. I remind Tawny to follow my warming instructions for the meals I froze. I remind Carly not to forget her homework on the kitchen table. I remind Ben to change his underwear. I was going to remind Logan not to drive too fast, but I guess I can do that on the way to the airport.

There are no prolonged good-byes. Happily, the days are gone when I have to fight or bribe to get away. Gone for a while, anyway.

Carly lifts my suitcase and says it's heavy, but it really isn't. There are only a few outfits that still fit me, and they are not my favorites.

"I can drive, Logan. You'll be driving back, anyway." I pray he likes the suggestion.

"Come on, Mom. You've never ridden with me on the highway before."

*Gulp.*

Ben follows me out to the van. He peers through the open window on the passenger side. He says he'll take good care of Rover. As Logan pulls away, I yell back to Ben that he should make sure the puppy does not eat Hobbit.

"Put your seat belt on, Logan," I order.

"Oh yeah."

The van screeches to a halt in the middle of the street.

Right now I wish the world were one big, empty parking lot.

# Chapter

# Twelve

Since there is another chapter to this book, I guess you figured we made it to the airport alive. It was a hair-raising experience, and now I get to do this three . . . no, *four* more times.

Two uninvented things I want in my new yellow Hummer (if I ever get one): passenger-side brakes and some sort of CD player that ejects the CD when the noise level goes over the legal decibel limit.

We arrive at the airport the designated two hours early, and security is a breeze.

Once on the plane, I close my eyes. Visions of Palm Springs dance in my head. I picture myself relaxing in a chaise lounge by the pool, being served refreshing drinks with colorful umbrellas. I picture the palm trees and mountains in the background. I picture . . .

*Stop.*

There's something wrong with this picture, and it's me. Me in a bathing suit.

After we land at John Wayne Airport and exit the plane, I notice that the pregnant women who seemed to be everywhere in Denver have followed me to Orange County, California.

"It's a psychological phenomenon," Allie tells me.

"This is an efficient airport," I say as we gather our suitcases in baggage claim.

We secure a Ford Escort for a rental car, since they are all out of Hummers (joking!), and the next thing I know, we are happy travelers, zooming down the freeway.

Allie drives since she slept on the plane. I sleep most of the way. She finds a classical radio station, and I dance to her music in my dream. I am a graceful ballerina, floating across a stage. I twirl in a sparkling pink tutu, up on my toes like I could never do in real life.

I tell Allie about my dream, and she says it has something to do with my desire for freedom. I ignore her.

We stop for a milkshake in some lizard town, along a less-traveled highway.

We pass a flock of windmills, and the DJ on the radio says it is seventy-four degrees.

"Optimum temperature," Allie says, satisfied.

Waves of nausea try to knock me down all of a sudden. I tell Allie I must be getting morning sickness, but Allie says it's strange that we just passed a sign that says Palm Desert, which just happens to be where my perfect sister lives.

"Couldn't we stop by for a spot of tea at Valerie's?" she suggests, trying to ruin my vacation.

"I'll tell you the first thing Valerie would say. 'So do you still live in that *same* house? Do you still drive that *same* van?' She just bought a brand-spanking-new house, and she'll want to gloat."

"I remember Valerie as being very nice."

"To everyone else on the planet. It's not just what she says, Allie; it's the *way* she says it."

"Okay, I hear you. But it seems a shame since we're right here in her backyard."

"Seriously, any time other than this, Allie. She won't even know that I was here."

And then I burst out in complaint. "Her address is even perfect:

twenty-five fifty-five Mountain View Drive. Isn't that a perfect-sounding address?"

"I like mine better," Allie says.

We don't talk for a long time. It takes me a long time to get over thinking about Valerie.

We reach Palm Canyon Drive after our desert crossing, and I'm sure we're in the Promised Land, because it's so unearthly beautiful.

The palm trees are what you notice first. I love all the images of palm trees in the Bible. Here they are, surviving the desert heat, their tall stems pointing toward heaven. I imagine Jesus's triumphant entry into Jerusalem and the great, spreading leaves welcoming him. *Remarkable*, I think.

The first thing I say upon reaching the hotel lobby is, "Can Doug afford this?"

The hotel off the main drag has an Italian villa setting that makes you feel like you're in the countryside.

"Doug loves you, Becca. He wants you to be happy."

I hear the sadness in her voice.

The second thing I say is that I'm dying of thirst. Seconds later I find a glass of pink lemonade topped with a colorful umbrella in my hand. I watch a flowered shirt leaving.

"Pretty cool," I say, like Logan.

Allie gives her name at the front desk, and our bags are whisked away by a bellhop.

"The only thing I have to do is brush my teeth. I don't even have to feel guilty about not making my bed." I twirl, conservatively.

Our room overlooks a dazzling pool that the bellhop says Cary Grant once swam in.

"This certainly is an oasis." I put my things away in the mahogany wardrobe. "I wish it were cold enough to light the fireplace. It's beautiful."

I sink into a leather chair and relax. I close my eyes but do not fall asleep.

"Caviar," Allie announces from our balcony as I watch the room-service cart disappear out the door.

I amble toward the balcony and close the screen door. I watch a beautiful desert sunset emerging across the sky in crayon colors: burnt sienna, Indian red, and eggplant.

"Can we afford caviar?" I scoop up the gold.

"It's my treat."

"Then can *you* afford it?"

"There's something I haven't told you," Allie begins. "When I lost my mother last year . . ." She chokes up.

"I'm sorry, Allie. We haven't talked much about it."

"No. It's fine. Mom was ready to go. She suffered so much through the cancer. She wanted to be with Jesus."

I so want to comfort my friend, to make all her hurt go away.

"My mother left me five hundred thousand dollars. That's why I'm able to start my own practice."

"You're half a millionaire, and you failed to mention it?" I ask, shocked.

"It's not going to change my life. After paying off some bills and taking a couple of trips, I've realized that what was important is still important, and what wasn't, still isn't."

I nod. "That's a good way to look at it."

"And money can't buy a good man. It can buy men, but not good men."

I wish I had some gorgeous cousin or someone at church to fix Allie up with.

*God, please. Sometimes she seems lonely.*

Wrapped in the thickest, most comfortable robes, my best friend and I share a special time together. There are long moments of silence, but even in the silence, words are being spoken.

And then I hear God, because I haven't taken the time to really listen in so long.

God is telling me that everything will be okay. *But not in one day, Becca. Flowers don't blossom in one day. They take time to unfold.*

I call Doug and the children. One by one they say they miss me and love me. One by one they pierce my heart that has grown dense, through stubbornness and will.

Doug tells me not to feel guilty about enjoying myself and not to think of them at all if I can help it. "Just keep our baby safe."

"Our baby," I repeat aloud after hanging up the phone. "You know, Allie, this is the first time I realize that I'm not in this alone."

# Chapter Thirteen

The gentle music of falling water from the fountain in front of the hotel saturates my brain with the strangeness of our travels. At the same time I wonder why it's all so strange to me. There were those days when Doug and I celebrated our love in reckless abandon. We were high-school sweethearts and married young, but we were adventurous souls, taking off to unknown places in our yellow VW bug. Is that what I miss?

The heat is immediate as we step out of the air-conditioned car and onto Palm Canyon Boulevard. We look the same as every other tourist (except not as tan or rich or fashionable, and I am missing my sunglasses). This is the kind of place you expect to run into a movie star, or at least a politician.

"Ever notice that the really rich try to be inconspicuous about their wealth? It's just something about the way they carry themselves." I catch myself. "Wait. Look who I'm talking to."

"Becca, five hundred thousand dollars is not rich these days. Not even close," Allie says.

I can tell she's embarrassed, and I'm sorry I said it.

*Sunglasses. Sunglasses everywhere.*

"I left my sunglasses in the car."

"You can borrow mine," Allie offers generously.

"No. You need yours. I'll buy another pair."

Allie pulls me into a trendy shop called The Tangent.

"They're DKNY," the sales clerk informs me as I look in the mirror and then down at the ring on her left hand that is not a diamond.

"It's an opal engagement ring," she explains. (Allie tells me later it's the latest fad.)

I take off the sunglasses. And then I look at the exorbitant price. "A hundred and seventy-five dollars?" I gasp, forgetting not to show my ignorance.

"We'll take them," Allie tells the sales clerk.

I smile at her, unsure. I want to say that is too much for her to spend on me, but Allie's love language is giving.

I put them on.

"Those look fantastic on you, girlfriend."

And they do. They actually do.

The flow of people walking on the sidewalk is constant but still pleasant company. It feels more like companionship than an intrusion.

"Can you tell me what time it is?" a woman dressed in all white asks, rattling her expensive-looking watch to indicate the piece isn't working.

I read my Eddie Bauer watch shyly. Back home in Denver, I'm rather proud of my watch, but here it feels like a Cracker Jack toy.

"It's ten o'clock," I reply.

"We haven't eaten breakfast yet. My stomach must be shrinking," Allie claims.

"You're right. But I have to eat. You know, the baby." I pat my stomach.

My cheese-and-avocado omelet is scrumptious. Avocados in California are as common as mountains in Denver.

Allie picks at her oatmeal. Oatmeal is hard to make wondrous. Even with walnuts and brown sugar, oatmeal is still oatmeal.

"Everyone looks so good in Palm Springs." I look around the room. "This is not good for my inferiority complex."

"You know, I'm intent on breaking you of your ridiculous habit of comparison. But, I have to admit, you do need a haircut," Allie says.

I agree with her, even without the benefit of a mirror. "You know, I've been so busy lately being soccer mom and basketball mom and all that, I've been getting my hair cut in kid shops when Carly and Ben get theirs cut. You know the kind of shop—little plastic chairs and toys everywhere. Isn't that pitiful?"

"Sort of." Allie sounds amused.

"I hardly get my nails done anymore." I examine my fingertips. "And I think my last pedicure was eight years ago, when Carly was born."

"Well, we did say we were going to pamper ourselves into oblivion."

"Yes, we did say that. But five hundred dollars here is a nickel in Denver."

"It will be my treat."

"Oh, Allie," I say, knowing she'll have her way eventually, even if I complain all day about it.

"Why don't you get your hair layered?" She plays with my dark hair.

"Hey," I protest, playfully flicking her hand away. "Pick on your own hair."

"I don't want any changes. Pregnancy is conducive to change; spinsterhood is not."

"You are not a spinster."

"Not in the historical sense. I'm not a librarian with glasses who wears her hair in a tortured bun—well, maybe sometimes. But I do wash my hair on Friday nights."

I wonder if spinsterhood is painful. I wonder if Allie gets lonely at Christmas with her mother gone . . . if she is ever afraid of living alone.

"You know, you're right," she says slowly.

"About what?"

"I *should* blow my diet. Eating oatmeal in paradise. Now that's something I wouldn't advise any of my patients to do."

"Is there a Baskin Robbins nearby?" I ask.

"Baskin Robbins is for kids, Becca. Besides, we don't want an ice-cream cone."

"We don't?" I ask, because *I* do.

"Tonight, after our full-body treatments, we'll have a high-powered feast," Allie vows.

It sounds good to me. Whatever it means.

⋘❀⋙

As Allie is getting a massage, I am being radically squeezed and plucked and soaked, as though I am a chicken.

*Has it been so long since I've been pampered that I've forgotten it's a pleasure?*

"I can't do this. I can't spend your money like this, Allie," I yell over the separator, hoping she'll agree.

"Yes, you can. I am allowed to treat my best friend. Besides, Doug paid for my trip," Allie yells back from her heated massage table.

"Where are you from?" my torturer in a silver apron asks.

"In a state that starts with the letter C," I mutter to take my mind off the piece of steel pressing on my face with great force. (The intent of the contraption is to extract blackheads that I've always been told I should not squeeze.)

"It can't be California," my new friend says. "You said you're not from California."

"That's right."

"I'll bet you're from Connecticut."

"No. Go farther west."

After several minutes of thinking very hard and continuing her ritualistic torture, the woman says, "Colorado. You're from Colorado."

"You got it, Chantal." I'm proud that I finally pronounced her name correctly.

"So do you get to see the presidents' heads a lot?" she asks.

At first I'm a bit confused, but then Chantal must be all the time. "Oh, you're thinking of Mount Rushmore. But that's in South Dakota. I live in Denver."

"And South Dakota starts with an S," she goes on.

"Yes, it does."

More pain, and hopefully some gain.

"You know, I like your name, Chantal. What does it mean?"

"I don't know. My mother named us all after mountains . . . or was it hurricanes?"

*Doug would never go for that.*

After the initial discomfort, I enjoy my full-body treatment. The flickering candles and wonderful aromas put me in a blissful state, and the pedicure and massage finish the job.

When it's over, I look great and feel relaxed, and I don't want to leave. "I'm not moving, Chantal. I'm sorry."

"But you have to," she says, looking immensely worried. "I have customers waiting."

She and her IQ may never be accepted in Mensa, but she is cute.

The desert heat dies. I put on a sweater and stand on the balcony. No one is at the pool.

"Look at that desert moon, baby." I pat my stomach.

"You talked to your baby!" Allie shouts from the bed.

"I'm not an ogre," I say.

"I know. It's just touching, that's all."

I come inside and eat my pillow chocolate, even though I'm still stuffed from dinner. "That meal was something, wasn't it? Especially the Norwegian salmon."

She walks into the night and I follow her.

"What's it like?" she asks, staring somewhere in the sky.

"You ate it too."

"I mean the baby. Carrying life inside you." Her voice sounds distant.

I think of how to describe the experience.

"I may never know it, Becca . . . except through you," Allie says softly. A lone tear spills down her cheek and glitters in the moonlight.

I choose my words carefully. "Apart from all the worries, the responsibilities, the fears—it is fantastic."

She smiles and wipes her tear.

"It's a privilege to carry a life inside you. A privilege I can't seem to grasp right now. I feel so terrible about it."

"It's okay. It *will be* okay." Allie reaches over and gives me a reassuring hug.

"When I stop to think about it, that's when it scares me. It's so much bigger than me."

"And you can't control it?"

"Is that what it is?" I ask.

"I don't know."

"Yes, you do."

"No, I don't. I get paid to analyze people's emotions, but some things are God's secrets, revealed in time. And until they are revealed, they're safe with him."

For a moment we listen to the song of the desert wind. It sounds vast and far reaching.

"I'm sorry for my frailty, Allie. I wish I were strong like you," I manage.

"Our human frailties do not discount God's gifts. And I am not strong or perfect or anything else."

"Are you going to blow your diet again tomorrow?"

"Yes," she says with certainty. "'Squeeze the sky into a thimble,' my mama used to say. And let me tell you something. My mama was always right."

She breaks into sobs, and I hold her.

"See—I'm not strong at all. Everybody just thinks I am." Her words come out muffled.

I sob with her. We are two rivers flowing together.

We finally break apart. I pull tissues out of the box on the tile-covered round table. We wipe each other's tears.

"Hey, let's go for a late-night swim," I suggest. "No one's in the pool."

"Right now?"

"Yes, now. I don't want to be seen in a bathing suit in daylight."

"It's not cold," I insist.

But it *is* cold. I inch into the pool that feels like a frigid ocean.

"Try it," I tell Allie, who is shivering at the edge of the pool. I pull her in, and myself in the process. We flinch from the temperature. And then we splash until our teeth stop chattering. Under the moonlight we forget about all our cares.

"This reminds me of being a teenager," I say, breathless. "Only then I weighed one hundred pounds, soaking wet."

"One hundred fifteen," Allie asserts.

We float for a moment, and then our eyes meet again.

"You were in love with Kevin Shriver, Becca. Remember?"

"I wasn't in love; I just liked his hair."

"He's bald now. I mean *totally*."

"And you, Allie, were in love with Frank."

"Frank Stevenson." She reminisces with pleasure. "We went to the same church all our lives. He even taught me to tie my shoes."

"He married Betty something, didn't he?"

"Bunny, not Betty," Allie corrects me. She sighs. "I should have married him when he asked me."

"Frank asked you to marry him?"

"In the seventh grade . . . or maybe it was the fifth grade."

"You would have been Allie Stevenson."

"He used to quote me a Robert Louis Stevenson poem. He said they were related."

"I'm just glad I didn't marry Kevin Shriver. I wouldn't have my incredible husband."

"Or beautiful children and wonderful life," Allie adds.

"Oh no." I sniff my wet hair. "I smell like lavender and chlorine." I close my eyes and dip.

When I emerge, Allie is pointing to the sky. "Over there . . . a falling star!"

"Catch it, Allie, quick."

"It slipped between my fingers."

"We'll try again tomorrow night," I assure her.

# Chapter

# Fourteen

Sunny morning. What else would one expect of April in Palm Springs?

"What's on today's agenda?" I line my lips in mango to accentuate my new glowing skin. I fling my freshly cut hair in the air.

"Breaking my diet, shopping, breaking my diet, a massage, then breaking my diet . . . ," Allie says, fully dressed and ready to go somewhere.

"Oh, I never want to leave this enchanting hideaway." I twirl in beige capris and a solid blue T-shirt. "Can we stay here forever?"

"Doug may not like that," Allie points out.

"The whole family can live here."

"I don't think so, Becca. This place is nearly three hundred a night."

"I guess not, then."

"Guess not."

"How about the Palm Springs aerial tram today?" I suggest.

"No thanks. I'm terrified of heights."

"It's only eight thousand feet."

"Oh, just eight thousand," she begins, sounding a bit frantic.

"Don't you want to 'ascend into a pristine wilderness'?" I ask, reading the brochure.

"Ascending is fine; it's the *descending* I'm worried about." She wrinkles her brow.

"Tell me, then, how you can fly thousands of feet in the air with no problem?" I bite into a banana for potassium and take a slug of cream for calcium.

"I'm fine on planes. But I almost flipped out on the *Queen Mary* last year when I was a bridesmaid and never a bride." She smiles, a crooked sort of smile. "I was standing on the bow looking down and, all of a sudden, developed a fear of high places."

"But you have to overcome your fears. That's what you tell your patients," I say, hoping guilt will be effective.

"I am not my patient."

After a continental breakfast, poolside, we walk downtown and browse the shops and galleries.

"I'm up for some more adventure. So what's to do around here?"

Allie looks at a brochure. "Spa hopping."

"Two days in a row?"

"I know what you mean. It would be like eating at a smorgasbord twice in one week."

"So why don't you buy something big, Allie?"

"Like what?"

"A piece of art, an expensive purse . . ." I begin to dream.

"To tell you the truth, material things don't excite me the way they used to."

"You mean that, don't you?"

"Yes, I do."

"Well, we could run barefoot through the desert," I suggest.

"And the purpose of plaguing our feet with cactus stickers would be . . . ?"

"The experience of it."

Allie laughs so loud she snorts. "Yeah, cactus stickers in your feet sounds like a blast."

"Okay, we'll wear tennis shoes."

Allie shakes her head. "You always did have odd ideas. Remember the time you made us climb that water tower for nothing?"

"That was before your fear of heights," I offer quickly. "And there was a view. Not a good one, but a view."

"And when we were eleven, you had the brilliant idea of painting all the neighbor's mailboxes in coordinating colors," she recalls.

"Are you sure that wasn't your idea?"

"I'm sure. But I got punished, regardless."

I change the subject. "I'm happy to go for a little walk, check out some of the side streets."

"I'll go for that."

A few blocks from downtown, I see a lit sign that says Bingo.

"Look—bingo." I point to the sign.

"I love bingo," Allie says, and she is serious.

"That would be about my pace," I agree.

We pass the senior-citizen center and walk another half block.

"My mom loved to play bingo. Sometimes I'd go with her," Allie says wistfully.

"We can do it if you want to."

"But it's silly, Becca."

"That's the point. Something different." I stop and look at my watch. "It's only eleven o'clock."

"Okay then."

We walk in the senior center.

"This is great, Allie! I feel centuries younger."

"Hello, ladies." A man named George introduces himself and says that he's a veteran from World War II. Then he tells us to find a seat and laughs hysterically for no reason.

George reminds me of my grandfather, who died when I was nine.

90

The room seems to be full of fun-loving seniors, but we soon find out they're rather serious about their game.

"Shh," a woman scolds when Allie asks if we can sit next to her. She's got three cards she's working at the same time.

"Go ahead," she offers. "But hold the talk until the next round."

"Have you ever played canasta?" I ask Allie.

"No, what is it?"

"I'm not sure," I admit. "But they play it on *I Love Lucy.*"

"I can talk now," the woman sitting next to Allie says and introduces herself as Geraldine.

"Hi, Geraldine. I'm Allie, and this is Becca."

I smile and wave.

"Sounds like a TV show," Geraldine comments.

"Do you watch a lot of TV?" Allie asks.

"Not very much. But I do admit to watching *Fear Factor* every now and then, when I'm not eating dinner."

I like Geraldine, because she's wearing purple and has kind eyes.

Across the table an argument ensues. Two ladies fight over who gets what bingo card, and the man distributing them sets his jaw stubbornly.

"You look middle age," Geraldine tells Allie.

"What does middle age mean to you, Geraldine?"

And I laugh, because I can picture Allie sitting in her counselor chair and taking notes.

I don't hear her answer.

The woman next to me whispers that I'm lucky to get Anna's favorite seat. She said Anna got a bee up her bonnet and took Marilyn with her. "One day she's going to have to learn to stand up for herself!"

"Who?" I ask.

"Marilyn."

"And how old is Marilyn?"

"Ninety." The feisty woman clears her bingo card. "No,

ninety-one. She had a birthday last week. I'm getting forgetful these days."

Allie and I each pay twenty-five cents for a card. Everyone pays attention as a new game starts.

"G-fifty," the caller says. After I place my piece of plastic, I study the caller's face, which does not match his voice. I study his face for a long time until I finally realize he reminds me of Ernest Borgnine with his caterpillar eyebrows and gap-toothed grin.

He waits for everyone to place their markers and then continues, "O-sixty-six."

"Bingo!" someone yells.

The caller ignores him, knowing that bingo is impossible at this point in the game. The game proceeds as sober seniors concentrate on the numbers. A few minutes later, Allie's card is dotted with plastic. Mine is sparse.

Eventually someone yells, "Bingo!" for real, and arms go up all over the room pointing to the winner, in case the guy with the goods is hard of hearing.

Allie purchases three cards, like Geraldine, and another game begins. I am more interested in the people than the game. I stick to my one card.

Across from me I watch a man falling asleep. A minute later he is facedown, snoring on his bingo card. When the man next to him taps his shoulder, he sits up straight and yells, "Bingo!" Then he starts reading his winning row, even though he doesn't have one.

Everyone laughs, and the caller yells, "Let's take a cookie break," right in the middle of the spin.

"He does that all the time, and it drives us crazy," Geraldine informs us in a confidential tone. "But at least he's honest. We've had some callers who weren't."

"They weren't?" I ask.

"No, they cheated so their friends could get the Froot Loops."

Two hours later the bingo session is over. We didn't win anything, but we had a good time.

The woman sitting next to me is drumming her fingers on her forehead and staring at me.

"Is your father the actor?" she asks.

"No, my father is a retired postman."

"Do I know him?" For a minute her eyes look cloudy, confused. "I don't think so."

"Is he married?"

"Yes, he is . . . to my mother." I somehow manage not to grin.

"What a shame." She clutches her black evening purse. "All the good ones are married." She collects her plastic bags of pills.

I smile at her, but she's looking somewhere else.

"See that couple over there?" She points to a man in a broad-brimmed golf hat and the woman with silver blue hair next to him.

"Yes," I say.

"They are tying the knot next week."

"Really?"

"He swept her off her feet. And she deserves it. She was so low after she lost Harry to cancer last year."

"Oh, that's too bad," I sympathize. "It must be hard after all those years to have to sleep alone."

"Naw. She has five more."

"Husbands?"

"No—cats, honey."

I turn my attention to Geraldine, who is telling Allie she wins at least once a week. "Last month they had a special prize day, and I won some tickets to the Palm Springs Follies."

"That's nice," Allie responds.

Geraldine's eyes sparkle. "You know, I'm a little jealous of those showgirls. The way they get to prance around in those colorful feathered outfits."

"Really, Geraldine?" Allie asks, with genuine interest.

"Especially my friend Doris. She can kick up some action, but then she's still in her seventies."

"Seventies?" I ask.

"Yes, all the cast members are seniors."

Allie puts her arm around Geraldine. "How old are you, Geraldine? If you don't mind me asking."

"Old enough for the follies."

"How old?" Allie pries.

"Eighty-one," Geraldine admits and smiles.

The seniors are taking up their gear. Slowly they exit the building. Some walk unassisted; others have wheelchairs; others have canes and walkers. All of the men are wearing hats.

Geraldine is taking her time.

"Can we drive you home?" Allie offers.

"Perhaps you can. I walked over here, but the old legs are a little tired today."

Geraldine's apartment is cluttered with clay. She is a sculptress.

"I started sculpting when I was seventy-eight, but I suppose the talent was always there."

While she and Allie chit-chat, I examine every inch of Geraldine's beautiful sculptures.

"Do you have children?" Allie asks.

"Yes, but they don't fool with me," she says, sounding forlorn. "I was what you call 'a career woman.'"

"What did you do?" Allie asks.

"I was the city clerk in San Bernardino. But I didn't spend much time with my children. Lots of late meetings and bad coffee. Anyway, they grew up resenting me and thinking my husband, Harold, was a saint."

"Oh, Geraldine." Allie holds the old woman's wrinkled hand.

"It's all right, honey. God has forgiven me."

We both hug her good-bye.

Geraldine shuts the door, and on the other side, we hear her loud, sad voice: "Treat your children well, ladies. Time is like a rocket."

*I hope you have a good life, Geraldine.*

# Chapter

# Fifteen

After a burger at the infamous Tyler's Diner, Allie seems in a reflective mood and suggests we take a drive. I wholeheartedly agree.

"Where do you want to go?" she asks as she turns the key to the ignition.

"I don't care, Allie. Anywhere."

Out of town the stretch of road is peaceful. But I cannot stay awake to enjoy the drive.

"Where are we?" I query some time later as I fight my heavy eyelids.

"Twenty-five fifty-five Mountain View Drive," Allie announces. Suddenly that address sounds all-too-familiar to me.

"Not my sister's house. You better tell me we are not at my *sister's* house!" I wail. I open my eyes wide and sit up as rigid as a column.

"I can't tell you that because we are at Valerie's house," Allie responds calmly.

I take off my DKNY sunglasses. "How did you even find it?"

"I was driving around, and there was Mountain View Drive right in front of me."

And then I am very upset with Allie.

Allie doesn't understand why I'm mad. It's evident by the surprise on her face, the look that says *I'm trying to do a good thing, so what's wrong with you?*

"What were you thinking, Allison Catherine Ray?" I fume.

"That you two could work out your differences."

"Oh no. Here she comes." I sit awkwardly, shoulders tense, as Valerie, looking graceful in a pastel sundress, takes steps in our direction.

Allie frowns at me. "She's your *sister*, for goodness' sake—not a terrorist who's going to blow you up."

"You don't really know my sister, then. She can demolish me with her words."

"I'm sorry," Allie says, but it's too late.

"Becca?" Valerie is peering in the window.

Allie lets the windows down. I would like her to drive away.

"It *is* you. What are you doing here?" Her voice is as syrupy as I remember.

"Allie and I are on vacation," I say casually and smile. But inside I'm bouncing off the walls.

"Oh, Allie. It's good to see you too. Come in, you guys." She walks toward her house.

I roll up the window.

"See," Allie whispers to me. "She's happy to see you."

"Just look at me. I'm a mess, Allie." I study my face and hair in the mirror.

"You look great," Allie soothes.

Valerie turns around and smiles. "I'll meet you in the house," she calls and waves slowly, royally.

Allie appears unsure.

I can barely find the handle to open my car door.

"I think you're overreacting," Allie says.

And that is so the wrong thing to say to a pregnant woman.

I smile, weakly, as we step into Valerie's generously windowed living room. When we were growing up, Valerie always said she'd have a house like this—one with a huge pool and spa and decorative accent tiles.

As we reach the French doors, Valerie waves like Carol Merrill on *Let's Make a Deal*, only more obvious.

"What is that supposed to mean, Valerie?" I ask, even though I know exactly what it means.

"It's overlooking the fourth green." It's clear she anticipates praise.

"I wouldn't know a fourth green from a fifth blue."

"No, I guess you wouldn't."

The thing is, I don't want a house in the desert; I don't even want a pool. I love my modest house and the tepee Doug set up in our backyard so we can pretend we're camping. So why am I bothered that my sister has what she wants?

"What are you doing these days?" Valerie asks Allie, an arm around her like she's *her* best friend, not mine.

"I'm a licensed professional counselor, starting my own practice," Allie explains.

"Impressive," Valerie says. Then she turns to me. "You have dry skin, Becca." She reaches for a bottle of moisturizer and squeezes too much peach-smelling lotion in my palm. I share with Allie.

"Oh, she doesn't need that. Her skin looks great." Valerie scrapes the lotion off Allie's hand. "I'll take the excess."

"Thanks," Allie says calmly, but her features look a little pinched.

I feel the big chill in more ways than one. Besides her frigid demeanor, Valerie's powerful air conditioning is trying to blast me out of the universe.

I start thinking about the past, about how Valerie always got straight As without studying while I had to study hard to get Bs; how she was president of her senior class, and I was only secretary;

how she had more boyfriends then she knew what to do with and still found it necessary to steal my only boyfriend.

"So I see you finally got a new car," Valerie says to me as she invites us to sit down on her plush sofa with another wave. "What is it? A Ford?"

"It's a rental car, Valerie. We flew into John Wayne."

"You could have gotten a direct flight into Palm Springs, you know. It is an international airport. Or you could have at least flown into Ontario."

"Doug planned this trip as a surprise for me, and I was just happy to be coming. No matter what airport, Valerie."

"But Palm Springs is right here. Why would you—"

Allie interrupts. "I'm flying back to Atlanta when Becca flies back to Denver, so Doug and I thought it would be better to fly out of Orange County."

"Oh, I see," Valerie says, like it suddenly makes sense to her.

Even though the couch is comfortable, I feel uncomfortable. I don't know what to do with my hands.

"So do you still live in that same house?" Valerie asks. "The one with the tepee in the backyard?"

*She knows we do. She just sent me a postcard from the Bahamas.*

"Yes. In fact, we redecorated since the family reunion last year," I say proudly.

"The tepee?"

"No, not the tepee. We added on a bedroom and turned the unfinished basement into a family room. Doug is doing very well in the firm now."

"Speaking of firms, my Randy is doing beyond well," Valerie interjects.

*Beyond well. What is beyond well?*

"He's a senior partner at the law firm now."

"Yes, you mentioned that in your postcard. Your last *two* postcards."

I change the subject before she goes into a two-hour brag session. "I'm dying of thirst. Do you mind getting us a glass of water?"

"Not at all. I'll get you some sun tea. I do wish Camille were here, though."

"Who is Camille?" I ask.

"Our maid."

"Well, if it's too much trouble, Valerie, I can get my own."

"No, of course not. I'll be right back." She points toward a thick leather photo album. "You haven't asked about your nephew. Luke is doing fantastic. He's attending Randy's alma mater, Stanford, in the fall. Is Logan considering community college when he graduates next year?"

She leaves the room before I have a chance to say.

I sigh, like I'm balancing an elephant on my shoulders.

"Maybe I won't even mention that I'm pregnant," I whisper.

Allie looks like she's trying not to say the wrong thing.

I flip through the creative memory album that is so much better than my attempts. "Luke really is a nice kid."

"He's very handsome," Allie says.

I sigh with exasperation. "I can't believe myself. I can't believe how little I've grown in spirit. Last year we went through a Bible study on letting go, and I thought I'd put all this pettiness behind me. But obviously I haven't, because I would like to wring my sister's neck right now."

"I'd venture to say that Valerie isn't as happy as you think she is. I think she's insecure."

"If there is anything that Valerie is not, it's insecure."

I thumb through the rest of the album pages and then shut Valerie's living memorial to her son.

My sister returns with the tea and sees the closed album. "Did you get a good enough look at it?"

"I sure did. It's beautiful."

We take a few sips of tea.

"I was thinking in the kitchen that maybe I should ship you some of Luke's used clothes for Logan. They're all still in good shape, and name-brand, of course."

"You mean castoffs, like we used to share when we were growing up?" I ask. The heat is rising in my voice; I just can't help it.

"Well, you and I really didn't do much of that. You and Lillie did more of that. You two are—"

"Shorter?"

"Let's say you take after Mom's side of the family, and I take after Dad's."

"Yes, I suppose I do," I say.

"Becca, stand up!" Valerie commands.

I oblige, without thinking. I drop my arms at my side and feel fat. She scrutinizes me. "Have you gained weight?"

"Well, actually I just found out I'm pregnant." I pat my belly and grimace.

"*Again?*" she asks, severely.

"You make it sound like I'm a breeding machine, Valerie."

"No. I'm very happy for you, really. If that's what you want. It's just *I* can't imagine it. For me."

"Well at your age, I guess not."

"I'm twenty months older than you, Becca, not a century. I was referring to the general monotony of it."

"In other words, your life is perfect just as it is?"

She thinks for a moment and then flatly states, "Yes, it is."

"How fortunate for you," I throw in.

"I am rather fortunate," she says, trying to make it sound like a joke.

I want to leave right now. But then Allie develops a sudden interest in golf. She points to the golf course and asks if it is a PGA golf course, and before Valerie can answer that question, Allie starts talking about golf, like she knows it.

"It sure is something that Arnold Palmer is retiring."

That conversation goes on for a while, because Valerie says her husband is very into golf, and she has to show us his boring trophy room.

And then Valerie leads us back to the couch and Allie leads us to common ground, because, after all, she is a counselor.

"It really is great," Allie begins, "that you all were raised in a non-Christian home, and yet most of your brothers and sisters are Christians now, even though they live in different places."

"It is amazing," I say, and Valerie agrees.

Allie asks how all that came about, even though she already knows.

For a time we uncross our arms and forget about ourselves. We discuss God's grace and how he works everything out for good.

To tell you the truth, I don't understand most of the reasons Valerie and I have this sisterly competition going on. Allie said it has something to do with competing for parental favor way back, and I don't know about all that. All I know is that my sister has my remote control and can push my buttons like nobody I know.

"I'm sorry I wasn't able to see Randy or Luke," I tell her as we stand at the car under fair skies.

"Well, I understand that your time is limited. After all, you do have a large family to get back to. Laundry and dishes and all that."

"Yes, I suppose I do."

"And, really, I need to select my meals for the week."

"Select your meals?" Allie asks, because I won't.

"Yes, Camille actually had a menu printed up with pictures and descriptions to select from. Salmon, shrimp . . ."

"It must be such a strain on your brain, trying to decide such important matters," I add, thinking myself witty.

"Not at all. After all I *am* the smarter sister." She cocks her head at Allie. "It's a private joke."

"I don't think there's anything you keep private, Valerie." I turn to Allie. "She saw it fit to share my diary with her class once."

"That was only after you stained my favorite blouse with ketchup, though," she counters.

"It was an accident, but somehow my sister would not believe that." I wag my finger.

"Only because you took it without asking."

I start in, intent on being right. "Look who's talking about taking things without asking! You seemed to help yourself to anything and everything, no matter who it belonged to!"

Unless Allie smothers these sparks of sibling rivalry, we will *never* get out of here, and she knows it.

"I think a very nice way to end this afternoon would be with prayer. Do you mind if I pray with you?" she asks, one hand on each of our shoulders.

"Of course not," I say.

"No. That would be fine," Valerie replies.

We listen as Allie speaks truth.

# Chapter
# Sixteen

Allie drives, because I am too emotional. We don't speak for at least five minutes.

Then I ask the obvious question. "*Now* do you see why I didn't want to visit Valerie?"

Allie belts out her answer. "My goodness, you two are strong-willed!"

"Just a friendly competition," I say guiltily.

"Friendly competition?" she asks in an even louder voice. "There is *nothing friendly* about your competition. You two make me ecstatic to be an only child."

I examine my fingernails and yawn.

"I'd love to attend one of *your* family reunions," Allie states sarcastically.

"The rest of us get along fine. It's just this thing between Valerie and me."

"That *thing* is a dragon, Becca. From ancient days."

"I know. I need a dragon slayer."

"We know a dragon slayer," Allie says.

I get what she's saying, but I'm not sure I'm ready for it yet. There's been too much water under the bridge.

# Tight Squeeze

We don't say anything more until Allie drives by Geraldine's condominium.

"Taking a shortcut?"

"I just can't stop thinking about Geraldine. She seems so lonely."

"We can visit her if you want," I offer.

"Now?"

"Of course."

Allie turns the car around and parks in front of Geraldine's condominium complex. Her eyes dim and lower, and a sad look comes over her face.

"Tomorrow is the anniversary of my mother's death."

"I'm know and I'm sorry." I pat her knee.

She turns off the motor and stares ahead in guarded silence.

*Was I there for her? Enough? Did I know how much she was hurting?*

Allie's mom was one of those moms everybody wants. My mom was a good mom. She did the laundry and cooked and all that. But with ten children, most of the time she just spread her love around.

Allie's mother raised her alone. She was there for all her daughter's significant moments, cheering her on, saying all the right things.

Things will never be the same for her.

Allie finally speaks. "My mother's love was like a blanket. She made me feel like I could do anything. I never once missed having a father."

I nod to show I'm listening.

"I still remember her bandaging my first skinned knee. The color of the bandage, the color of her fingernail polish even. Everything good that I am came from her."

To say that I understand wouldn't be true. How could I understand?

Again, silence reigns. I watch a gardener working in the cactus garden. Two birds land in a fruit tree.

105

I sever the silence and the sadness with my brilliant idea. "Let's take Geraldine to the Palm Springs Follies tonight. She would love it."

"You know, she would at that." Allie smiles at me appreciatively.

✐⚘✐

Geraldine looks changed in the three hours since we've seen her. Her makeup has been removed, and she is wearing curlers and a bathrobe. But she is happy to see us.

"Come in, ladies." She pulls off her scarf and rips curlers out of her hair, then stuffs the curlers in her terry pockets, exposing her gray ringlets.

We sit down. Allie and Geraldine take the floral couch; I take the rocking chair. Allie holds Geraldine's blue-veined hand in hers.

After Geraldine goes on awhile about the sale on canned vegetables and plant fertilizer, Allie shares our idea.

Geraldine hesitates. "I'd love to, but I can't afford—"

"Our treat, Geraldine. Our treat," Allie insists. "That is, if you don't mind seeing the show again."

"I can never get enough of those high kickers."

"Great," Allie and I chime.

"We'll even take you out to dinner beforehand," Allie adds.

A smile spreads over Geraldine's face. She squints at the clock. "Would you mind if I excused myself to take a shower, ladies? I am stickier than honey."

"We have plenty of time. Plenty of time," Allie says quickly, then turns serious for a moment. "Geraldine, can we invite your children to come along? You said they live in San Bernardino."

"That's right, they do," she states flatly. But she's seemingly unmoved by the suggestion.

"Can I call them?" Allie asks.

"They won't come, I promise you that. But Linda's number is on the front of the phone book over there." She points.

"Can I try?" Allie continues.

"Do what you want, honey, but be prepared for an earful, and I do mean an earful." She hesitates, then concludes, "There's no use even trying to call my son."

Geraldine's slippers flop away, and a missed curler falls and bounces. When the door shuts, I whisper to Allie, "Is this a good idea?"

"We have to try, Becca. If we don't, we'll be thinking of it for weeks."

"*We* won't, but *you* will."

"Would you call Linda, Becca?"

"Me? Why me?"

"I don't know if I can get through it without getting too emotional."

"Well, sure . . . okay."

I sit on the end of the floral couch, holding the frayed phone book, and dial the black rotary phone.

"Hello."

The voice on the other end is pleasant.

"Linda?" I ask.

"Yes, this is Linda."

"My name is Becca. You don't know me, but I'm a friend of your mother's."

"You don't sound like a friend of my mother's."

"A younger friend, a new friend."

"Listen, if you're from her church . . ." Linda's voice takes on an edge.

"No, I'm not. I just wanted to invite you to the Palm Springs Follies tonight. My friend, Allie, and I have invited your mother. It would be our treat. We could have dessert afterward and talk."

"Listen, Becca, or whatever your name is, hear this: my mother did nothing for me. My whole life she served us TV dinners. It was my father who was there. If you look through all those picture albums of hers, my mother took hardly one of those pictures. It was my dad who was there for us. When he died, my brother and I were orphans as far as I'm concerned."

"I know you feel—"

"And I wouldn't go calling my brother, by the way. He won't be so nice. He has a more colorful vocabulary than I do, and his temper is much worse."

"But . . ."

"Waste your good deeds on someone who needs it."

"Linda, your mother is old. When she's gone, there won't be a chance for reconciliation," I try.

"My mother shut me out of her life for years. Now she knows what it feels like to be alone."

"Do you realize that she could die and no one would know?"

"She's got that stupid parrot of hers. Let *him* mourn her. Have fun at the show!"

*Click.*

"Becca. Becca . . ."

I flinch. I've been in la-la land again for a moment. There's a grievous look on Allie's face.

Suddenly the heat seems unbearable.

"Allie, please turn up the air conditioner."

Allie does.

I swing the phone in small circles . . . and then bigger circles.

Allie eyes me expectantly.

"She was *awful*, Allie." I return the receiver to its cradle.

"What did she say?"

"She said a lot of things. She said don't bother calling her brother. To let Geraldine's parrot mourn her."

"Her parrot? She doesn't have a parrot."

An empty wrought-iron birdcage sits in the corner of the room, partially covered by an old burnt-orange cloth.

Allie lowers her head. I am more concerned about her than

Geraldine. Her tears fall like raindrops, watering the commercial carpet.

"Poor Geraldine," she utters sorrowfully.

Doris Rawley's voice rings out as sure as Liza Minelli's. She dances with vigor, dignity, and attitude.

"Isn't she something, ladies?" Geraldine is on the rim of her seat, wearing a purple dress that looks hand-sewn, as the vaudeville sisters join Doris, dancing to Rockette-style music.

"Did I tell you? Did I tell you ladies they were something?"

"You certainly did, Geraldine." Allie smiles at me, a most excellent smile.

Watching Allie and Geraldine arm in arm gives me more pleasure than the show. It seems Allie has found herself a substitute mother.

When I had told Geraldine her children weren't coming, she had simply said, "As you sow, so shall you reap." And those were her only words on the subject. Before more could be said, she had gone to the kitchen to arrange a plate of Triscuits and Velveeta. And then she had shared, in great detail, the background of the dancers—beginning with Emma Lee, age fifty-five, and ending with Mary Jo Bruckner, age eighty-six.

The three-hour extravaganza, with jokes in-between, is a great diversion from my earlier bout with Valerie. It also gives me hope that I still have some good years left, because these ladies can kick higher than I can.

A standing ovation ends the evening.

When we drop Geraldine at her door, she urges us to come in for tea. We thank her but decline the invitation. The whole condominium complex is asleep, and I wish Allie and Geraldine would hurry their good-byes. I've already said good-bye, but Allie lingers at the threshold of Geraldine's door. Her eyes rest on the old woman's face.

It's clear Allie doesn't want to leave.

"I'll be in the car," I say as I walk away.

"I might have been one of those high kickers. Harold always said I had the legs for it. What did you think, Allie? Do you think I missed my calling? That I might have been a dancer?" I hear Geraldine ask.

I walk slower, to hear Allie's answer.

"You *are* a dancer, Geraldine. In your heart you are a dancer."

# Chapter

# Seventeen

*Free movies tonight*, the pink slip on our turned-down bed says.

We pick up two DVDs at the front desk. I pick one for Allie; she picks one for me.

Allie watches *The Princess Diaries* first, which my family owns and I've seen a million times, but Allie hasn't. She cries through a great deal of it, and I laugh because she's crying. I am so entertained by watching the usually cool Allie blowing her nose and bawling.

"You'll enjoy this one," Allie tells me as she puts on the DVD.

I adjust my pillows and settle in for theater surround sound.

By some fluke I've never seen *Ever After*. I remember all the mothers of the daughters on Tawny's cheerleading squad chastising me for not seeing it. I'm hoping it's as good as they say.

A few minutes into the story, I get that this is a Cinderella thing. Not exactly what I need to see with my own sister complex, but well done for a Cinderella remake.

Allie falls asleep with a devotional book. I gently tug it from her fingers and tuck her in like I do my younger children—and occasionally my older children when they have a bad day.

I go back to watching my movie.

Poor Cinderella is the ridicule of her sisters and stepmother, and although it has a simply wondrous storyline and I know the happy ending by heart, I am mostly mad at Cinderella's unfair circumstances and wish I had popcorn so I could throw it at the horrible stepsisters.

It is the next morning, the sunshine tells me.

"What time is it?" I ask, not fully awake.

"Eight o'clock," Allie replies, too happy for me.

"Why so early?" I moan.

"Because we're on vacation."

"Aren't you supposed to sleep in when you're on vacation?"

"Not when you're with me," Allie proclaims. "I feel like eating something solid. That rich man's dinner didn't cut it for me."

With our car running in the parking lot I ask, "Why Denny's?"

"Because there are three of them in Palm Springs," Allie answers.

I'm not sure that having three Denny's is a valid excuse for eating there, but because I'm so tired, I relent. "Why are there three of them?"

"Maybe not everybody in Palm Springs is as rich as we think. Plus they have the Grand Slam Breakfast. Two of almost everything a diner could possibly want." Allie spouts the words like she's doing a commercial.

The hostess seats us and gives us menus.

"Oh goodie," I exclaim. "We get to select our meals from a menu like Valerie does."

"The Grand Slam or the French Slam?" Allie asks.

"The French Slam sounds more sophisticated."

"The Farmers' Slam looks good. But it has gravy," Allie says.

"So what, Allie? Live it up."

"I'm back on my diet as of today. Remember, the class reunion is coming up."

"In a couple of years." I roll my eyes and catch myself doing it. Allie flips the menu.

"Five pounds, Allie. You told me, and I quote, 'I can handle five pounds.'"

"I think it's more like ten with the way I've been eating."

"I've accepted the fact that I'm going to get fat," I say.

"Well, your fat is for a worthy cause. I'm ordering the Slim Slam." Allie closes the menu with determination.

I can't make up my mind, but I put the menu down anyway. "I'm having a strange thought."

She grins. "How unusual."

"Stranger than *usual*," I counter. "I'm coming up with this incredibly creative way to forgive my sister, because I've thought of nothing but my sister since yesterday."

"Haven't you heard of prayer?"

"Seriously, Allie. I'm like a pretzel over Valerie, especially after that movie last night. And I think I have the solution: making myself a gift basket."

She looks puzzled. "Why not just send yourself flowers?"

"You're not getting it, Allie."

"So explain."

"I'm not sure how."

"Try. Just try."

"All right. When we were growing up, Valerie always made me feel less than perfect."

"You mean you *allowed* her to make you feel less than perfect," Allie analyzes.

I wrinkle my nose. "Whatever. Anyway, I'm taking back what I *allowed* Valerie to take from me—in a symbolic way. The gift basket would have all the things that Valerie stole from me."

"For instance . . ."

"Like how she always made me feel dumb. I'll buy a really smart book to read, like *War and Peace*."

"Hmm. *War and Peace?* That's a very long novel. I've read it, and it was a challenge getting through it."

"She tore up my favorite Donny Osmond poster, so I'll buy a new one."

"I don't think you're going to find one." Allie stares at another diner's plate and licks her lips. "Besides, Donny has crow's-feet now, you know."

"It doesn't have to be Donny. It can be anything I like."

"I think I'm getting it." Allie cleans her teal glasses with her napkin.

I continue. "And you know how she's always referring to how short I am, compared to her? I'll buy a pair of shorts in her favorite color."

Allie chuckles as she puts on her glasses. "Shorts with a stretch panel? How fun."

I hadn't thought of it.

An hour later we're in Longs drugstore. My shopping cart is full of economical treasures.

"Oh, a football key chain!" I exclaim.

"Football? What for?"

"The boyfriend Valerie stole from me. Roger Bedford."

"You told me you didn't even like him, Becca."

"And a hairbrush," I say, excited (even though I already own three because Tawny is always borrowing mine). "Valerie was always taking my brush and claiming she didn't. Like I didn't notice her long hair strands stuck in the bristles." I throw it on the pile, not even trying to disguise my resentment.

"You can't fit all this in a gift basket; you're going to have to get a big box for all this stuff." Allie examines a bottle of dark blue nail polish among my goodies (long story).

I ignore her. "And chocolate." I throw a couple of Hershey bars in the cart.

"Valerie stole your chocolate too?"

"No. That's for comfort. A girl needs comfort when she has a sister like Valerie, you know."

"Well, okay." Allie adds a couple of Dove bars to my greed.

On the next aisle, I reach for a Barbie dressed in a rock-star outfit. "Oh, and she cut my best Barbie's hair into this pitiful Dorothy Hamill haircut."

"A Barbie? Now this is getting ridiculous."

"You're right. I'll take Scrabble instead. Valerie was always better than me in Scrabble, and she loved to flaunt it."

"You already have Scrabble," Allie says, perturbed.

"Not Super Scrabble."

"You can't take Scrabble on the plane; it's too big. Get a grip, Becca."

We spend the rest of the morning downtown, hobnobbing with the rich and famous, even though they don't know we're hobnobbing with them.

We browse the eclectic shops and boutiques, and even though we aren't hungry, we eat an Auntie Anne's pretzel and a Penguin's frozen yogurt.

I pick up a T-shirt for Logan, a bracelet for Tawny, a book on art for Ben, and some cute socks for Carly. *I still need to buy Doug his favorite gourmet lollipops, the kind that don't melt,* I remind myself as we sit on a stone bench.

*Melt.*

"Oh no, that chocolate I bought is going to melt, Allie."

"Yes, chocolate usually does melt in the desert."

"Did you think of it?"

Allie smiles like a fox.

I sigh for my foolishness.

She tilts her head. "So do you feel better? Did your spree help you forgive your sister?"

I shrug, a little mad at Allie for being so direct.

"You have enough beauty products to host a cosmetologists' convention."

"Well, Valerie was always taking my stuff," I fire back in defense.

"Listen, Becca. I don't mean to sound like a counselor . . ."

"You are a counselor, and you always sound like a counselor." I cross my arms, sigh, and then uncross my arms. "But I love you anyway."

"That shopping spree isn't about your sister, is it?" she asks, looking straight into my self-centered eyes.

"It isn't?"

"No. It's about your own insecurity," she explains. "You and Valerie are a lot alike."

"But you like me better, right?"

"I'm not even going to answer that," she says.

I sigh again.

"You know John 21?"

I squirm. "Not off the top of my head. Do you?"

"Well, it was in my devotional last night. In it Jesus tells about Peter's death and then talks about John's future."

"I know it now."

"But the part that's important is when Peter asks Jesus, 'Lord, what about him?' And Jesus says this to Peter, 'What is it to you? Follow me.'"

I feel small—smaller than small.

Diminutive.

Miniscule.

You couldn't find me with the most powerful microscope in the world—that's how small I am.

"And I would ask *you* the same question," she says, sounding exactly like a preacher. "What is it to you? What is it to you that your sister, or anyone else for that matter, has more than you, is smarter than you . . . is more organized, or more beautiful?"

I finally get it.

"You know what?" I ask, feeling awful. "Suddenly I don't want any of that *stuff*."

"I didn't think you would." Allie smiles.

"Do you think Geraldine would enjoy it?" I ask.

"All but the football," she says.

"Let's drop it off at her apartment."

"We can do that tomorrow as we're leaving. I want to say goodbye again, anyway."

Allie says she needs to pick up a present for her new receptionist and she'll be right back.

So there, on that stone bench in Palm Springs, I confess my sins to God and how ruefully ashamed I am for my lion's share of pride.

# Chapter

# Eighteen

Forgiven, cleansed, and free, I call Doug. He gives me a rundown on everything, including the puppy tearing up Tawny's Skechers and Logan's Doc Martens.

I wince. "Oops. I meant to tell them."

"What?"

I explain.

"I've just made a decision," Doug informs me.

"What?"

"As of this moment, Blessing is an outside dog. He's got my slipper in his mouth."

"Give him the other one, Doug. Those scruffy slippers deserve to be torn up."

"Not my corduroy beauties?" he says, with affection.

"Yes, your corduroy uglies. You wear those out in the street, and someone will be dropping you off at the soup kitchen for a good meal."

We laugh together, his laughter lasting longer.

"Carly and Ben made a tent out of sheets in Carly's bedroom. They're under it now playing Trouble by themselves because my palm is sore from hitting that plastic bubble. Tawny and Logan are out with friends."

"That's nice." I miss my family. "How are you handling both home and the office? That's a tall order."

"You do much more than I ever knew, Becca."

"Thank you. I appreciate your noticing."

"I can't wait until you get home. My feet are cold at night."

"Not mine. But not because they don't miss you." I tell Doug about seeing Valerie but not about my shopping spree.

"Don't take yourself too seriously, sweetheart. And take care of our baby."

I hang up the phone. "Our baby," I say dreamily as I walk out on the balcony. "Oh, Allie, I think I am falling in love."

"With Doug, I hope."

"With Doug and our four children . . . and this one on the way." I drop into an iron chair and sigh, long and hard.

"Here." Allie hands me a pillow chocolate from her pocket, the way you would hand a baby a pacifier.

"I don't want chocolate. I want my craving."

"Fried green tomatoes?" Allie asks.

"No, that is my lost craving. I want my new one."

She raises an eyebrow. "And what's that?"

"Sushi. I saw a sushi bar downtown." My eyes search her reaction.

"Sushi. Isn't that raw?" She makes a face.

"Not all sushi is raw. Not a California roll. It has avocado, cucumber, and other edible stuff," I say, trying to sound convincing.

"Since we're in California, why not?" Allie agrees. "But let's wait until they're open tonight. No more peering in the window, if you don't mind."

⊱✿⊰

"Why is everyone so crazy about rice?" Allie asks at the sushi bar as another customer enters and the bell chimes.

"*Irasshaimase*"—the employees state their perfunctory greeting. Even the sushi chef behind the chrome bar joins in.

119

The waitress provides us with hot towels, and I wipe my hands, proud to know sushi bar etiquette.

"Are you sure this isn't the bathhouse?" Allie teases.

"Just follow my lead."

"Yes, Becca-san."

"And don't talk to the sushi chef," I warn.

"I wasn't planning to. He's pretty handy with those Ginsu knives."

A few minutes later, Allie is cautiously biting into a triangular piece of pressed rice wrapped in seaweed.

I am biting into my delicious California roll. "Don't you think sushi has a mystique about it?"

"To some, I suppose," she replies with an indistinguishable face.

"This place is authentic. You saw the look I got when I ordered the California roll. And did you hear the way everyone pronounces *wasabi*? That's horseradish, you know."

"Remember when we were sophomores, and we had to write a haiku in Mrs. Benson's class?"

"Like yesterday," I joke.

"Let me see if I can remember mine." She concentrates.

"Brown leaves drop from trees
Laughing as they hit the ground
The season is gone."

"You're joking, right?" I ask, seriously.

"I don't think I'll tell you, Miss Smarty Pants."

"Here's mine." I make it up as I go along:

"Green stuff on my plate
Strong as it blasts my sinus cavity
Glad for water around
waaa-sah-bee."

"Don't you think that's pretty good?"

"It's supposed to be five syllables, seven syllables, and then five syllables. And you added an extra line," Allie says, like some expert.

"Well, excuse me," I fire back. "Why don't you rap my knuckles with your ruler, Teacher?"

"Think I should ease up, huh?" She smiles.

"If you want to be technical, Allie, your first line rhymes, and it's not supposed to."

"No, it doesn't."

"*Leaves* and *trees* do so rhyme," I counter.

We say nothing for a time. I listen to the music, old instruments of Japan strumming peacefully. Then I take a sip of bitter tea.

The door chimes.

"*Irasshaimase*," the greeting ignites again.

"I think my sister is about to walk in the door," I say, panicking. "There's my brother-in-law, Randy in his fancy-schmancy suit."

"Now, Becca. Be nice. We can invite them to join us."

"Okay. I'll be nice." But I'm shaking all over. I can barely stand to look again, but I do. "Wait. Who is that with Randy?"

"Not your sister. That much I know."

The pair sits down. Randy is facing the window to the street. The petite waitress presents them with hot towels and menus and walks away in miniature steps.

"Maybe she's a client," Allie speculates.

"Maybe," I say, hopefully, but I peer more closely.

They hold hands across the table. They whisper and giggle, and whisper and giggle some more.

"I don't think so," Allie states. "I don't get that close to my clients."

All doubt is erased when the blond bombshell stands up and runs her long red fingernails through Randy's dark curly hair. He pulls her on his lap and kisses her ear, and she tells him, "Stop it, Randy. I need to fix my makeup."

I pray that God will give me the wisdom to handle this unpleasant situation. I mean, it can't be an accident that we're here tonight.

"Hold yourself together," Allie says, knowing me all too well.

The *other woman* walks right past us and beyond the cotton curtains with bamboo designs that lead to the restrooms.

"I'm going to talk to Randy. You go to the bathroom and detain . . . that, that . . . woman," I say in a soft voice. Inside, anxiety is raging like a bull.

"How am I going to do that?"

"I don't know, Ethel Mertz, but do it anyway."

Allie puts lipstick on; don't ask me why. Then she gives me a toothy grin with lipstick on her teeth and disappears.

I casually walk over to Randy.

"Oh, Becca," he says, suitably surprised.

"At a loss for words?" I ask, displaying my own toothy grin.

"Not at all. Valerie mentioned you were in town. I'm here with a client."

"Oh, a client, huh. A very *close* client?"

"I'm helping her through a divorce, if that's what you mean."

"No, that's not what I mean." I sit down in his "client's" chair. "I was sitting right over there at the bar when you kissed her."

He gives a guilty look, but not guilty enough to please me.

"I think I'll have a talk with my sister," I state, the tone of my words sour like vinegar.

Randy turns his head downward and then raises it again. He locks eyes with mine and then says the most unexpected thing. "Go ahead. It's not like she doesn't know already."

"What?" I gasp, amazed. "You mean you make a habit of having girlfriends on the side?"

"Listen, Becca. It was over a long time ago between your sister and me. Why do you think I didn't go to the family reunion?"

I'm absolutely stunned. "And where is God in all this, Randy? What about your profession of faith?"

"Yeah, answer that question for me. Where *is* God? I'd like to know myself."

I want to say, "Guess who's moved?" but it would sound so bumper sticker.

"Here comes Katie. Would you mind . . . ?"

I walk away and hear her ask about me.

"Just a client," he says.

She gives me a look that could wilt a bird of paradise. "Let's get out of here!" she tells him.

He throws a bill on the table, and they walk out arm in arm. The bells chime behind him.

*"Domo arigato gozaimasu."* The employees bid him thank you.

And I feel bad for all the times I didn't love my sister properly.

# Chapter

# Nineteen

That night I lie under a yellow flowered duvet, wishing it were dark and quiet and that the world would go to sleep.

"What on earth *could* you have done?" Allie asks.

"I could have been nicer to my sister," I wail in pure despair.

"And that would have stopped her husband from having an affair?"

"No, I guess not."

Allie throws me a chocolate, and I deposit it in my mouth.

"I want to go home," I say with my mouth full, and mean it. Then I fling my head on my pillow.

"Don't do anything drastic, like smother yourself." Allie tries to cheer me up.

"I won't," I promise, not cheered up at all.

Allie slips between the sheets in her melon green nightgown, smelling of aloe vera lotion. She takes her Bible off the stand and reads a psalm to me, but I don't really hear it.

I stare hypnotically at the ornate ceiling.

Allie fluffs her pillow.

There is a long conversational gap as I consider all the mean things I've ever said to Valerie—most of which, I rationalize, were deserved.

Allie turns to me and yawns. "You've learned something very important through all this."

"What, counselor?" I sit up, because I want to know what very important thing I learned.

"You learned that Valerie's life is not perfect. Nobody's life is." Allie closes her eyes. "You can leave a small light on; it won't bother me."

*Hint. Hint.*

"I can't sleep anyway. I'm going to sit on the balcony and write in my journal," I say, since I'm feeling on the brink.

"Write about Geraldine . . . so we don't forget her."

I hesitate. "I'd like to, but I only write brooding thoughts in my journal."

Allie opens one eye. "Why?"

"Because that's the only time I feel like writing."

"Well, then, I'm buying you a happy diary, so you can write about Geraldine."

"Good night, Allie."

"Good night."

I put on a coat over my pajamas. I take my journal and pen and open and close the sliding glass door.

A few minutes later, I peer into the room to see that Allie has achieved her goal. She sleeps like the happiest baby.

I am amazed she can fall asleep so easily. Allie amazes me, period. I'm glad to have a best friend like Allie. I don't deserve her. I take up my pen, my instrument of truth.

*Dear Journal:*

*The teenage voices from the pool remind me that I am getting older, less tolerant. I remember how I said I would never be like the*

*older people, the ones who glared at us when we were just having fun.
I thought how little they knew then. And now I know they knew a
little more than I thought . . .*

The night is long, and the anarchy that surrounds me suffocates
my thoughts so they never reach fruition. I mostly sit, and pray in-
between. I pray for revelation and peace and wonder if one can be
achieved without the other.

About 1:00 a.m. I lie in satin. Sleep finally comes, sweet and
deserved.

"Good morning," Allie says softly in my ear.

"What time is it?"

"Eight o'clock."

With eyes bleary from lack of sleep, I look up at her. "What is it
with you and eight o'clock?" I moan.

"It's our last day here, and we need to make the best of it."

"Okay. Okay." I run my fingers through my unruly hair.

"Since both our flights don't leave Orange County until
tonight, we don't have to rush. So why don't you choose something
you want to do, and I'll chose something I want to do?"

"You first." I yawn.

"It's a simple request. I want to go to an art gallery and then
have a frozen yogurt. The same thing I do back in Atlanta; isn't
that crazy?"

"I don't think so."

"And you want to go clothes shopping, right, Becca?"

"Normally, yes; for maternity clothes, no. Besides, the prices
here are outrageous."

"So what, then?" she asks.

"First breakfast, then your art gallery and frozen yogurt, and
then let's drop off the stuff at Geraldine's."

She smiles. "And then?"

I put on my robe and move to the balcony. "I just want to think of someone else for a change. I've been so stuck on myself lately."

"You have someone else to think about, Becca."

As you might have guessed, Geraldine loved the loot. I wanted to tell her where it all came from, but Allie said it was unnecessary to tell everybody everything all of the time.

Geraldine gave us each a sculpture, and I promised to stay in touch. Allie promised more than staying in touch. She told Geraldine she wasn't getting away from her so easily. That she was in her life forever.

As we ride around in our rental car, trying to decide where to go next, I examine my sculpture. It's a mother with a daughter at her knee.

"Allie, the mother's eyes are so sad, and the daughter's eyes are staring at the flower on the grass."

"I think that says a lot. What does Geraldine call that sculpture?"

"Lost Time," I say sadly. I think of my own children and vow to make every moment count.

So now we are in a quaint little shop on a Palm Springs side street, the kind where you put together your own gift baskets. I go with a pink theme, because pink is Valerie's favorite color.

Allie likes my idea of making a forgiveness basket for my sister with her favorite things. It's more productive than my last idea, she says.

I examine a silver bracelet with kittens and put it in the frilly basket, already nearing the brim.

"Why the kittens?" Allie asks.

"When Valerie was seven, the kitten she picked out of the litter died. Mine lived nine lives."

Down the aisle I spot a beautiful butterfly made of handblown glass, crafted in Sweden.

"Are you considering that for Valerie?" Allie asks.

"I was just thinking that when we were in high school Valerie was supposed to go to Sweden with the choir but wasn't able to."

"I remember that."

"She got mono and had to stay in bed all summer. I didn't think much about it at the time, but it must have been hard." I feel a twinge of empathy.

"I'm sure it was." Allie nods sympathetically.

"And she loves butterflies."

A few minutes later, I spot a rack of tiny cups. I pick up one that says *Rachel,* and I start to cry. I start to cry because I had truly forgotten.

"What?" Allie puts her hand on my shoulder.

"Valerie had a miscarriage once. She wanted a girl and wanted to name her Rachel. Oh, Allie, how could I have forgotten that?"

"It's okay. It's called 'selective memory.'"

"Do you think it would make her sad if I buy it?"

"Yes," Allie says, "but I think it would show her that you care."

We continue down the rows selecting things for Valerie, and with each gift, I pray for my sister.

"You know, Valerie has experienced a lot of loss in her life," I admit. "Maybe not tragic loss, but loss is loss."

"None of us are exempt," Allie concludes.

"No, none of us are, are we?"

⋯⋯

Valerie cries when I give her the basket. She invites us inside, and we sit cross-legged on her Persian rug examining the goodies. It's a friendly atmosphere, the way it should be with sisters.

When Valerie sees Rachel's cup she weeps uncontrollably.

I hold her; she drenches me with her tears. Then she looks at me with the loneliest gaze ever.

"Becca, I wanted a house full of children like you. But after the miscarriage, Randy said one was enough. All these years I've resented you for your children. I'm sorry."

"I have a lot to be forgiven for too, Valerie," I say.

My hands find themselves on my belly as Allie drives toward John Wayne Airport. The drive is mostly quiet, with occasional thoughtful comments. I'm emotional, but it's sweet emotion.

"Valerie says she wants to come when I have the baby," I tell Allie. "I think that will be a good thing. I *think* it will, anyway."

"I plan to be there too." Allie smiles.

"I'm a little thick, but once I get it, I get it for the long run," I say, speaking of Valerie and myself.

"We never really *get it*, Becca. We just reach for the next lesson."

"We reach?" I ask. "Sometimes I think lessons just drop out of the sky and bonk you on the head."

"It may seem that way, but all our lessons are by design."

I turn off the air conditioner and roll down my window because I'm tired of fake air. We listen to the sounds of the freeway, the cars speeding by.

I offer Allie an Altoid, and she declines after saying they are stronger than *wasabi*.

"So, we didn't do anything all that daring—except maybe bingo and sushi," I say after a long silence.

"Not much. But I'd like to think we painted some rainbows in the sky by being true to ourselves."

"Rainbows in the sky . . . how beautiful, Allie. You should be a poet."

She makes up a poem.

"Rainbow in the sky
Touching the ground with color
The rainbow is gone."

I give her a doubtful look.

"Or maybe I should stick to counseling?" Allie laughs.

"Definitely you should keep your day job."

"And your day job, Becca?"

I grin. "I think I'll keep my day job too."

Our time together is short, and I feel the sting. At the same time, I'm excited to see my family, and even Blessing. (Doug is building him a doghouse to match our tepee.)

"I'm sorry that Longs drug was out of *War and Peace*," Allie jokes. But I know she means it too.

"I have a confession."

"What?"

"I told you I wanted to read *War and Peace* because Valerie made me feel dumb. But it's not true."

"It's not?" Allie looks surprised.

"No. I want to read it because when it was assigned in our senior year, I didn't. I got an incomplete grade because of it."

"Now I remember that assignment." Allie rolls her eyes.

"I'll bet you got an A on it. I'll bet you did."

"Does it matter to you?" she asks.

"No," I say.

"Good." She smiles. "By the way, Becca, you are very smart, and I think you already know that."

"I'm learning that life doesn't have to be as complicated as I make it," I say.

"It's true—we do complicate things. It's hard being a counselor sometimes. I feel like I have to have an answer for everything."

"You don't, you know."

"No, I don't; do I," Allie comments, as if she's somewhere far away. A minute later she announces, "I think I'll let my hair down more often."

I pull the chopstick out of her bun, and her long, silky hair cascades like a waterfall.

"I didn't mean it literally," she says.

"It looks good down," I counter. "And you look good in glasses."

"You know, I don't think I mind looking intelligent after all." Allie glances in the mirror.

"Why should you mind looking intelligent when that's what you are?"

"I think I'll wear my glasses all the time," she adds.

"That would solve your contact problems."

"No more contact-lens drop soup." Allie laughs boisterously. "That would make a good *Reader's Digest* story."

"My life would make a good *Reader's Digest* story."

We laugh, and I love the sound of our laughter.

"Ooh, speaking of food . . . there's a Cheesecake Factory not far from the airport," I suggest happily.

"What was that cheesecake you had?"

"White Chocolate Chunk Macadamia Nut," I say, as though I can taste the words.

"Wow. The name of that dessert is longer than the entire novel of *War and Peace*!"

I am craving sweets big-time when we walk into The Cheesecake Factory.

"Wouldn't you rather have sushi?" Allie teases.

"Sushi was a passing craving. And fried green tomatoes is a summer craving. Cheesecake—now that's a *respectable* craving."

"You do know that you have an unhealthy fixation on food," Allie says, looking reasonably concerned.

"Yes, I know. Will it ever go away?"

"Without question."

"You know what I've always wanted to try but couldn't because I was so stuck on having cheesecake?"

"What?"

"The Giant Brownie Ice Cream Sandwich." I envision it in a massive dish, with a cherry the size of an apple on top.

"At least I'm almost sure it will go away," Allie says, back to her former thoughts. "Oh sure. It's a typical pregnancy thing." She looks like she's trying to convince herself.

"Well, I don't care. I'm enjoying it for now."

While waiting to be seated, an older woman smiles at me in that telling way. "When is your baby due?"

"In November," I state proudly.

And then she starts in on the advice. I just smile.

Allie searches in her purse for nothing, trying to contain her laughter.

# Chapter

# Twenty

## Four Months Later

Just as I gather my shopping bags at my feet and plop on a bench in the corner of the mall, my cell phone rings. I expect that it is one of my children with a miniature crisis because of the way my day started, but to my delight it's Allie.

"I can't believe it's late August already," I tell her. "Just yesterday it was April, and we were lounging by a pool with palm trees and mountains in the background. I only wish we had taken more pictures. I was actually skinny then."

"Funny, how you say that now."

"You've been to the Macy's Thanksgiving Day Parade, Allie, right?"

"A couple of times. Why?"

"What would you say is the biggest balloon?"

"The Statute of Liberty is pretty big."

"Rounder than that," I hint.

"The M&Ms chocolate-candy guy is pretty round."

"That's me." I sigh. "Only without the chocolate coating, and I can't dance as well."

"Does he dance?"

"I'm not sure. But I bet he doesn't have feet the size of Texas." She laughs.

"How are you doing on your diet?" I ask.

"I'm maintaining. Those last five pounds have taken up permanent residence."

"And it's less than two years to the reunion. Be nervous, Allie. Be very nervous."

"I'll ignore that comment. So, where are you? And what's all that noise in the background?"

"I'm at the mall. I need to buy a new pair of shoes. My size elevens are too small."

We laugh.

"Just be happy that you don't have to stand on your size-eleven feet all day," Allie chimes in. "Some women do, you know."

"Oh, I'm happy, Allie. Especially since I've been writing in that furry purple 'happy diary' you sent me. I've even given it a name."

"What?"

"I can't tell you; it's too embarrassing."

"Fine. I won't tell you mine, either," Allie teases.

"You already did."

"I did? I told you about Mr. Zeeks?"

"You did now." I laugh.

"I fell for that one," she says in a self-deprecating tone.

"Anyway, it's hard to write only happy thoughts, but I've retired my cranky journal. I'm allowed to write an occasional unhappy thought in Ducky, I hope."

"Ducky?" she asks.

"Oops. Accidental spill."

"Ducky? As in a web-footed creature that eats stale bread, pond scum, and invertebrates?"

"Don't ask," I say.

"I won't."

"Good."

"Well, I suppose, Becca . . . *occasional* unhappy thoughts should be permitted. But only if necessary."

"It is necessary. I was crunching ice chips when I was stressed, but then the icemaker died."

"Sorry."

"It's okay." I try to find a more comfortable position on the hard, wooden bench. "It had a good life as far as icemakers go."

"Happy anniversary, by the way," Allie says.

"That's nice of you to remember." I panic momentarily. "Oh no! I bought myself a canvas maternity tent and these tiny little earrings that I now realize will look hideous on me, but I forgot to buy Doug an anniversary present. That is so like a guy." I groan, mad at myself.

"Or a pregnant woman," Allie adds.

I sigh.

"Maybe Doug will take you out for dangerous crab tonight."

We laugh, remembering the Chinese restaurant.

"I think Doug's got something planned, but I just want a footbath, you know. I'm getting tired of food."

"Or better yet, one of Chantal's pedicures," Allie says.

"I'd go for that . . . except that Palm Springs is one hundred–plus degrees right now."

"I know. I talked to Geraldine last night."

I watch the people pass by as Allie tells me about her new receptionist and how she has no concept of client confidentiality.

I squirm. My baby is a three-hundred-pound weight on my bladder (and they say she or he weighs less than three pounds. Balderdash!). "Hey listen, Allie, it's been ten minutes since I've been to the bathroom. I have to go kick some old lady or toddler out of the line."

"You don't really do that, do you?"

"Only once." I laugh. "After I had a thirty-two-ounce carrot juice."

"Why did you have a thirty-two-ounce carrot juice? You can't stand carrot juice."

"Because Carol said I was lacking beta carotene."

"You can get too much beta carotene, you know."

"I know. I was turning orange."

"Don't listen to Carol," she advises.

"I *try* not to listen to Carol, but it's hard. She calls me all the time. I tried disguising my voice once . . . Not really, but I wanted to."

We both laugh.

"I'll bet your skin and hair look great."

"They do. I'm as shiny as the M&M guy."

"So, later M&M."

"Bye, Allie Oop."

After relieving my bladder of its misery, I wander through the mall in search of Bozo shoes. I walk in a shoe store, thinking that the purse on the mannequin is really cute . . . and big enough to hide my pregnant body.

While admiring the scenic needlepoint, the mannequin moves. I startle, because I think I've knocked it over.

Apparently this lady thinks I'm going to mug her. She grabs her purse and holds it to her chest, then looks at me, reasonably shaken. "Well!" she exclaims, like Mrs. Howell from *Gilligan's Island*.

"I was just admiring your handbag," I say, at a loss for other words.

"Well," she says again and leaves.

"Can I help you?" The young salesman approaches me suspiciously.

*How embarrassing! They don't even have mannequins in shoe stores. What was I thinking?*

"I'm looking for a comfortable shoe."

He raises an eyebrow. "One shoe?"

"*Shoes*. Sorry, I'm pregnant," I say, using my continual bad excuse for brainlessness.

"No reason to be sorry."

I exhale, clutter the floor with my load of bags, and sit down.

"It's good that you came in the afternoon," he tells me.

"Why, are you having a sale?"

"No. Because your feet are apt to be largest this time of the day, and more your natural size."

"Thank you for that." I wiggle my fat little piggies and look around the store.

"So, do you have backaches? Pain at the heel, arch, or ball of your foot? Edema?" he asks, rapid-fire.

"All of the above," I say, resigned.

"Then it is critical we accomplish proper-fitting footwear."

*Accomplish? I never thought of buying shoes as an accomplishment. I think he takes his job way too seriously.* This eases my embarrassment about the mannequin incident.

"So what size are you?" he asks behind glasses that are too big and a beard I'd like to trim.

"Size seven and a half."

He looks at me doubtfully, removes my right shoe, and measures. "You're a size eight."

"My feet have grown, I guess." My face contorts, because eight sounds so much bigger than seven and a half.

He excuses himself and comes back with a couple of shoeboxes. He fits me with some black square-toed shoes and informs me that they are the preferred footwear for pregnant women.

"They are?" I ask, thinking they are the ugliest shoes I've ever seen in my life.

"And the rubber sole will be easier on your knees. You see, your center of gravity has shifted."

"No kidding."

He holds up my flattened Keds by the dirty laces and stares at them, as though they deserve lengthy examination.

*These shoes are comfortable*, I reason to myself. *And I would only be wearing them for a short time.*

I stand up; I walk across the floor; I look in the low mirror. *U-g-l-y.*

I stand dreamy-eyed for a few minutes, shifting my gravity, trying to decide.

*Comfort. Looks. Comfort. Looks.*

"Bex."

I turn around. "Manhattan. What are you doing here?"

"Shopping, of course." She drops her bags near mine and pulls me toward a display of high-heeled shoes. "Oh, I have to show you the most adorable shoes, Bex." She picks up a shiny pair and flashes them under the lights. "Try these. These would be great on you."

"I don't think so, Manhattan. I'm seeking comfort, not thrill."

She looks down at my feet. "Obviously."

"Unless you don't like your friend, you should not be suggesting those shoes," the salesman warns.

Manhattan looks at him like she wants to say something out of line.

"You see," he explains, "your friend is suffering from overpronation, and you're not helping her by suggesting footwear that could magnify her problems."

Manhattan places a hand on her hip. "From what?" she asks, her Brooklyn accent stronger than usual.

"Overpronation. It's a condition that occurs when a person's arch collapses upon weight bearing," the salesman clarifies.

"You mean flat feet, don't you?" Manhattan asks. She towers over me in giant high-heeled sandals, making me feel like a fat midget.

"That is the layman's term." The salesman takes a step back and adjusts his glasses.

"Did you go to school for that?" Manhattan fires at him.

Belatedly, the salesman answers no and frowns. Then he goes on to say that he never went to college, even though he had a scholarship.

Manhattan eyes the salesman's ringless finger. Suddenly she seems interested in the stranger. She smiles. "There's nothing wrong with selling shoes."

And then he says his name is Steve, compliments her sandals, and says she has a good arch.

"My name's Manhattan."

"Manhattan . . . what an interesting name." He smiles back.

I walk back to the mirror and am jolted by reality.

*These are past ugly.*

I shuffle over to the Keds.

*Nothing wrong with Keds. They'll go with the canvas tent I just bought.*

It takes some obvious body language for Steve to notice the Keds I am swinging in front of him.

*Hint. Hint.*

Finally he notices and brings out a size eight but only puts them on halfway. He will not break eye contact with Manhattan.

She follows him to the cash register.

"Would you like to go to our church barbecue this Saturday?" Manhattan asks with a flirtatious smile.

"Barbecue?"

"A singles' barbecue."

"Sure." Steve adds that his grandfather was a minister.

I take my change and my bag as Manhattan rests her elbows on the counter.

"My mother's name is Luna, and Luna means *moon* in Spanish."

I don't know why Steve says that. Maybe because Manhattan is an unusual name.

"My mother's name is Helena," Manhattan adds.

Steve turns on the charm. "I'll bet she's beautiful like you."

"She has a nice arch," Manhattan says, and they both chuckle.

I interrupt. "Well, I have to go pick out a present for Doug. It's our anniversary."

There is no response.

"Eighteen years," I say, like they should be impressed.

They maintain unyielding eye contact as I gather my belongings.

"Bye," they finally say so I will go away.

# Chapter

# Twenty-One

It's a rare occasion that Doug insists I drive his PT Cruiser. I'm having fun with the top down, sporting my DKNY sunglasses and wearing darker lipstick than I normally wear.

The power is nothing close to my dream Hummer, but the retro look and classic dashboard makes me feel I am of another day and age, maybe even a movie star like Greta Garbo or Carole Lombard.

I love playing Doug's jazz collection. I'm driving down the boulevard singing "Summertime and the living is easy" . . . when the light apparently turns green. Somehow I don't see it, the way I don't see so many things right in front of me these days. The car behind me lets me know the light is green with his tooting horn. I glance up, feel dumb, and accelerate in park (how did I get in park?). Eventually I get it right.

Suddenly I feel pregnant instead of sophisticated. I grab a tissue and wipe off my magenta lipstick (Carol sells Mary Kay too). I can no longer pretend I am Greta or Carole, or even Helen Kane (she played Betty Boop). I stick the tissue in my purse, because trash is not allowed in Doug's car.

My brain starts drifting, like it tends to do every other minute. Right now I'm thinking of an article I read about how babies are being named after inanimate objects—Almond and River, and such—and am wondering if it really is as bad an idea as I thought it was when I read the article. We've settled on Jake for a boy, and my father is thrilled. But there are so many girl names to choose from.

Cayenne. Paris. Silver. Strangely, these names sound beautiful to me. Echo. Phoenix . . .

I tell my brain to cut it out or ruin my child's life. I just entered my third trimester, when pregnancy hormones begin drowning brain cells. Babies should be named in the second trimester, when pregnant brains are in their prime.

When I pull in the driveway, my children are waiting for me. This is very unusual, particularly for a Saturday when we all tend to go our separate ways.

I step out of the Cruiser loaded down with my purse and bags, my hair a jungle from the wind.

"Hi, guys."

We stand there facing each other. Sly smiles forewarn me that something is up.

"I'll help you with those, Mom," Logan offers and whisks my purse and bags away.

*Logan offering assistance. Huge red flag.*

"Can you lay them on my side of the bed, Logan?"

"Sure, Mom," he calls back from the front door.

"They're heavy, Logan."

"I'll say. What's in this one? A bomb?"

"We'll save that mystery for later," I say.

Tawny, Ben, and Carly stare at me but don't say anything.

"Are you wondering what's for dinner?" I ask finally.

"No." They all smile. "We know what's for dinner."

Doug comes out of the house wearing jeans, a crisp white shirt, and a sporty blue tie, which is as dressed up as my cowboy ever gets . . . unless he's going to work or church, of course.

I gulp.

# Tight Squeeze

*They're not throwing us an anniversary party. Naw.*

"Happy anniversary!" He kisses my forehead and wipes a smudge of lipstick off my chin.

"I did say that this morning, didn't I?"

"Yes, you did." He even looks freshly shaved.

He holds my hand like you see on those diamond commercials. I only hope he doesn't have a diamond for my fat fingers. I can barely stand wearing the one I have. It's like dressing a worm.

Ben takes out his kazoo and starts blowing. "Follow me," he orders in-between his kazoo solo.

Ready or not, Doug and the girls express me down the sidewalk. I close my eyes as Doug opens the gate to the backyard, fearing the worst.

I imagine a party, much like the Nelsons' anniversary party a few months ago. It was church potluck style, followed by Bandit.

Bandit is this game that we really don't know who made up. That's the joke. It's a card game, but whoever loses the round gets a smear of makeup on their face. The thing about this game is that I always seem to lose, and someone always seems to have a digital camera handy as I am being tarnished in eye shadow and lipstick, promising myself never to play again (but I always do). The next Sunday at church, my goofy speckled face ends up on the widescreen during announcements for what seems an eternity as everyone laughs hysterically and the person next to me whispers, "You lost *again?*"

I close my eyes tight as I hear the swing of the gate. Then I open them.

The news is good: a yard absent of visitors.

Doug announces we are spending the evening alone in paradise, and I see that paradise is our tepee. A banner reads *Happy Anniversary!* and the tepee has heart-shaped balloons floating at the top, announcing to all the neighbors that we are celebrating tonight.

"Build a fire and the whole world will know," I say.

Doug smiles at me and runs his fingers through my hair. He doesn't care that it is a jungle.

My children hug me and then whisper to their father, "We'll be out later with dinner."

Like a queen, I am directed to the interior of our nomadic dwelling, where a dozen wilting roses sit in a waterless vase and melting candles sit on a low corner table.

The beanbags are alluring.

"This is great." I drop in one, throwing my old Keds off my over-pronated feet.

"I suspected you didn't want to go out tonight."

"You got that right, honey," I say, relieved. I kiss the air, which is so much easier than getting up.

Doug places a beanbag next to mine and kisses me way better than the air.

Just then Blessing assaults us, and Ben rushes in and grabs him. "You leave them alone, Rover."

After a few romantic moments, my children return in black-and-white outfits to serve us.

Logan supplies warm, wet washcloths, like at the sushi bar. I wipe my hands and face and feel revived. We discard the towels in a basket, and he takes them away. I laugh at the red napkin hanging out of his back pocket, meant to lend ambiance. Tawny's signature is all over it.

"Chicken Madeira from The Cheesecake Factory," Tawny announces as she places the paper plates on our laps (I cannot be trusted with china these days).

Carly enchants us with her flute solo, and Ben scatters heart confetti in the air. Tawny lights the candles and then turns over the etched glasses and pours sparkling apple cider.

"Anything else . . . Sir? . . . Madame?" Tawny asks.

"No, thank you." Doug is smiling and proud.

"You have all the romantic niceties covered," I murmur.

Logan comes back with a steel bucket of dry ice. The vapors rise in a billowing cloud, and the effect is surreal.

"Be still my heart," I say.

Our children beam as they stand over us, and we beam back.

"Good job, kids," Doug tells them as they bow and leave. "It was their idea, you know," he whispers in my ear. "And mostly Tawny's."

"That touches me, greatly. You kids are something else," I call as they walk back in the house.

We eat our dinner. I remove an occasional piece of confetti from my dinner plate.

The Chicken Madeira is better than it ever was at The Cheesecake Factory, even though it is cold and the noodles are stuck together.

After dinner, and without asking, our plates are gathered and a Giant Chocolate Brownie Ice Cream Sandwich is set before me.

"We can share," I offer.

Doug and I feed each other bites. I make a bigger mess than Doug, and the kids forgot the napkins.

Under the canvas we watch the patch of sky turn to dusk.

Carly takes away the dessert dish and leaves fuzzy blankets in the corner.

"Thank you, Carly." I smile at her, and Doug nods in appreciation.

"I didn't buy you an expensive present this year," he says, trying to read me.

"Good. I don't want an expensive present."

"This is totally from the heart. I'm hoping a thoughtful gift might mean more to you than dollars. Just this one time," he adds.

"That is so sweet," I tell him—and I really mean it.

He motions for Ben, standing near. Ben gives him a box and leaves.

The night is still, except for a dog or two barking in the distance. Blessing answers their call from the garage.

Under the glow of the candle flames, Doug opens the floral box and takes out a sheet of yellow-lined paper. "Fifty reasons why I love you."

I look down, shyly.

"Number one reason I love you, Becca Joy: because you love God with all your heart, soul, and mind."

"That's beautiful," I say, and meet his gaze.

Doug smiles. "That's number two."

"What?"

"Number two reason I love you: because you are beautiful inside and out."

I tear.

Doug pulls a tissue from a strategically placed box and hands it to me. I dab my eyes.

"Number three: you think of us before yourself."

"I feel like I don't. Not enough," I counter.

"You do," he says reassuringly.

Doug continues gifting me with praises. "Reason number fifty," he concludes. "You are a *joy* to me."

I sigh. For all the wonder of the night, I sigh. I think of Doug's beautiful present and suddenly feel very foolish for mine. "Oh Doug, I bought you two of the most lame presents ever."

"Lame?" he asks.

"I sound like Tawny, don't I?"

"Yes."

"As she would say, they are off the lame-o-meter."

"They can't be that bad, baby."

"They are, Doug. I bought you two of the most poorly thought-out gifts, and I'm not giving them to you." I start to cry. I lean into his chest, drippy eyed. "At the time they seemed reasonable!"

"Tell me, then." He lifts my chin.

I lower my eyes. "First, I bought you car seats. Isn't that ridiculous? You have those beautiful heated leather seats in your PT

Cruiser, and I bought you sheepskin. I can't believe I did that."

He laughs. "That may not have been the best idea, but you can take them back."

I moan and then look at his peaceful face.

"Maybe the other one is better," he says.

"Not much."

"Try."

"I bought you night-vision goggles. 'Experience the night' it said on the package."

"Night-vision goggles. Wow." I can tell he's trying not to laugh.

"Surveillance in our backyard. Oh, Doug."

"I can use them camping. Logan and I will have a blast with them."

"I didn't have a chance to wrap them," I say, realizing it only now.

"That's okay, Becca. I'll see them later." He kisses my cheek and turns away to further mask his amusement. "I'm really excited about them. See?" He shows his teeth. "I am so excited I can't contain myself."

I start laughing. I laugh so hard I fall off my beanbag because of my lopsided body. Doug tries to lift me, but he falls over too.

We lay on the swept dirt for a long time, laughing and matching hands. When it grows dark, we take the flashlight and make animal shadows on the canvas.

I pull off his cowboy boots, dust off his ruined white shirt, and for the rest of the night, I lay on his large chest and under blankets on the beanbags, talking about everything and slapping mosquitoes.

"Ouch," I say.

"Bitten again?" Doug asks.

"By the lovebug."

"Just think. We'll be having our own little bug again soon. Are you sorry we didn't opt for the three-dimensional ultrasound so we could see the baby's face?" Doug asks, touching mine.

"I was disappointed when we couldn't tell from that initial ultrasound if we were having a boy or girl. But I'm not anymore. I figure

God is still knitting our little bug in the oven, and when he or she is baked . . ." I choke at the thought.

"It will be a nice surprise, won't it?" Doug's voice sounds like first love.

The baby kicks.

"What time is it, Doug?"

He checks his nightglow watch (last year's anniversary present). "Ten thirty," he says, surprised, for the night has passed too quickly.

I see the lights are on in the house.

"Doug, do you think the kids are still awake?"

"I just saw a couple of faces peering out the window."

"Then would you mind if we invited them out for popcorn?"

"I would treasure it," he says.

And I see the sky in his eyes, despite the night. I tell you, it's the most amazing thing.

# Chapter

# Twenty-Two

Dear Ducky!

I am feeling rather daffy today. Most mothers do on the first day of school.

Contrary to what some may think, most stay-at-home moms do not sit on the couch all morning eating bonbons and watching Regis and Whoever. We are what you call overwhelmed, except Judy, of course. Judy made blueberry waffles. Judy was back home before I secured my children in the van. And then she took my children to school because they wanted to ride to school in a yellow Hummer—for once in their life . . . please, Mom, please.

Really, Judy isn't an issue for me anymore; I adore her now. I just haven't had time to do my devotions yet this morning. What a bad excuse.

Besides, my icemaker is broken. Another bad excuse.

I need to get my priorities straight. Hold on, Ducky, while I do my devotions and pray some more.

*❧❧❧*

I'm back, Ducky. Hebrews 11 is good stuff.

So the first day of school was huge for me when I waved good-bye *to Carly as she entered her kindergarten classroom four years ago, wearing braids and carrying a Tigger backpack. There was separation anxiety on both our parts. It's hard not to laugh now, watching the kindergarten parents recording the moment with camcorders and trying to keep their emotions in check, like their life has ended. And the kids all have an apple.*

*I want to tell Mrs. Puccinelli's class that her family owns an apple orchard in Washington, and they ship her cartons and cartons of apples every year. But why spoil it for the new kindergarten families?*

*Yes, I am emotional because my babies are not babies anymore, and Logan will be leaving us for college soon (which would solve the baby-space problem—but don't tell him that). But I am feeling guilty, because it feels like freedom, as well.*

*I haven't been alone in so long. The truth is, I'm not sure what to do first. The truth is, I feel a little lost.*

*Quickly, Ducky.*

*Carly's teacher just called and said that Carly has a headache. (Poor thing gets a headache every first day.) So I have to go the office to sign a permission slip so she can take Tylenol, and while I'm at it sign the volunteer sheet her new teacher thinks I may have "overlooked." Like I overlook stepping in dog mess.*

*Maybe I'll stop by McDonald's for a cup of ice. Or, I just had a thought . . . I can make my own ice. I don't need an icemaker; all you need is an ice tray. Brilliant.*

*Yours, Daffy*

By eleven o'clock I am bored. Bored with cleaning and laundry and dishes, and too antsy to read a book. I'm going to have to work into this relaxation thing.

The Bible study is tomorrow, we have plenty of groceries, and coffee is not allowed. The gym is out, obviously. Walking would be good, but I tell you my belly is massive. I know I'm having quadruplets, but Dr. Christy insists there's only one baby in there. Do you think Judy would steer the wheelbarrow for me? Maybe we could plant some tulip bulbs as we walk.

I think I'll think from the couch.

*Man, this couch is comfortable. One day I'll have a beautiful couch. But for right now, ribbed velour is just a dream.*

I close my eyes.

The phone rings. I reach for it and say "Hello," nearly falling off the couch. You gotta love gravity.

"Hi, Becca."

"Hi."

*Am I supposed to recognize the voice?*

"How are you feeling?"

"I'm feeling pretty good. And you?"

*Who is this?*

"So, is anyone giving you a baby shower?"

"Not that I know of."

*Who is this person? I should know who this is.*

"Great. Then I'll take the job."

*Oh no. It's Carol. Of all people, why Carol?*

"You don't have to, Carol."

"I want to. I love organizing."

*And controlling and irritating . . .*

"And games; I love games. The one where people try to guess what's in the baby food jar makes for some outrageous facial expressions. I'll bring my camera."

*I hate that game.*

"But Carol, it's my fifth baby."

"I know, and normally a fifth baby would not constitute a baby shower, but with eight years in-between, you qualify, Mama."

"You don't have to. Really."

"I am anyway, and you won't talk me out of it."

Silent sigh and a bit of dread.

"Carol, would you mind if we skipped the dirty diaper game? The one where the person with the chocolate Kiss wins?"

"I suppose." Carol chuckles.

I don't know what else to say.

"So, Becca, you just give me a list list, and I'll send invitations out out."

*What's this with the double words?*

"Oh, and what do you think about sticker tattoos? Wouldn't that be fun fun?"

*I get it. Baby talk.*

"Tattoos?"

"That's Vanessa's idea. Oops. The planning is supposed to take place behind the scenes, so you didn't hear that, okay?"

"Okay."

"Call me back with the list of names and some dates that will work for you."

"I'll do that, Carol. Thank you."

"Now go take a nap or something, Mama."

"Okay. Good-bye."

It's 1:30 and I've folded the laundry I did this morning, had lunch, and loaded the dishwasher. Now what? Put together a creative memory scrapbook?

I think I'll water the lawn.

"Becca," Judy calls and waves.

I walk over. "Thank you for taking the kids this morning."

"You're welcome."

"What are you doing?"

"I'm planting bulbs for spring. Daffodils and crocus." Judy looks fresh as a daisy under her gardening hat, holding a spade.

"No tulips?" I joke.

"Tulips do better in indirect light," Judy explains. "I'm planting them tomorrow."

I want to laugh. "I still feel bad that Blessing ruined your garden. We have a lock on the gate now."

"It's all right. It gave me a chance to get acquainted with the Farmer's Market. I may set up a booth next year."

I sit on the brick planter.

"Becca, I'd love to give you a baby shower."

"You're a couple of hours too late. Carol is giving me one," I say, disappointed.

"Where are you going to register?" Judy asks.

"Register?" I play with her fertile dirt.

"What store?"

"I haven't thought of it, Judy."

"I go to a lot of baby showers. A Diaper Genie is a must. Oh, and the Hebrew language baby video is the rage."

"Why?"

"Research shows that when babies are exposed to second languages they become more creative when they're older."

"It's all so foreign to me," I say.

"You'll pick it up again," she soothes.

"And again . . . and again . . . and again." I laugh.

"You are hilarious, Becca. Do you sit up all night writing jokes?"

"No, I stay up all night using the bathroom. I'm thinking of sleeping in the bathtub."

"Well, you must keep your family in stitches all day with your quick wit."

"I'm afraid that you can't be a comedian in your own home."

It's 2:30. I've watered the lawn and had a snack, and now I'm bored again.

"Allie."

"Becca, hi!"

"Can you talk?"

"For a minute. Sure. What's up? This isn't your usual calling time." Allie sounds busy.

"Carol is giving me a baby shower."

"That's nice," she says.

"No, it isn't," I state flatly.

"It isn't?"

"No, Allie. I wanted *you* to give it."

"But I live in Atlanta, Becca. There is a slight location problem."

"Can you at least come?"

"I don't know. I'm already taking off time when the baby is born."

"If I have it on a Saturday, could you come? Just for the weekend?"

"I don't know."

"Please, Allie. I'll pay for your ticket."

"You know it's not a matter of money."

"Then you can come?"

"When?" Allie asks.

"Whenever you say."

"Let me check my calendar at the front desk and get back to you later, okay?"

"Please come, Allie. My mother-in-law is returning from Death Valley in a couple of weeks."

"Death Valley? Are you joking?" Allie asks, like it's the sun she's returning from, which it practically is.

"No, I'm not. She's the only person who lives there from March through September. She's got an air-conditioned trailer there. It gives her a chance to work on her crafts undisturbed."

"Rather strange, don't you think?"

"Not for Irene. You know, Irene, don't you?"

"As a matter of fact, I do," says Allie. "In high school we used to call her the 'Silk Dragon.'"

"That sounds like her. She's half hillbilly, half drama queen, and I'm not joking either. You know how hard I try not to talk about her because I get depressed. But being pregnant, I don't think I can help it." I laugh nervously.

"I do remember that when Doug and I were in a play together, Irene insisted his suit be pressed by *her* dry cleaner and that the school pay for it," Allie reminisces.

"That's mild compared to some of the stuff she pulls."

"But will she even come to your baby shower?"

"Are you kidding? Not even a broken fingernail would prevent her from ruining my special day."

"That's too bad. It shouldn't be like that."

"You'll visit me in the hospital if I have a nervous breakdown, won't you?"

"I'll pray that you don't have a nervous breakdown."

"But if I do," I continue, "will you read my mother-in-law haiku and tell me it's really, really good—even if it doesn't make any sense?"

I can hear the smile in her voice. "I'll even write you a couple of poems—but not about mother-in-laws, because, unfortunately, I don't have one."

"You can have mine . . . for free."

"No thank you; I'd like to pick out my own."

# Chapter

# Twenty-Three

I wave good-bye to Doug and the children as the van disappears down the street. Allie, my supporter, stands near, because today is my baby shower, and there are so many things that can go wrong at baby showers.

"It's a joyous celebration of mother and baby," Allie says as we walk into the house, which is sparkling clean because Doug hired a maid for me. I smile at the living room, which is jam-packed with padded steel chairs borrowed from the church.

"The house looks great, Becca."

"I know; Clara did a fantastic job. She even washed the windows."

"And you had a good conversation with Valerie this morning." Allie looks smart in a powder-blue suit.

"I did, didn't I?"

"And Carol and Vanessa have the baby shower under control," she says.

"They said they'd be here at one o'clock."

"Your mother-in-law has you terrified, doesn't she?"

"Yes, she does. Feel my hands." I place them on Allie's cheeks. She shivers. "They're like ice."

"And my left eye is twitching like a belly dancer."

"Becca, this is *your* baby shower, and no one else's. Just remember that, and you'll be fine."

"I will," I say determinedly, but a second later, I cry, "Oh no! I better pull the birdhouse out of the basement storage closet."

"What birdhouse?"

"This humongous wood and wire disaster she made at a craft workshop in Pigeon Forge, Tennessee. It's seven stories tall and takes up half the living room."

"Doesn't a birdhouse belong in the backyard?" Allie's question is reasonable.

"She says it's decorative," I counter.

"What happens when you don't have it out?"

"Irene gets all panicky and demands that you fix her some snapdragon tea 'to settle her nerves.' I have some if you want to try it."

"No, thank you."

"Stick with Irene, and you'll be eating watercress for this and hanging an onion poultice around your neck for that. And she seriously believes in them all."

Allie's eyes scan my face with surprise.

"See, she grew up in the Appalachian Mountains and clings to the home remedies handed down by the old folk. Her father was a moonshiner, and she's always sharing inappropriate stories with the children. I'm always having an inside fit and biting my tongue to pieces."

"Goodness. Doug is nothing like that."

"Doug's father was a journalist from Charleston. They met when he was doing a story on Irene's poor mining town. He always felt he rescued her, and she let him keep rescuing her all his life."

Allie clucks her tongue. "She sounds like a high-maintenance woman."

"Charlie treated her like a kept woman. I mean," I add, "he

cooked and cleaned and even cut her meat, and still she was never happy. And after he died of a heart attack three years ago and she moved back here, she expected Doug to take over the role."

"I see what you're up against, Becca. I knew Irene was difficult, but I didn't realize . . ."

"The worst is that she never forgave me for not having the huge wedding *she* planned for us back in West Virginia. She forgave Doug easily enough, but not me."

"Did she actually tell you that?"

"Let's say she hints at it rather strongly. When your husband gets a leather jacket for Christmas and you get a pillowcase—and I mean *one* pillowcase . . .

"Yes, I know about all that," Allie says quickly. "And being nice doesn't help?"

"I've *been* nice," I complain. "I've taken her out to plays and on shopping sprees. I couldn't do any more for her than I've done, and still she treats me like I'm Doug's petty-officer third class, or whatever the bottom rung is."

"I see that a lot in my practice."

"For example, she had to reimburse me for something last year, and she made the check out to my maiden name."

"Ouch!"

"Yes, ouch."

"Well, let's forget about Irene for a while. I'm sorry your own mother couldn't make it."

"I am too."

"We have an hour yet."

"So how about some tea and conversation, Sista Ray . . . to calm my battered nerves? I'm feeling giddy from all the excitement."

"Snapdragon?"

"No, not snapdragon. Tangerine Orange Zinger."

"In that case, it sounds like a mighty fine idea, Sista Joy."

"Hip action!" I say, and we go at it like we did when we were young and used to know some dance grooves.

"Whoa, girl! You've got some mighty big hips there." Allie laughs between bumps.

"They have been spreading lately, that's the truth, Sista Ray. But hush now, or I will bounce you back to Atlanta like I bounce a basketball."

"I'm not worried, Sista Joy. You never could bounce a basketball very well."

"Stop breathing on the windows; you're fogging up Clara's work." Allie wipes off my breath with a napkin.

"I'm trying to figure out what Carol and Vanessa are unloading from Carol's Suburban."

"It looks like a movie set, doesn't it?" Allie comments.

"Like a *Gone with the Wind* movie set."

"Are those pillars?"

I squint but can't quite make it out. "They hinted that they were doing some sort of a theme party."

"I have the distinct impression that this may not be your typical baby shower," Allie warns.

A thought hits me. "Oh no! Vanessa asked me what my favorite Disney movie was, and since I wasn't sure, I told her *Sleeping Beauty*. You don't suppose . . ."

Allie opens the door.

"Surprise!" Vanessa is wide-eyed and carrying what appear to be posterboard cutouts.

"Wow, Vanessa. It looks like you guys went to a lot of work."

"We did," she announces.

Carol walks in, juggling rolls of lavender and pink crepe paper. "I'll bet you won't be able to guess what we're doing."

"Throwing me a baby shower?" I say, deadpan.

"Funny, funny," Carol says in her double-word talk.

"It's your favorite movie. Do you recognize this guy?" Vanessa asks, displaying the artwork.

"It looks like the prince."

"Prince who?"

"Caspian?"

"Becca, I'm surprised at you." Vanessa waves a playful finger in my face.

"Oh, Prince Philip," I say.

"That's better." Vanessa puts down the posters and takes off her coat.

"Happily for you, my nephew is an artist, and Disney is his love," Carol adds. "I love Disney too, but they need to get rid of Michael Eisner. Roy Disney would be shocked at what he's turning his dream into."

Fifteen minutes later my living room is a princess zone. Strands of lavender and pink flood the room. Cutouts of Princess Aurora and Prince Philip hang from the ceiling. Sleeping Beauty party favors, along with matching paper goods, lie on pink tablecloths. Even the cake is Sleeping Beauty, lying on her cushioned bed awaiting her awakening kiss.

"They do realize you could be having a boy, don't they?" Allie whispers when they leave the room.

"I have no idea."

"If Sleeping Beauty was pregnant—maybe. But Becca, this is out there." Allie shakes her head, horrified.

"Oh, Allie, what am I going to do?" I ask under my breath.

"Be brave, Becca. Be brave."

But I am not brave. I am a wreck. And when Allie announces that my mother-in-law just drove up in her white Cadillac, I hope for Willy Wonka's elevator to come rescue me . . . straight through the roof.

"What is this mess?" my mother-in-law asks as she walks in the door.

*What happened to hello and how have you been the past six months?* I fake a welcome. "Irene. It's good to see you."

She leans her overblushed cheek in my direction, and I peck it obediently.

"This mess is called a lot of work," Carol announces as she steps out of the kitchen with Vanessa right behind her.

"Carol. Vanessa. This is my mother-in-law, Irene."

Irene ignores the introduction and launches in. "You must be joking! This can't be for your baby shower, Rebecca. Are you sure this isn't Carly's birthday party?" She looks down and gathers a handful of rose petals. "And what's this? Don't you know if someone steps on these rose petals they could permanently stain your carpet?"

"So how was Death Valley, Irene?" I ask, caring more about my sanity than my carpet.

"Hot, but productive."

I open and close my eyes, then open them again. But everything is the same. My mother-in-law is still draped in red silk and matching alligator shoes.

"Why didn't you just do *The Hunchback of Notre Dame* theme?" she snaps. "It would be about as appropriate. Imagine—my grandson with a *Sleeping Beauty* shower."

Carol is discouraged, but not defeated. She walks away waving a pink wand and muttering to herself. Vanessa follows her.

I steady my voice. "We have no indication the baby is a boy, Irene."

"What do you mean no indication? Why, you're carrying that baby higher than a king on a throne."

I want to drag Allie in the other room for a good cry, but I have to be a big girl.

# Chapter
# Twenty-Four

A million and a half years later, the guests arrive.

"Did they charter a bus?" my mother-in-law asks, peering out the window and picking her teeth with one of her homemade cinnamon toothpicks.

It does seem that every single woman in my church is here. Marguerite Zwicker is being assisted with a curiously large red package. I see Alda Meyers has her standard dollar-store bag, and I know what's inside.

When everyone is seated, Carol waves her wand and makes an announcement. "*Ladies*. Every woman wants to feel special, and today our princess is none other than Princess Rebecca." She pauses. "Rebecca . . . What's your middle name, Becca?"

"Embarrassment."

Vanessa's mouth drops. "Really?"

"No, not really. I don't have a middle name."

"So, our princess is none other than Rebecca NMI Joy," Carol announces with rare humor.

"What is NMI?" Vanessa asks.

"No middle initial," Alda explains.

Everyone laughs, and Alda sits up straighter, thinking herself very clever.

"*Sleeping Beauty* is Becca's favorite movie," Carol says, and I want to deny it, because I'm not sure if the fairy/witch thing might make the more reserved church ladies stumble.

I turn my face to the gleaming windows, missing the sunshine. I watch the leafless branches of my maple tree.

I feel a rustle; Vanessa is trying to put something on my head.

"What is that?" I ask.

She shows me a gold sequined hat.

*Please, nobody take a picture.*

"May I take that hat, Vanessa? It would cover up Becca's beautiful French braids," Judy says tactfully.

*Thank you for the rescue, Judy. I didn't even realize you were here.*

"Aren't French braids such an ideal hairstyle for pregnant women?" she says to the group.

There is unanimous agreement. Several of the women compliment Judy on her floral dress and ask her where she bought it.

"Oh, I made it," she responds and then changes the subject.

"I tried to French braid my Barbie's hair once," Vanessa says dreamily.

And I stare out the window again, wondering if this day will ever end.

Carol starts us off with the string guessing game, the delightful game where everyone tries to guess the size of your stomach. Over half the participants guess me the size of a battleship. Judy's daughter, Amanda, however, boosts my ego. Sharing her mother's good manners, she guesses my belly is ten inches wide.

"Thank you, Amanda," I say. "Give that girl a prize."

Carol hands her a scented candle.

I am on autopilot through the rest of the games. I have this smile on my face that feels harsh to me, but Allie, sitting next to me, whispers that I am doing well. Very well. Very, very well.

When I awake from another long daydream, we are playing a *Sleeping Beauty* trivia game, and Irene does great with it. She guesses all the fairies' names and their colors and even knows that Aurora means "the dawn." (Irene does community theater.) When she wins a Ghirardelli chocolate gift set, she tears up royally. And then, to my complete surprise and slight resentment (because she's never once apologized to me), she apologizes to Carol and Vanessa for her abrasive manner.

The trio hugs, and everyone seems happy. The ladies munch on pink cookies shaped like Princess Aurora's baby cradle and drink pink punch with floating sherbet.

Cherri VanDitte starts in with her told and retold labor stories, which starts a wildfire of labor comparisons.

I relax in the velvet purple chair, one of the props Carol brought with her, and stare at the stack of presents since I'm tired of staring out the window. I'm wondering what could be in Marguerite's big red box.

Suddenly, and without provocation, Manhattan runs out of the room, crying. Everyone asks what's wrong.

"She told me she wants a baby," Alda blabs.

All the women *ahh* in sympathy and then go back to their labor stories.

Allie, heart mender that she is, follows Manhattan, and Vanessa passes out stickers, the kind Carly outgrew last year, which I suppose is better than being pressed with temporary tattoos. (Alda hid the tattoos because she said they were unbiblical.)

I stare at the clock.

Carol suggests cake as a happy diversion and heads for the kitchen.

We hear a bloodcurdling scream, and I race to the kitchen to find Blessing, dirty paws on the table, massacring the princess cake. *Carly must have left the back door open. Carly. Oh, Carly.*

Vanessa, who owns a pet shop, pulls Blessing and his cake-

covered face across the floor and out the door because I am dysfunctional at the moment. Someone I don't even know wipes the
table with the wrong sponge.

"Well, this beautiful cake is unsalvageable," Carol says, bitterly
disappointed.

"It's not a problem," Judy chimes in. "I just made two cakes this
morning. Would chocolate velvet do?"

Carol sighs with relief. "If it's anything like your buttermilk pie,
it would be wonderful!"

"I'm so sorry, Carol. I am so sorry," I murmur.

Carol looks ready to cry.

"I'll be right back," Judy announces. "This would be a good time
to open gifts."

Vanessa directs my titanic body into the other room and yells,
"Gifts!"

The women turn to me as I settle clumsily in my throne.

Manhattan walks in the room and sits down next to me. Allie
is right behind her. I smile at Allie; she smiles back.

"I'm feeling better," Manhattan says.

"You sure are something," she tells Allie.

"She is, isn't she?" I hug Allie.

"Allie says I don't need a man or a baby to complete me,"
Manhattan explains. "That I am complete because God and I are a
majority."

"That's right, Manhattan." I touch her knee as affirmation.

"Yeah, yeah," she says, because she does not do well with out-
ward shows of affection.

"Hey, Manhattan. Whatever happened with you and the shoe
salesman?" I ask cautiously.

"The romance connection went nowhere. I found out he was
kind of a nerd."

*And you couldn't tell that right off?*

"Besides, he lives with his mother."

"I'm sorry, Manhattan."

"Don't be. It all worked out well. We're trading places. He's going back to school, and I'm going to take his job at the shoe store. Twenty percent discount." There's a gleam in her eye as she bobs her purple stilettos up and down like a water pump.

"Let's open those gifts. I'm not getting any younger," Marguerite says dryly.

Laughter rolls through the crowded room.

As I open each present, I express my pleasure and smile excessively.

Alda records the names and the gifts with gratuitous interest. "Four silver picture frames and three yellow baby blankets," she whispers from two seats away. "You'd think people would be a little more imaginative."

*More imaginative? You gave me baby washcloths and a pacifier.*

The mysterious red box contains cloth diapers from Marguerite Zwicker. Carol gives me some Melaleuca products she's peddling. And my mother-in-law gives me boy clothes with little fire trucks and construction equipment. (It takes a wee bit of control to look happy for that one.)

But I'm thrilled with the rest of the presents, including Judy's Hebrew language baby video (I want to learn Hebrew myself) and Allie's Diaper Genie. I can't wait for Doug and the kids to see it all. Now I wish the girls had stayed.

After Judy's cake receives rave reviews, Carol announces the baby shower is over, in case the guests don't notice the cups being collected from their hands. Everyone who can assist in tearing the castle apart does, but the princess is told not to lift a finger.

After the quick and thorough cleanup, I try to balance my lopsided body to say my formal good-byes.

"Don't stand up," I'm told, as though I am an invalid. So I sit down again.

A line forms, and one by one I smell my guests' perfume. Some pleasant, some overbearing, some that should be against the law.

Obligatory comments are made about how great I look and how I won't even know I'm in labor, it being my fifth baby.

Carol and Vanessa receive extra hugs for their efforts.

Then the church ladies make a mass exodus. Only Maggie, the lawyer-turned-stay-at-home-mom, remains, gathering her baby and her diaper bag.

"You'll be doing this again, Becca. Are you ready?"

"Is there such a thing, Maggie?"

"Good-bye, Sleeping Beauty." She hugs me.

The smile I give her is masked in uncertainty.

"Remember, Carol did my baby shower too. It was everything baby bottle."

"I do remember now." I grin.

"We even drank lemonade out of baby bottles, remember? And we played that game with lollipop pacifiers."

I laugh.

"Lemonade is not a good idea in baby bottles," she says.

"The pulp?" I ask, and she nods as her baby fusses.

I walk Maggie to the door.

"What's this?" I read the note taped to one of three jumbo trash bags: *Keep these to remember the happy occasion!* And there's this big smiley face. "Oh, decorations from the party," I realize. "How did they all fit in there?"

"You gotta love that woman," Maggie says. "I know I couldn't do what Carol does, and even if I could, I don't know that I would. Take care." Maggie steps down the sidewalk with a little less spring than at her own baby shower.

"So," Allie says, coming out of the kitchen in my apron. "What are you going to do with the party decorations? Burn them?"

"No. I would feel guilty. I'll probably put them in the basement closet along with the birdhouse."

I gasp. "Oh, Allie. Where's Irene?"

"In the bathroom. Why?"

"I forgot to put out the birdhouse."

"Did I hear 'birdhouse'?" Irene asks, walking in the room. "I make and sell birdhouses." She touches her bouffant hairdo, which resembles a bird nest.

"There's this birdhouse store in Atlanta, Irene, that has the most unusual birdhouses you have ever seen."

I know it has to be true because Allie never lies.

"I would like to know where the birdhouse I gave you is, Rebecca."

The ground is shaking in formidable terror, along with me.

"It's in the closet," I say sheepishly and prepare for a 10.5 on the Richter scale.

"*Safe* in the closet," Allie clarifies, before my mother-in-law can put me in my place. "You know, Irene, it easily could have been broken today with all the foot traffic."

"I suppose," she says.

There is a long silence, stretching my endurance.

"You better get started on my son's dinner," my mother-in-law demands. "You said he'd be home soon."

I dutifully drag my body to the kitchen. I make a lot of noise rattling the pots in the cupboard, possibly giving the impression that I am a proper housewife. Truthfully, I have no idea what I am serving for dinner.

Maybe one day she'll realize that her son was just as skinny when I married him as he is now.

"You went to high school with Doug, too, didn't you, Allie?" I hear Irene ask from the other room.

"Well he was a couple of years ahead of us, but we were in a play together."

"Do you remember how big and strong he was back then? He was the quarterback on the football team, and the girls . . ."

Then again, maybe not.

# Chapter

# Twenty-Five

Dear Ducky:

   I just went for a pickle and the pickle jar was empty, so I drank the pickle juice straight from the jar. One of my brothers used to do that, and I used to call him a horrid, horrid creature when he did. Am I now a horrid creature?

   This last week has been a stream of embarrassments. I really shouldn't be waddling around in public; it's not safe anymore. Last week I took Carly into the men's room with me. You know how scatterbrained Carly is—well, neither of us noticed the urinals. We were happily chatting away—me in the stall, of course. And then Carly asked how come the sinks looked so funny. I tell you, I moved rather quickly.

   We stopped by the shoe store to see Manhattan after that. She made me try on these shoes that only you and other web-footed creatures could look good in, Ducky. As she was sliding the monster on my right balloon, she asked me why I was wearing two different socks. Of course, I used my standard defense. "I'm pregnant. I can't see my feet." But it was true.

   Then Carly and I ordered lunch at Wendy's, and I forgot my change.

*"Ma'am. Ma'am. You left your change," the young man called after me.*

*Later I couldn't find our van in the parking garage. We went up and down and around and around. I coveted several yellow Hummers, but I could not find my ugly brown van. Finally we prayed. Duh! There it was, in front of us.*

*And one more story, though, trust me, I have more. Yesterday Doug and I went out for lunch after church, because Tawny was having a nice day and insisted on making macaroni and cheese and chocolate-chip cookies for the kids (I know she eats the dough, even though we tell her repeatedly that eating cookie dough depletes you of B vitamins). So, of course, we went to The Cheesecake Factory, and, of course, I had Chicken Madeira and a Giant Chocolate Brownie Ice Cream Sandwich.*

*Anyway, as we were walking out the door, I felt for my purse, and it was gone. I ran to the booth, leaving Doug wondering what on earth was wrong with me. "Becca, what are you doing?" he asked as he caught up with me.*

*"Someone stole my purse! Do you think it was that strange man across from us who was staring at me?" I whispered, intent on retribution.*

*"It's right here," Doug said, pulling on the black purse strap on my shoulder that matched my black blouse.*

*I couldn't believe it was right there. "And by the way," he said gently, "that man was staring at you because you have fudge sauce all over your face."*

*End of embarrassing stories. Stay tuned; there will be more.*

*RebeccaJoyEmbarassingStories.com*

*Yours, Daffy*

I am thirty-six weeks pregnant and had my first really fun exam today (and I see all those heads out there nodding . . . knowing what I'm saying).

Now, like every other mother, and particularly those over thirty-five, I hope my baby will come early.

At thirty-six weeks, things turn really funny on you. Everywhere pregnant females gather in a herd, they share statistics. For me the statistic is I'm 70 percent effaced and dilated one centimeter. Now I know what that means . . . but what does it really mean? Does anybody know except the doctor?

You might think this private information should be kept private, especially when you think of it too hard. But I'm thinking Alda Meyers might casually slip in my statistics in the middle of a prayer request. Apparently it's public broadcast info in the twenty-first century.

Case in point—I know Angela is 90 percent effaced and dilated three centimeters, and I've never even met Angela. Her mother told me this as we picked out the best cantaloupes at the grocery store.

Don't be all that impressed with my statistics, ladies. Some girl I met at the car wash told me she has been effaced and dilated for about two months. And then she asked me if I had experienced a Braxton Hicks yet.

Now, I know a Braxton Hicks is a contraction that scares you silly in your first pregnancy, but don't you think it sounds like the name of an old boyfriend?

The mucous plug . . . now that's fun conversation. And then there's the old favorite: "Has your baby dropped?" It makes pregnant women sound like child abusers.

There are so many things that make me laugh at this stage in the game that I wonder why we don't see any pregnant comedians out there, except that I think I know the answer already. It would be pretty uncomfortable standing on stage with legs swelled to the size of a sumo wrestler's. Besides, you'd have to take a potty break before you even delivered your first joke.

My firm belief is that the reason pregnant women journal is

because everyone (except other pregnant women) is tired of hearing their pregnant woes. I'm happy for my Ducky, I can tell you that. But more than anything, I can't imagine being pregnant and not having the Holy Spirit, my internal guidance and 24/7 conscience. I would be so mean.

I wake up next to Doug on a Sunday morning with two pillows under my abdomen and another three between my legs.

I look at my thirty-eight-weeks'-pregnant hand and lament my ringless finger. I can't wear my wedding ring anymore.

Doug consoles me with a pat.

I arrange my pillows and sit up. I pull up my nightshirt and examine my pregnant belly. "Will you rub some of that olive oil on my belly?" I ask Doug, pointing to the headboard.

"What are you making . . . an omelet?" He laughs.

"I'm preventing stretch marks."

"Rats, I like stretch marks. They're like a map." He outlines a patch with his finger.

"On second thought, let's save the olive oil for the omelet. I don't want that cold oil on my stomach. It looks like it might snow."

"The weather does look iffy today, doesn't it?"

"I'd like to stay in bed all day." I sigh.

He hugs me. The baby kicks.

"Who are you?" I ask my stomach. "Are you Jake? Are you Rachel?" I say unthinkingly.

"Rachel, huh?"

"Doug, what do you think of the name Rachel?"

"I think it's better than Espresso and Mocha. But not quite as poetic as Tiramisu and Caramel."

I laugh, because the names I suggested have been about as ridiculous. "That was just a phase I was going through. I was missing coffee."

"Well, please don't go through any more phases, Becca. We have enough phases with four children."

"No more phases now. We're in the homestretch."

"You know, I actually do like the name Rachel," he says thoughtfully.

"I think it would be a great name too."

"Rachel *Irene* Joy," Doug adds, grinning.

*Grrr.* A scowl comes with the growl.

"You do this to me every pregnancy, Doug, and every time you do, it isn't even funny."

"Okay, Rachel *Elizabeth* Joy," he counters.

"Better. Much better," I say, scowl-less. "Rachel is the name Valerie had picked out for the daughter she never had. She'll be so happy when I tell her."

"When is she coming, again?" Doug asks, because men never remember such things.

"The week before I'm due."

"Are you sure you want her visiting in your condition?" Doug draws ticklish lines on my tummy.

"Why wouldn't I? She's my sister!"

He smiles, but only a little. "Because I know how sensitive you are around Valerie."

"But honey, I told you that we're okay now."

"Yes, I know what you told me, Becca."

"Lillie and Mary both want to come when the baby is about three months, but I haven't heard from either of them lately."

"What about Sherri?"

"Didn't I tell you that Sherri is living on a kibbutz in Israel, growing tea?"

"You might have. In the middle of a football game."

I change the subject. "Mom and Dad are going to try and make it out, but they have two grandchildren ahead of us they have to visit."

"That's too bad," Doug says.

I play with my nails.

"I don't suppose any of your brothers are coming," he says.

"Are you kidding? The most I get from them is a Christmas card once a year signed by their wives. But I realize they're just guys."

Doug defends the male species. "I have to admit babies aren't the uppermost thing on a man's mind in the fall."

"But in *your* mind, it's babies, right, Doug? Babies are more important than football?" I eye him, just to make sure.

"Our baby . . . sure. Definitely. Without a doubt." And then he talks to my stomach. "Just don't be born on Monday night, kid."

I sulk.

"I'm kidding, Becca. I'm only kidding."

*Sure you are.*

Men can be so maddeningly male.

⋆⅋⋆

The nesting instinct is kicking in. I have this impulsive urge, stronger than any food cravings (which have greatly diminished), to clean anything and everything. I'm up every night until midnight rearranging furniture and scrubbing the walls, feathering my nest for our little bird.

Doug's worried I'll take the refrigerator apart so I can clean those hard-to-reach spaces.

I tell him it can't hurt. Valerie is coming tomorrow, and she detests dirt. At our family reunion, she went around picking pieces of lint off my carpet and bought me a new microwave because she said mine had spaghetti-sauce splatters.

I have packed and repacked my hospital bag, reorganized my billing system, and organized the garage, arranging Doug's tools in alphabetical order (kidding on the alphabetical order).

To tell you how wacky I am, I even took Irene with me to do some

174

early Christmas shopping. She bought Doug seven hundred dollars' worth of fishing gear and asked me if I wanted the George Foreman rotisserie (I must be moving up in her world).

I told her I preferred to buy my roasted chickens from the grocery store, but guess what I'll be getting for Christmas anyway?

# Chapter

# Twenty-Six

My house is spotless when Valerie arrives at my doorstep a week before my due date. She insisted on taking a taxi, because she said she wasn't "used to vans." I told her we had a PT Cruiser, too, and asked her if she would prefer it. She said, and I quote, "I wouldn't ride in one of those hearses if I were dead."

This is a huge clue that Valerie is still Valerie, despite our understanding.

When the taxi driver drops a big box on my living-room floor, Valerie forgets to tell him thank you or good-bye. "Logan should appreciate these," she says proudly.

"Thank you," I answer.

*What were you thinking, inviting your sister at this delicate time, macaroni brain?*

Five minutes into our exchange, I excuse myself and head for the bedroom. I grab my cell phone I left in my purse the day before and call Allie.

She picks up immediately.

"Allie. Oh, Allie. Valerie is still her horrible, mean self. Do you realize that this is a very bad time to have a horrible, mean sister staying with you?"

"I didn't think it was a very good idea," she says cautiously.

"When are you coming, Allie?"

"As soon as your water breaks."

"Could you send me a hatpin by Federal Express?"

"Becca, drama will not help here. You need to think on your feet."

"I can't even *stand* on my feet; how am I going to *think* on my feet?"

"Stop swinging like a pendulum and think logically," she orders.

"I haven't thought logically once through this entire pregnancy, and you want me to start now! I'm not going to make it, Allie. Seriously."

"Just agree with everything Valerie says and compliment her a lot. Remember, she's been through a lot with her husband and her son at college and all."

"Yes, Saint Allie."

"I'll ignore that because of your condition and the promise that in the near future, you will revert to your former pleasant personality," says Allie.

"I'll apologize later, when I'm normal. But I'm in a crisis, girl-friend."

"I can walk you through this the way I do my patients, but you have to hear what I'm saying. And you cannot make any jokes."

"No jokes?"

"None."

"Okay."

Allie takes a huge breath. "First you need to start thinking in terms of . . ."

Silence.

"Allie?"

Silence.

"Allie?"

Nothing!

"Oh no. This lousy battery. A-l-l-i-e!" I scream hopelessly. Then I throw the phone on the bed.

"What? What?" Valerie rushes in the door.

"I think I'll freshen up," I say.

Valerie eyes me. "You always were strange." Then she adds, "Do you have a *TV Guide?*"

"No. Why?"

"I wanted to watch *Pyramid.* Donny Osmond hosts it, you know. Do you remember how crazy we all were about Donny when we were growing up? Ahh . . ." She floats out of the room.

*I remember how you ripped my Donny Osmond poster in half after you said you loved him more.*

"Better?" Allie asks an hour later when my cell-phone battery is recharged.

"Slightly. I prayed."

"Good. Then you don't need my advice."

"I don't have time for lengthy advice. Valerie is primping and will be back in a minute. We're going to the health-food store because my meat has hormones." I sigh. "I would make a hormone joke, but nothing is funny right now."

"Maybe I can come sooner," Allie says, like she's seriously considering it.

"Really, Allie? Really?"

"When do you think the baby is coming, Becca?"

"When do you think the stock market is going to crash, Allie? I don't know."

"Your due date is November eighth?"

"Yes. November eighth," I confirm.

*God, make her come . . . please.*

"And you always have your babies on time."

"So on time, Allie. Really."

"Becca, this is such a critical time with some of my patients. It would be better if you called me when you were going into labor."

"I have one word for you, Allie."

"What is that, dare I ask?"

"Medication."

"Becca, you have been an absolute cat during this pregnancy."

"Oh, I know. I do feel so sinful all the time. 'Amazing Grace' is my favorite song these days. I just vary the words."

"Again, dare I ask?"

"I change 'wretch like me' to 'beast like me' and 'loser' and 'worm' and 'hormonal disaster.' It makes the time pass quicker."

"I get the picture. I'll do what I can to get there," she says.

"Oh, thank you, thank you, thank you."

"You're welcome, welcome, welcome."

She sounds like the goose in *Charlotte's Web*.

"Hey, Allie, do you want me to pick you up in the hearse or the van?"

"Hearse? You have a hearse?" she asks, doubting.

"Well, it is occupied at the moment."

"Occupied?" She sounds worried.

"No dead bodies, just Doug driving back from Boulder. He had a seminar there today."

Silence. Allie is thinking.

"It's a private joke, Allie Oop. Hey, here comes Valerie. Call me later with your flight info."

"And a prescription for a big yellow pill?" she asks.

⚭

It is November eighth, the date I have been waiting for, thinking about, literally dreaming of for months. But I've seen more action watching grass grow.

Allie and I are seated in the van in the airport parking lot. She is holding a Styrofoam container on her lap.

"So, nothing yet?" she asks.

"Nothing."

"You better have that baby soon."

"Tell the baby that."

"Hey, Boo, it's a virtual paradise out here, so hurry!" she yells.

"Don't lie to the kid, Allie."

"Okay, it's a rotten, sinful world, but there's chocolate on this side."

"Better," I say, satisfied. "This baby has been so calm during my whole pregnancy, I've hardly gotten to know him or her." I rub my itchy tummy.

"He or she will have his or her say when he or she has lungs."

"Don't you just hate that?"

"Hate what?" Allie adjusts her pink wire-rimmed glasses.

"Saying 'he or she.' It takes up so much time."

"But 'it' sounds like a creature and could give the kid a complex."

I start the van. "So tell me what's in that container so we can go."

"A special treat for my best friend." Allie opens the box and lets out an elongated moan. "It was fried green tomatoes; now it's mush!" she says, disappointed.

"That's a shame."

"I was committed to saving it for you, no matter the cost. I was intent on fighting off hijackers and airport security dogs so you could have your respectable craving."

"It was a kind thought, Allie. But don't worry about it. I don't have much of an appetite these days."

She lays the pottage on the backseat. "Why isn't your sister here?"

"Valerie is at home watching *Pyramid*."

"That game show with Donny Osmond?"

"Yes, that game show with Donny Osmond. Don't even get me started."

"But you two have been doing better . . ."

"Sort of. We went to church yesterday and held hands during worship."

"That's great," Allie comments.

"It was, until she pointed out my one age spot and whispered, 'You can have that removed, you know.'"

"Oh dear."

"But I overlooked that and enjoyed the sermon on forgiveness . . . until we were leaving."

"What happened then?"

"Alda Meyers, the snoop, asked what I was like as a child."

"And?"

"Valerie started firing ammunition posthaste, but I'm not going to tell you what she said because it could be used against me in a court of law."

"And you started firing back."

"No, I didn't."

"And aren't you proud of yourself?"

"I am very proud, but my tongue is bitten to pieces."

Not being used to the weather, Allie shivers, and I turn up the heater.

"Besides that, we've done fairly well. We've been doing devotions together at night."

"Is that bringing you closer?" Allie asks.

I chuckle. "Well, we did get into a little argument."

"Is nothing sacred between you two?"

"It was that pesky little passage, Genesis 6. It should be disallowed from devotionals."

"Oh, 'There were giants on the earth in those days . . .'" Allie says in her scholarly tone.

"That's the one." I chuckle again. "We went through that whole 'sons of God' bit and whether 'man' is a descriptive noun or a primary noun."

"I'm glad I wasn't there." Allie loosens her gray lamb's wool scarf.

"Doug finally had to referee. 'Does it really matter?' he said.

'The point is, there were giant offspring, and you two can agree on that, can't you?' So we became friends again and made taffy like we did when we were children."

"Taffy. Yum," Allie says longingly.

"Well, not exactly like when we were children. Valerie pointed out that too."

"Are we going to sit in the parking lot all day talking?"

"No, we are not." I back out too quickly, just missing another car.

# Chapter
# Twenty-Seven

"You have a *mouse* in your house!" is the first thing Valerie says as we pull up in the driveway.

"A mouse? Are you sure?" I ask, disbelieving.

"Yes, I'm sure, Becca." Valerie is wearing my warmest coat and looks angry. "The thing scurried across the living room and went into hiding."

"Was the door left open, Valerie?"

"I propped it open for a few minutes while I was hunting in your garage freezer for some ice. Do you know that your icemaker isn't working?"

"Yes, I know."

"I already called an exterminator for you. He's coming out first thing in the morning. You'll have to clear off your counters and put everything away in the kitchen."

"What company did you call?" I ask, disturbed.

"Lloyd's Pest Control. I got it out of the phone book."

"Lloyd's. I don't know him from Adam."

"Trust someone for once in your life, Becca," she replies irritably.

"Valerie, we haven't had a mouse for a couple of years. It's probably only one mouse, and a trap would have worked; we don't need an exterminator."

"Those traps are vicious. Besides this thing was gigantic—of the King Kong variety. And don't you know mice have diseases? Lloyd said you could have a mouse infestation if you don't take care of it right away."

"Did you happen to think that I'm pregnant, Valerie, and the exterminator's chemicals may not be good for my health?"

"It's some sort of a gas that dissipates quickly. Lloyd says it's harmless; he breathes it all the time. They tent the house, and then you have to be out for twenty-four hours. It's that simple." Valerie jumps up and down to warm herself.

"And where are we supposed to stay?"

"You can go stay in a hotel or something," Valerie says casually.

"Eight of us in a hotel?" I think of the expense.

"Judy said we could stay at her house. She invited me for lunch and served scallops. She's a fantastic cook!"

"I am *not* going to impose on Judy."

"Suit yourself, Becca. I've already accepted her invitation."

I sigh. By now I'm completely annoyed. "Well, let's get started."

"*You* can get started," Valerie says. "I am not stepping foot inside your house until that monster is destroyed."

I look at Allie; she looks at me.

"Oh, and would you please bring my suitcase over to Judy's before you leave for the hotel?"

Valerie chooses not to notice my furious expression. "It's freezing out here, Becca. Why do you have to live someplace so cold? I could be lounging in seventy degree weather right now."

❧

"My sister is going to be the death of me; you realize that, Allie," I say in the kitchen, trying to decide what to start bagging first. "When we were growing up, our house was full of mice."

"Maybe that's why she doesn't like mice," Allie offers graciously. "Here I am with my life turned upside down over one stupid little mouse."

Allie looks ridiculous wearing a pair of my old jeans that look like capris on her. When she packed she wasn't expecting housework. I almost want to laugh at her, but at the same time, I'm irritated at her because she doesn't seem upset by Valerie's behavior.

Two hours later, however, as we've worked our fingers to the bone, her irritation starts to show. "I have to say, Becca, that your sister *is* rather exasperating. I thought her calling and asking you to bring over a box of Cheez-Its was uncalled for."

"Thank you, Allie. Thank you for finally getting it."

"It's not that I don't get it," she clarifies. "It's just that I try to avoid conflict whenever possible."

"That's because you are an only child."

"No, that's because Paul says in the Bible that whenever possible we should live peaceably with all men."

"That may be part of it, but being an only child, you didn't learn that it's normal to have conflict."

We stop and hear ourselves.

"Do you feel like a stretched rubber band, Allie Oop?"

"I'm just exhausted from traveling all day and your sister's antics—"

We hear the front door slam. Tawny steps into the kitchen, smelling of my best perfume and wearing my favorite sweater.

"Hi, Mom. Hi, Allie," the rest of the children call as they come in the door and tear down the hall.

"I hate taking that bus home, Mom," Tawny says. "Why do you drop us off in the morning but refuse to pick us up after school?"

"One of the privileges of adulthood, Tawny. Now we're going to have a family meeting. Spread the word," I say.

"Without Dad?"

"Yes, without Dad."

"Can't it wait? *Sponge Bob* is on," Ben complains as we gather in the living room.

"There will be *no* television this afternoon," I insist.

"Why?" Logan asks.

"Let me explain, kids," I say, as Allie leans back in the La-Z-Boy and closes her eyes.

When I finish my explanation, Tawny shrieks. "You mean there's a *mouse* somewhere in this house? Maybe even a *flock* of them?"

"Mice don't come in flocks, bonehead," Logan declares.

"Do they have a pool at the hotel?" Carly asks.

"And who's going to watch Rover?" Ben cries.

"Yes, they have a pool, and Blessing will be fine alone. Now no more questions; go pack your bags. Your father will meet us there later."

The majority leave.

Tawny lingers. "Mom, I will positively *die* if I see a filthy little mouse. Can't you just pick me up at the Andersons' house?"

"You need to pack first."

"Oh, *Mom*. Can't you *please* pack for me?"

She runs out of the room calling, "Thank you!" before I can answer. I don't have the energy to fight it.

"Say hello to your Aunt Valerie at Judy's house," I yell. "Tell her Allie and I had a wonderful time doing all the work." I think about the expense again. "There goes our vacation to Estes Park," I mumble under my breath.

I wake up Allie because I don't want to be cranky alone. "Allie. Allie. How about a cup of tea?"

"I think we could both use a cup of tea."

Fifteen minutes later Allie and I sit at the breakfast nook, getting over the day.

Ben almost knocks over my cup of tea. "Mom! Mom!"

"What Ben? What?"

"Hobbit is missing."

"Again?"

"I don't know how he got out. He was there this morning." He twists his face as he says it.

"Hobbit . . . Oh, Allie, you don't suppose . . ."

"I do suppose. At lightning speed Hobbit could resemble a rodent, if you were half-blind."

"Lloyd's Pest Control," I say, reaching for the phone book. "All this work for nothing."

"Becca, may I join you in disliking your sister for a moment?"

"You may."

With three children on the job, Hobbit is located within a few minutes.

"Where was he?" I ask.

Ben looks hesitant to answer but finally does. "In Tawny's shoe in the living room."

"Just where Valerie spotted him," I say to Allie, and her eyes widen.

"We don't need to mention this to your sister, Ben. She has an aversion to Hobbit droppings."

We laugh, because crying won't help.

"And Ben, we need to make it a priority to get a lock on that cage."

"Okay, Mom."

Valerie is looking out the window feeling sorry for herself after a macaroni-and-cheese dinner, which is all I had the energy to prepare.

"You are so unfair, Becca," she hisses.

"I'm just saying that a sugar glider looks nothing like a mouse, Valerie. Have you ever seen a mouse that size, and with a bushy tail like a squirrel?"

"Well, that thing is positively dreadful. If I had known you had such a pet, I might not have come to visit." With a *humph* she folds her arms.

I've just about had it. "Well, you are free to leave anytime you are unable to endure my abhorrent household."

"Where did you come up with such a big word, Becca?" Valerie says patronizingly.

"Scrabble, anyone?" Allie interjects—and only she laughs.

"Okay, let's just drop it," I say. "Does anybody want to go out for an ice-cream cone? Or we could stay here and make taffy."

"Allie, unless you've had Becca's taffy, you haven't experienced taffy. I have third-degree burns to prove it." Valerie shows a miniscule red spot on her right thumb.

"You just didn't have enough butter on your hands," I stress.

"Besides the injuries, you didn't put vinegar in the recipe. That's why it didn't turn out like Mom's," Valerie says to me.

"Vinegar? That would ruin it. Don't you think, Allie, that putting vinegar in sweet taffy would ruin it?"

"Would you two please stop for five minutes?" Allie nearly yells, uncharacteristically bold. "You're giving me a headache."

The phone rings.

"Mom, it's Grandma Irene." Logan gives me the phone.

"Speaking of headaches," I mouth to Allie, then answer pleasantly, "Irene."

Irene starts in, and I partially listen and answer, "No, not yet . . . Yes, I know . . . Maybe it was that way back then, Irene, but now . . . Ouch! Hold on, Irene."

"Are you all right, Becca?" Allie asks.

"I think I'm having a contraction. You talk to my mother-in-law."

Allie takes the phone. "Irene, Becca is having a contraction, so she has to go."

I shake my head no to Allie, hoping she understands that means

I'd rather eat a raw quail egg at the sushi bar than have my mother-in-law over here now.

"No. Don't come over," Allie says firmly. "Irene! . . . She's coming over." Allie drops the phone on the chair.

"Oh great," I whine as Allie leads me to the bigger couch. Valerie takes her time surrendering her comfort.

"This is definitely a contraction," I say weakly. "Call Doug."

No questions; Allie does her job.

"Are you okay?" Valerie asks halfheartedly.

"No, I'm not okay," I answer, doubled over.

"I think I'll have a Coke," she says. "A Coke with no ice."

The news of my condition filters into the bedrooms, and one by one children come to my side.

Ben brings me a glass of water.

"Thank you, Ben, but I'm not thirsty."

A minute later Carly stands at the couch with my suitcase.

"Just put that in the corner, sweetheart." The words are strained.

Logan comes in with a washcloth and hands it to Carly, who wipes my brow. "Do you want me to drive you to the hospital, Mom?" Logan asks.

"No," I say abruptly, then add, "thank you for asking."

"Do you want me to go get Tawny?" Logan continues.

"No. But you could get me a clean toothbrush from the front bathroom medicine cabinet and put it in my suitcase."

"Sure, Mom." He walks out of the room backward, worry showing on his face.

"Doug will be here in five minutes," Allie reports. She takes off my shoes and rubs my feet. "It will be okay, Becca. It's going to be fine."

"Thank you, Allie."

Ben strokes my hair; Carly continues to wipe my brow.

Pain sweeps over me, and I wish I had some ice.

Valerie stares at me from the loveseat and says to the children, "You guys look so cute over there taking care of your mom."

I moan, but softly, so as not to alarm the children.

"I can't believe that thing wasn't a mouse," Valerie says. "It looked so much like a mouse. I wonder why God made mice. They serve no purpose I can see."

I close my eyes and take a deep breath. *This is so much like my sister. I'm lying here in excruciating pain, and she's asking why God made mice.*

# Chapter Twenty-Eight

My legs are in stirrups, and since I am not a cowgirl, I guess you know where I am.

We are in the same labor and delivery room at Shapiro Community Hospital as when we had Carly.

The nurse says I am 80 percent effaced and six centimeters dilated.

"Yee-ha," I say, like a rodeo queen on Labor Day weekend. I feel like I can take on anything: barrel racing, calf roping, bull riding, back labor. I feel invincible.

Rodeo queen status is a fleeting thing. All that *bull* about fifth-time labors being a cakewalk; I think people in the stands make that up. An hour later my water has broken, and my contractions are coming five minutes apart. Doug is at my side, adoring me with loving eyes.

The cowgirl's enthusiasm is fading fast. In fact, now she's feeling more like a mean mama cow in active labor. The animal instincts are taking over. She would like to kick somebody, but she's trying to keep herself in check.

*How long can the cowgirl hold on to that rope?*

"You know, eight years isn't all that long ago, but I can hardly remember what it's like," Doug begins.

"Doug, please bring me some ice."

*Holding on. Holding on.*

He comes back with a bucketful and slides an ice chip across my dry lips.

I grab the piece of ice from him. "I want to eat it, not wear it," I say impatiently and start chomping on it violently.

*The cowgirl has let go of the rope. The cowboy is in trouble now.*

"I think my memory is coming back to me," Doug says.

I glare at him, and a contraction follows. "What was my focal point the last time we were in this room, Doug?" I ask, almost screaming.

He hesitates. "The wallpaper."

I remember it now. It had teapots. "Why did they change the wallpaper?" I ask my nurse, through raging pain.

"It made people nervous," she replies.

I grimace. "Jumping monkeys, how could teapots make people nervous?"

"It was too busy." She adjusts the monitor belt around my abdomen.

"And yellow stripes aren't?" I fire back, aggravated.

"The yellow is supposed to make people cheery," she explains.

"These stripes are supposed to make us cheery? This wallpaper makes me dizzy, not cheery. I would be more cheery with gray walls in a prison cell. Who makes these decisions anyway? Does the hospital have a committee, or does some wallpaper guy open his wallpaper book and point randomly?"

"Do you think it's time to give your wife some pain medication?" she asks Doug.

"Why are you asking him?" I hiss. "*I'm* the one in labor, in case you haven't figured it out."

"I've figured it out all right," she says to the air. "So would *you* like some pain medication, Mrs. Joy?" she asks, as pleasantly as if she were Florence Nightingale.

"Are you kidding? This is my fifth child."

"Understood." She tiptoes out of the room to get the anesthesiologist.

"Honey, you're giving Elizabeth an awfully hard time," Doug says carefully.

"Is that her name? Elizabeth? I don't want my baby named after my labor nurse!" I exclaim. I raise the bed. "I want to see my children," I demand.

"They're not here. I decided it would be better if they didn't come after all. Judy was kind enough to offer to fix them dinner."

"I want them here now!" I'm whining like a spoiled child, and I know it.

"I'm not sure they're allowed. Besides this isn't a good time for them to see you, Becca."

"Why not?" I pout.

"Because if they see you now, they may decide not to have children of their own, and you do want grandchildren, don't you?"

"Well, all right," I say. "Can I at least have Allie?"

"I'll call the ladies in."

"The ladies?"

"Sure—you can't have Allie and not have my mother and your sister."

I do some *hee hee* breaths.

Ten minutes later the gang walks in.

Allie puts a vase of roses on my bedstand. "How are you doing?"

I look at her sluggishly. "I've been better."

My mother-in-law stands at the end of the bed. She pats my foot obligatorily and asks Doug if the chair he is sitting in is comfortable enough.

"It's great, Ma," he replies.

"Do you want to watch Monday Night Football?" she asks him.

I glare, big-time.

He says no, though hesitantly.

"What about a bite to eat?" she continues. "I can pick you something up at the cafeteria."

"No thank you, Ma. I'm fine."

"Fork over that stress ball, Allie," I say.

She tosses me a ball that says *I can do this!*

I squeeze my bad thoughts away. Finally, I notice that Valerie is waving a book.

"What do you have there?" I ask, because she'll wave it all night if I don't.

"It's called *Laughing through Labor*. I got it in the gift shop. It says here, 'When you laugh, it releases natural chemicals in the body that create a feeling of pleasure and have a pain-relieving effect.'"

"That should be right up Allie's alley," I spout, thinking myself humorous in-between contractions. "She loves endorphins."

"I don't get it," Valerie says.

Doug massages my shoulders as I ride another labor wave. I concentrate on the yellow roses Allie brought me and pray one of my favorite psalms.

When I look up, Valerie is telling labor jokes that make me want to spit at her.

*Jesus, help me be a better person,* I pray.

The anesthesiologist comes in and relieves me from Valerie's comic relief. The women are asked to leave.

Allie squeezes my hand. I don't want her to go.

"You know I love you," she says.

"I love you back."

Irene and Valerie say they'll see me later.

"I'll see you two later," I call back.

"Will you be okay, Son?" my mother-in-law asks my husband before she leaves.

I squeeze my stress ball several times.

The anesthesiologist explains the epidural and administers it efficiently and painfully.

Doug coaches me through my contractions as we wait for the medication to take full effect.

"Tawny is in the waiting room. She wants to come in," Doug tells me.

"Are you sure I won't traumatize her?" I ask flippantly.

"I'll be right back," he says, already looking worn.

A few minutes later he returns.

I feel much better. "I'm sorry, sweetheart. Come sit down on the bed and talk to me."

"Medication is a blessed thing." He kisses my forehead and sits down.

As the needle on the machine moves up and down, Doug asks if I can feel the contraction.

"Hardly," I say.

He is amazed.

Tawny arrives with a picture from Ben, a beanie baby from Carly, and a hello from Logan. Her contribution is music: specifically, Christian rap. We bop to the beat until the music starts giving me a headache.

Doug goes to the cafeteria for a cup of coffee. I ask Tawny to turn off the music so we can talk.

We share a few moments of intimate conversation. Tawny says she wants to wait until she's thirty to have children, and then she only wants one.

I don't offer any advice. I remember being fifteen.

Doug is back with ice chips. I crunch on them.

I have no concept of time. I made Doug take the clock down,

and the new nurse hasn't said anything about it. Since I am nicer now, I feel sorry that I was testy with Elizabeth. I like the name Elizabeth again. My new nurse's name is Jill, and she seems so nice. I wonder if maybe Elizabeth was nice too.

Time passes slowly, despite not knowing the time. Doug asks me if I am ready for delivery.

"Like a girl scout is ready to deliver cookies," I quip.

We laugh, and the endorphins make me feel happy. Either that or the medication.

At 11:40 I am ready to push, but the doctor is not here.

Jill pours mineral oil on my stomach, and I ask her to apologize to Elizabeth.

"Don't worry about it," Jill says. "It happens all the time."

Dr. Christy comes into the equipped room in surgical attire. He is calm and smiling and says he will try not to do an episiotomy.

I am wildly ecstatic for that news. Save the Ginsu knives for sushi.

After four sets of hard pushes, my baby's lungs are inflated for the first time.

I close my eyes and hear the most beautiful sound I have ever heard in my life since the last beautiful sound I heard eight years prior, and the three times before that.

"Where's the clock?" the doctor asks.

"It's 11:59 exactly," the nurse reports.

"You like to live on the edge, don't you, Becca?" Dr. Christy teases.

"Is it a she or a he?" I ask. The most important question in the universe right now.

"It's a she," Dr. Christy announces as he checks her. "Ten fingers, ten toes . . . Hair is a little lighter than the others, though. Has the milkman been around?"

"Lighter?"

"Not really." Dr. Christy grins. "Dark as midnight, and lots of it."

The nurse whisks her over to the warmer and suctions her.

"Do you mind?" Doug asks.

"No, go ahead."

"Seven pounds, two ounces, and nineteen inches long." The announcement is made by one of the nurses.

"And she's more beautiful than sunshine," Doug exclaims.

"She scores a ten," the nurse says, referring to the APGAR.

I am finally handed my bundle of joy as Doug touches my shoulder, speechless with emotion.

Elation is my first emotion, my second emotion, and my third.

All the worrisome thoughts evaporate. Every bit of pain was nothing.

I am a musician composing a glorious symphony; I am a poet writing inspired prose; I am an artist painting a beautiful work of art. In this moment I am everything I have ever hoped to be, will ever hope to be.

God is speaking to me, words I've heard all along. *Flowers don't blossom in one day, Becca. They take time to unfold.*

And now I understand.

I feel like a flower holding a flower—the most beautiful flower in the world.

# Chapter

# Twenty-Nine

*November 9*
*Ducky . . . oh Ducky:*

*Words cannot describe how I feel. One might think that, after the fifth birth, this baby stuff might become old hat. Absolutely not.*

*I am melting all over the floor. I am so full of pride and love and a hundred other emotions that are seeping out of my abundant soul.*

*Yes, there are other mothers all over the world in other hospitals, claiming their babies are the most beautiful. But, Ducky, Rachel is more amazing than any of them. (And Daddy agrees.)*

*(She is asleep now, so shh!)*

*Dear Ducky:*

*I was in a tizzy a couple of hours ago. I started thinking how different Rachel looks than our other children. Her nose is not like my other children's; it is slightly upturned—rather perfect, however; and her lips are thinner, her face is rounder. Because of these differences, I checked her wristband several times to ensure that Shapiro*

*Community Hospital had it right. When he was making his rounds, I mentioned it to Dr. Christy, but he made another milkman joke. He has way too much fun for a physician.*

*So then I asked the nurse on duty about the possibility of a baby switch. She said it has NEVER happened. I told her it has; I saw it on Dateline.*

*My nurse is a stern woman. Everything about her is tight, including her uniform. And her name is Irene. Doo doo doo doo (Twilight Zone music).*

*After my second . . . okay, thirteenth inquiry about the possibility of hospital negligence relating to the baby switch, Nurse Irene said, rather rudely, I thought, "The call button is for medical purposes, Rebecca. Not for purposes of persecution."*

*"When is your shift over?" I asked.*

*"In another hour."*

*"Then I shall save my questions for the next nurse," I said haughtily.*

*"That is an excellent idea," she said. "Gloria is on shift next."*

*A trail of laughter followed her out the door.*

*Do nurses have tenure like college professors? I mean, after being a nurse for a certain amount of time, they can't be fired, or something?*

*Dear Ducky:*

*Remember the pride and love and hundred other emotions seeping out of my abundant soul? Well, there are others now, just as strong, but far less productive. Allie says all these strange emotions I am feeling— paranoia, anxiety, tearfulness, and wanting to murder people—is postpartum blues.*

*I asked her if it will get worse or better, because I didn't remember having this malady in my former pregnancies (but Doug said he did).*

"*Worse for a while, and then better,*" she said.

"*Promise you will be my friend no matter what?*" I ask her, tears flowing against my will.

"*I promise,*" she said and waved a piece of Godiva chocolate in front of me that she said would ease my distress.

"*My lactate consultant says 'no chocolate.' That chocolate will make Rachel gassy and fussy,*" I whined.

"*Listen, Becca, you went through a lot for that kid. One piece of chocolate won't bother her.*"

So I opened the gold wrapper and sucked for about two seconds, then spit it out. I handed it off to Allie, because I didn't want it.

"*Yuck!*" She tossed it in the trash can like it was a snake.

"*Sorry, Allie, but I can't do it.*"

So she took a piece, unwrapped it, and ate it.

"*I'll start on my diet again tomorrow,*" she said, her eyes closed and her face peaceful, like she was in love.

Gotta go, Ducky. My plastic food has arrived.

$\sim \infty \sim$

Dear Ducky:

Judy came by with roses, sweet-smelling lavender everything, and a 1928 locket (my favorite brand of jewelry). Glory, I love that woman.

Carol and Vanessa came next. You know that silly discussion they had on baby gift etiquette? Well, this time they discussed hospital etiquette. The social graces of what? I'm still trying to figure it out.

Manhattan came by with the shoe salesman. "*He's moving out of his mother's house,*" she whispered as she left.

They all saw Rachel through the glass. Carol and Vanessa said she looks just like me; Manhattan said she looks just like Carly.

Allie, Valerie, and my mother-in-law came by. Irene said Rachel *looks just like Doug. She can't see any me in her—none at all. Allie passed me the squeeze ball without me having to ask.*

*"Why do you keep squeezing that thing?" Irene asked, irritated.*

*I smiled but didn't answer.*

*Valerie said the baby looks nothing like any of us, which made my anxiety bubble again. And then she said I don't look like I even had a baby.*

*Hmm.*

*Doug came after everyone left—but he didn't bring the children. I threw a fit, wagging finger and all.*

*He held my finger and kissed it. "You're coming home in the morning. Besides, I wanted to spend some time with you alone."*

*That made it instantly better.*

*I decided on a lacy pink outfit for when Rachel gets to go home. Doug and I talked for twenty minutes about how she will look in her new outfit, and then we got real mushy.*

*Later, Ducky. Alda Meyers just arrived. I'm going to hide you under the mattress. Don't quack, okay? You're our little secret.*

So, Ducky:

*I am such a writing machine today. I've never written so much in one day, but then it's not exactly exciting here between visitors and the nurses checking my blood pressure, pulse, temperature, respiration, and all that private stuff. Oh, and bathroom visits.*

*They just took Rachel away to the nursery, and I miss her already.*

*Had a few more visitors since Alda. Pastor Ramsey and his wife were pleasant, as always. They brought me flowers and a devotional book on motherhood.*

*Al Samson came by in his blue polyester suit. He said we need to get life insurance on the baby right away and recommended the Gerber Grow Up plan. He also brought flowers from Doug's office, along with a card. The card was full of fake signatures. (Marge, the receptionist, signed for all the guys, trying to make each one look different; I know the trick.) Ursula's note was real. "Babies are a Joy!" All of the fifty people who wrote that on their card think they are so clever.*

*I'm exhausted but on an adrenaline rush too. I want to run a marathon, but I want to take a nap. My body can't make up my mind.*

*Dr. Christy is extending my hospital stay, so we're not leaving for another day. He mentioned edema and winked. I caught on right away that he's doing me a favor. You see, Rachel is jaundiced and she has to stay. If I had to go, that would really mess up the breast-feeding schedule.*

*All my babies were yellow babies.*

*Irene had lots of advice on that.*

*"Wasn't Doug a yellow baby?" I asked—respectfully, of course. I'm not sure what she said. It sounded like blah blah blah to me.*

*I'm getting a roommate. I think that's super-inconsiderate, don't you? I think fifth-time mommies should not be required to have a roommate.*

*My new nurse, Gloria, is a Christian, and we're having lots of fun. She likes Judy's cookies. (Doug brought half of them by.) She wants the recipe.*

*So I have to go to the bathroom—Gloria said so. I'm not waddling anymore, Ducky. I am sauntering. Tomorrow I hope to be moseying.*

*November 10*
*Dear Ducky:*

*If my nurse Irene was tight, my roommate is taut. I mean, no slack whatsoever.*

*She's young, but she takes everything so seriously. She asked me if*

*I could refrain from my cute jokes. (And they were some of my best.)*

*I mean, you have to make it fun here or it isn't any fun, especially when you have a yellow baby who looks different than your other children, and you are suffering from postpartum insanity.*

*I asked my roommate if she spoke French, since her name is Antoinette and I figured it wasn't an Irish name. Plus she has a thick accent.*

*"Of course. Oui, Madame."*

*I told her that Nurse Irene had said something to me in French I didn't understand, and then I pronounced it as best as I could remember.*

*She laughed. For several minutes, in fact. But then she wouldn't tell me what it meant.*

*If you ask me, she is being très difficult. Moi needs some sleep, so I don't lose my American/Irish temper. See—I know some French. I know lots of French restaurants are named Chez something. Like Chez Gerard and Chez Tony.*

*French food sounds good right now. Cheesecake sounds better.*

*Dear Ducky:*

*I just fed Rachel, and she latched on like a leech. Her bilirubin count is down, and my spirits are up.*

*Doug brought me smuggled cheesecake. (I am never eating another Giant Chocolate Brownie Ice Cream Sandwich in my life.)*

*We were having a good time . . . laughing, laughing, laughing, when Antoinette asked if we could "hold down the noise." She was watching General Hospital.*

*Doug said he had to go home and feed the kids anyway. He's making the chili recipe that won the church chili contest.*

*After Antoinette's soap operas were over, and I stopped gagging from the seedy drama, I put on a Tammy Trent CD in Tawny's boom box.* Antoinette asked me to turn it off because she wanted to take a nap. I was really mad until Allie came by.

"How many visitors has she had?" she whispered as Antoinette snored in French.

"None. Why?"

"She may not even be married. Have you thought of that?"

"No."

When Antoinette woke up, Allie rubbed her shoulders, and they became instant friends. Then she gave Antoinette my chocolate (since she is bottle feeding). A few minutes later they were laughing hysterically.

"What's so funny?" I asked.

Antoinette said it was Allie's joke, which was my joke that I had already told her and she didn't laugh at all.

Antoinette taught Allie some French phrases and then took another nap. While she was napping, I begged Allie to find out what that French phrase Irene said to me means.

When she woke up again, Allie asked.

"I have no idea." Antoinette laughed like a bowl full of the Jell-O they serve us here. "Your friend's pronunciation is very bad."

Why that little rat, I thought, but didn't say it because Allie had me feeling really sorry for her.

Eventually Antoinette and I became friends. She said she was sorry for her bad attitude, but that she had postpartum depression. With her accent, depresheon sounded really cute. Like it was something you wanted to have.

I found out that Antoinette's husband had gone back to France with another woman. Poor girl.

Antoinette and I are going to meet at Mimi's Café in one month. I asked her if eggs Benedict is French.

"Oui, Madame," she said.

# Chapter

# Thirty

It's Saturday . . . five days after the blessed event. And I've just discovered a terrible secret. The scale says I weigh only five pounds less than I did when I was pregnant. I come out of the bathroom in a blue robe, feeling blue.

Valerie says it's no secret, and then all my children leave the room, except Rachel, who can't talk.

"You mean it's no secret I'm still fat!"

"Well, maybe not fat."

I take a relieved breath. "What, then?"

"Hefty," Valerie announces.

"Hefty? Isn't that the name of a trash bag?"

"It's just water gain," Allie assures me. "It will all flush out of your system in the next few days."

At this point I am so happy my mother-in-law isn't here. She's on her way to a craft show somewhere. What a shame. I so need her input the next few weeks on these touchy matters.

Doug says we're having something very special for dinner next Saturday.

I'm quick on the draw. "Not chili, I hope."

"No, not chili. No, no, no, no, no, n-o, no, not chili," he emphasizes.

I choose not to ask him to elaborate on that.

So, speaking of yesterday (which we weren't but I am now, because I have no concentration), Doug went to work, the kids went to school, and Allie went to buy me a couple of in-between outfits. (I burned my maternity clothes—or wanted to anyway—and my other clothes are too tight.) So it was just me, Rachel, and Valerie, in order of maturity.

Anyway, I wasn't feeling well. I was feeling swollen from breast-feeding and achy all over. The exhaustion finally caught up with me, and now "sleep deprivation" is my middle name. But don't tell Vanessa, or she'll believe it.

Seriously, I could not move.

Since everyone in the household had helped out with Rachel, I thought my sister, who had traveled umpteen miles to "help me out," might actually do it for an hour while I slept.

Ten minutes or so into my nap, I hear a rap on my bedroom door.

"Becca," my helpless sister called, "Rachel has a stinky diaper."

"So, change it."

"Ooh, yuck. And besides, I don't know how." (I guess Luke changed his own diapers.)

"You unfasten, wipe, grab a new diaper, and fasten. It's real easy," I said, massively cranky. I tucked my head under my electric blanket and went back to sleep.

After I got my hour nap, I was pretty cheery, considering that it was a bleak and sunless day. Then I heard some voices coming from the living room.

This part is so entirely predictable you won't believe it. There was Judy rocking Rachel in my new Cracker Barrel rocking chair that Allie bought me.

"You have an angel here." Judy gave me the baby, who smelled good and was fast asleep. "But I really have to get back home. I have dinner in the Crock-Pot."

When she left, I gave Valerie the most exasperated look. "You couldn't change your niece's diaper? What did you do—go knock on Judy's door and ask her to change Rachel's diaper?"

"I called her on the phone. She doesn't care; she has six kids," Valerie said.

Sometimes I cannot believe my sister and I are from the same gene pool.

"It was the most disgusting thing," she added, holding her nose to prove her point. "It was yellow-green." Then she went back to reading her magazine and drinking the pink Snapple that Doug was saving for our special dinner.

✿

As I cuddle Rachel, I imagine this new world is a shock to her. A week ago she was floating in her warm balloon, tranquil, swallowing amniotic fluid in her cushiony paradise and being comforted by the sound of her mother's heartbeat.

And now she's in this other place wearing a bulky diaper that has to be restricting—a place where temperatures rise and fall, and children yell in your ear. In this strange, new environment, it must be upsetting to have everyone prodding you awake to be fed and changed, when all you want to do is sleep.

And now it's up to Doug and me to do better than her private swimming pool. Is that scary, or what?

One day, not too far away, she will discover her new world. She will try to figure out how things work. Already she opens her dark blue eyes and sees me; she smells me and knows me.

One day, when she gains control of her little body, she will roll over, then sit and play, and then she'll crawl. And on that most special of special days, when she takes her first steps, we will be there, urging her on like a sea captain guiding a ship.

We'll play peek-a-boo somewhere in-between, and then she'll learn to wave bye-bye. And then one sad, sad day she'll kiss me squarely on the lips as she heads into the kindergarten classroom, and I will feel like my life is over—for a while. (I feel bad now for making fun of the parents taking their children to the first day of kindergarten.)

And one day, very, very far away, she may be doing the same thing. Kissing her child squarely on the lips and telling him or her that life changes, like the seasons, but be happy anyway.

Life is a funny, funny thing. A repeat in many ways.

But a gift . . . oh, Rachel, if you only knew the things that God has prepared for us.

"Please tell me, Doug. Please tell me what we're having," I beg, as the snow falls, the biggest flakes so far this fall.

"It's arriving by UPS." He smiles and walks away.

*What would arrive by UPS?*

"Oh, Allie. You know what the special meal is, don't you?"

"Yes."

"Tell me. Tell me now." I grab her blouse.

She unfetters my fingers. "That would spoil the surprise. Now please don't ask me again."

In the hall I see Ben and try a third time. "Ben. Ben, darling. Do you know what Dad is up to?"

"Yes . . . only because I overheard him telling Aunt Allie. But he told me not to tell anyone."

"But you will tell me. Your own mother, won't you?" I cajole.

"Dad said you were tricky, Mom. But I didn't believe him." He walks away, the elastic waistband of his Joe Boxer shorts showing above his Target jeans.

In the living room I make one last attempt, testing my sister's loyalty.

"Don't even ask, Becca," Valerie snips back, "because I don't have a clue. I'm leaving anyway. Judy is dropping me off at the Smile Brighter clinic while she goes shopping."

Back in the bedroom.

"Rachel. If you were able, you would tell me, wouldn't you?"

Baby gurgling noises.

"Thank you, little lamb. I knew you would."

"The UPS truck is here!" I yell in full-blown hysteria, demonstrating my need for a good outing.

I grab my biggest coat and put it on.

The family congregates on the dead lawn hidden by snow; the UPS man looks overwhelmed.

"What is this? The whole neighborhood?" he asks, his dark hair dusted white.

"Cheaper by the dozen." I zip my coat.

"You mean there are more of them in the house?" he asks.

"Yep!" I say. "But only one."

My children, improperly attired for the freeze, run back in the house as Mr. UPS presents me with a lumbering package.

I waver under the size of it. When I turn around, the brown truck and the UPS man are driving away.

Doug turns to me. "Here, let me take that package. You've just had a baby."

"Don't touch it!" I scream and dash into the end zone like an NFL quarterback.

A touchdown has been scored in the kitchen.

Curious faces all around, I try to read the sender's address, but the name is smudged from the moisture.

"All right, you can go ahead and open it," Doug says, because he has no choice.

I grab a knife and tear into it, ripping into the cardboard, but there is nothing edible in the box.

"What is this?" I ask, pulling out a monstrosity: a moss-covered birdhouse.

"Let me see that box," Doug says.

A second later he says, "This isn't our dinner; this is from Mom. Hey, Allie, it's addressed to you."

"To me?" Allie asks, surprised.

"This thing is taller than ours." I feel a mixture of disbelief and hilarity pass over my face.

"That's like a totally boring package," Tawny comments.

"I'll say," Logan agrees.

They leave the room.

"That's big," Carly says. "Bigger than my Rapunzel tower."

"That's not what we ordered, huh, Dad?" Ben offers, under-statedly.

"No, it's not, Son," Doug answers, and he and the children walk away.

"Allie, let's have some tea and write some mother-in-law poems." I head for the tea cupboard.

"I did say I like birdhouses," Allie says, troubled. "But I meant in tree branches. I can't take that on the plane!"

I laugh even harder as Allie continues to mumble to herself. "What am I supposed to do with that thing?"

# Chapter

# Thirty-One

So the package didn't come by UPS, and Doug is feeling terrible about it.

"I'm going to go clean the bathroom." He grabs cleanser from under the kitchen sink.

"Why is he going to clean the bathroom?" Allie asks.

"Have you seen our bathroom?"

"No."

"If you had, you wouldn't be asking."

After being up all night with the baby, my nerves are unraveling. The surging tide of baby blues ain't helpin', if you'll pardon my bad grammar.

"So how long until these hormones go away?" I'm despondent, practically on the ground.

Allie pulls out *Baby's First Year*, which was a gift from Maggie, who said it tells you everything you need to know about the first year.

"There's a big truck in front of the house!" Carly announces, dragging Rapunzel's flaxen hair across the floor.

Allie closes the book. I look hopeful.

"Federal Express," Logan says.

211

"Dad! Dad!" Ben calls and wakes up Rachel, who was sleeping in her bassinet in the living room.

Since I am a good mother, I attend to my baby.

⚜

"Now for the big reveal," Doug says, smiling, as I nurse Rachel under a blanket.

"Our feast has arrived and is in the kitchen, waiting for me to work my culinary craft."

"What is it? What is it?" I ask, impatient.

"Maine lobster," Doug says with pleasure.

"Oh! Maine lobster—that's even better than Dungeness crab!" I exclaim.

"And more expensive," Doug adds. "Dozens of recipes to choose from, sweetheart. Take your choice." He gives me recipes, neatly written in calligraphy.

"Judy?"

"Yeah, Judy. I couldn't find it in our old Betty Crocker cookbook. Is that the only cookbook we own?" Doug asks.

"Yep." I eye my choices, one-handedly.

Lobster Thermidor. *That sounds messier than eggs Benedict.*

Lobster Cantonese. *I'm not over my Chinese trauma yet.*

Lobster Bisque. *I don't want soup; I want something to sink my teeth into.*

"I think, Doug, that good, ol' fashioned butter and lemon is what I want."

"Are you sure?" he asks.

"Absolutely."

"You and Allie go down in the family room and watch an *I Love Lucy* video while the kids and I prepare your feast," Doug instructs, collecting the recipes.

"Sounds good to me." I wipe thin milk off Rachel's mouth and lay her down with all due vigilance.

Warm and cozy under a blanket, Allie and I laugh heartily. The on-screen hilarity redirects my focus from the lobster feast being prepared by my personal chef.

Lucy's fake nose is on fire, and I am telling Allie how Lucy dipping her nose in the coffee cup was not in the script when I hear a scream.

"What kind of scream is that?" Allie asks.

"Let's see," I say, trying to discern the particulars.

We hear it again, only louder and longer.

"It's Tawny, and she might have seen a mouse. You don't suppose Valerie might have been right—that we actually do have a mouse?"

Allie doesn't answer. We throw off our blankets and tear up the stairs.

The whole family is in the kitchen, except Rachel, of course, whom I am delighted to say slept through the commotion.

"Oh, Mommy!" Tawny holds on to me like she's three years old. "Daddy is a *murderer*."

This is surprising news. I've had five children with a murderer.

"Look!" She points to a big stainless steel pot bubbling on the stove.

Since we don't own a big stainless steel pot, I deem that it's on loan from Judy.

"Oh, my," I say, more for Tawny's sake than mine.

"Did you think lobsters cooked themselves, sweetheart?" Doug asks Tawny ever so patiently.

"It's . . . it's just so awful."

"What about cows and pigs? Did you think they were meatless animals?" Logan asks, making sense to me.

"No. But, you don't murder them right in your kitchen." Tawny releases me and covers her face in horror.

"Look at those buggy eyes," Carly says, amazed.

"It's brutal; positively brutal," Tawny continues and shudders.

"Have you ever tasted lobster, Tawny?" Logan asks.

"No," she admits.

"Well, I have, and it's fantastic."

"Where?" we ask.

"At the Andersons' on Brett's birthday."

Ben is silent, and I wonder what he's thinking.

"I am *not* sucking lobster guts of murdered lobsters!" Tawny insists, flailing her arms.

Valerie walks in just then, white teeth gleaming, complaining about the snow and the mall, and the world, and hardly noticing anything is out of the ordinary.

"Aunt Valerie, look what they're doing," Tawny says pitifully.

"Is that your surprise, Doug? Murdering lobsters for fun?" my sister asks, aggravating the situation and me.

"You may find some comfort in knowing that lobsters have no central nervous system," Allie tells us.

"So, Valerie," I reason, holding Ben, who is reasonably confused, "are you going to tell me you have never been to a lobster restaurant?"

"Sure, I've been to a lobster restaurant. Randy and I eat at Red Lobster all the time," she says matter-of-factly.

"So then you are a murderer too," I say.

"We don't do the murdering." Valerie ends her sentence with a heavy sigh.

"People are paid to murder, so that's okay?" I ask, drained from the exchange.

She goes into some politically correct explanation, and Doug says something reasonable back. Allie adds her academic opinion.

Tawny picks a piece of fancy green out of the salad bowl and eats it.

The rest of my children just watch the exchange, like watching a ping-pong ball bounce back and forth.

Finally we agree that it would be better for everyone (except the lobsters, Ben points out) if we had our lobster dinner here and sent Aunt Valerie and Tawny out to eat.

Doug extracts a fifty-dollar bill from his wallet and says to my sister, as nice as it can be said, "Call a taxi, and you and Tawny go out somewhere."

"I get the hint, Doug. You don't want me driving your car," Valerie says, offended.

"I think Doug is being very generous," I tell Valerie. "Besides, you called his car a hearse and said you wouldn't ride in it if you were dead."

"She did?" Doug asks, murdering another feisty lobster.

Tawny shrieks. "Did you hear that?" She wails. "The lobster is screaming."

"That is the sound of steam escaping from the carapaces," Allie says calmly.

I don't ask what a carapace is.

I don't even care what a carapace is.

After the meal is over, Allie and I are told to relax, and we take Doug up on his kind offer. We sit on the living-room couch, our stomachs amply full from the lobster, which I cannot even begin to pretend was not succulent and wonderful.

Rachel wakes up, and I feed her again. She burps like a sailor, and I lay her down in the back bedroom.

Allie and I talk over the clangs and activity of the cleanup.

Valerie and Tawny walk into the room. At least they're not as sour faced as they were a couple of hours before, because they have been pacified with Doug's fifty dollars. But the look on their faces is still slightly regrettable. They're feeling sorry for the lobsters.

Doug sets our fine bone china around the dining table and announces dessert. The whole family congregates, but little is said until I ask Valerie where they ate.

"We didn't," she says, stone-faced.

Tawny shows us her whimsical beaded earrings, the ones I have
been telling her for months cost too much. At Tawny's insistence,
Valerie shows us her opal ring, which Tawny says is Peruvian. I expect a portion of Doug's money financed the stone, and that annoys
me since Valerie could afford to fly to Peru to buy it.

"So I guess you're hungry then," I say to Valerie, peevishly.

Tawny answers, "I'm starving."

Valerie wipes her marble brow, as stoic as a statue.

Allie puts on a classical CD.

Doug brings out a carrot cake with cream-cheese frosting on a
fancy platter; he says it's from my favorite bakery.

Everyone agrees that the dessert looks good, but no one seems
excited about it.

Doug looks positively beaten down with disappointment. He'd
intended to make this a special night for me, but now all we have
is a botched dinner party.

Tawny is oblivious to it all. She cuts herself a huge piece of cake
and starts eating it.

Allie cuts for everyone else.

The other children play with their cake, their spirits lower than
the Dead Sea.

*This expensive evening has been ruined!* I lament inwardly.

I can't tell you how irritated I am, and particularly at Valerie,
fair or not.

What I do now is most out of character and highly unexpected—
some might say even cruel, but others may say deserved. I lob a
piece of my cake at my sister.

"That is for ruining my otherwise perfect evening," I say, satisfied.

"Whoa, Mom," Logan exclaims.

"Good aim," Ben says with admiration.

Valerie is gaping incredulously; her mouth is open so wide you
could drive a fishing boat in it.

*Chalk it up to hormones,* I chuckle to myself.

Tawny, next to me, is looking stunned, like, *Did my mother really do that?*

Doug and Carly, sitting on the other side of me, say nothing.

There's an awful moment of silence.

"That was rather effective in relieving my stress!" I say, excusing my bad behavior.

Valerie regains her senses and lobs a piece of cake back.

"That was rather effective in relieving my stress as well," she says and sighs. Then she pings again.

I laugh and lick off the dripping excess.

"It's a good thing you have Pergo floors," Allie interjects.

This may have been the wrong thing to say, because all at once forks become slingshots; cake flies from all directions. The accompanying music aids the war.

The only nonparticipant is Allie, a.k.a. Switzerland. She is sitting at the end of the table, probably thinking, *Peace treaty.*

Everyone else seems to be enjoying the fun. Even Tawny—despite the fact that she is the main target, at least for Logan, Ben, and Carly. Doug, after fair play with the children, joins me in lobbing Valerie.

Back and forth the cake flies over the white tablecloth. More pieces are cut and thrown.

And we all start laughing hysterically, until we are falling off our chairs.

We are a complete mess when the cake symphony is over. I sit on Doug's lap and we kiss, smashing cake between us. It is an absolute riot; we are having the best time ever, and nobody cares that anybody murdered anybody, or who said what, or who did what. We truly do not care.

Blessing tears in the room at that moment, like he has a cake-smelling device planted in his nose. (I don't even care how he got in here.) He gleefully eats the cake off the floor.

And Ben, in his typical dry humor, says he wants to do this on his birthday instead of having a party.

# Chapter
# Thirty-Two

It's almost boring with everyone gone. Allie left over a week ago; Valerie left last week, after staying for Thanksgiving.

You see, Luke wasn't able to come home from Stanford for the holiday, and Randy had a business meeting scheduled on Thanksgiving. (I told Valerie that didn't sound right, but she said it was entirely believable and then ran crying to the bathroom.)

I felt so sorry for her that I begged her to stay for Thanksgiving, and she did. But only after she made a big deal about having to think about it for a couple of hours.

Miraculously, it was an incident-free Thanksgiving. I didn't even care that Valerie played Scrabble with Ben while I ran around the kitchen sweating profusely. It truly did not bother me that she took a two-hour nap after the turkey dinner while I did the cleanup. I am completely serious; it didn't. I know now that's just Valerie, and that laughing about it is better than getting mad.

Accuse me of being simplistic, but throwing cake worked.

After our cake warfare that lobster night, Valerie and I got along fabulously. It was as though she and I were able to release these unidentified emotions from childhood and have fun at the same time.

Allie said she never would have believed it. Now she's going to add a room onto her office—a concrete room with a drain—so that it can be hosed down after cake fights.

I would not try this at home, however. I had to call Clara in for a thorough cleaning. She didn't ask for an explanation as to why the chandelier and windows were covered in cake, and I didn't tell her. Now she probably thinks we are weird.

Sometimes I wish Allie were not so smart, because she told me something I didn't want to hear. She told me that the word *weird* in Old English means, "Of, relating to, or suggestive of the preternatural or supernatural." (I wrote it down and memorized it so I could show other people how smart I am.)

And now I feel weird about using the word *weird*, and Tawny is down in the dumps about it, because she uses *weird* "like all the time."

I didn't bother to ask Allie what she was doing hunting around in Old English dictionaries, because she might have thought I was alluding to her spinsterhood, which may be an Old English word as well.

She brings it up a lot more these days . . . being single, that is. I guess with her mother gone, it's harder to ignore, especially around the holidays.

On Thanksgiving Allie sounded really down, and I worry about her being alone at Christmas. I told her that Denver is still here waiting for her, and now that her mother is gone, there is no reason to stay in Atlanta. I reminded her that Denver is one of the best places to live, according to multiple surveys. It has a low unemployment rate, affordable housing, recreation, and it is safe.

"I know. I used to live there," she said.

"May I remind you, then, that Denver has no humidity and Hotlanta is, like, one hundred percent humidity?"

"And Denver is cold," she threw in.

"But Atlanta is swarming with crime," I countered.

"How would you know?" Allie asked.

"I did my research."

"Then you would also know that Atlanta is referred to as 'the jewel of the South,' has a thriving economy, and is teeming with culture?"

"You can start up a practice here, Allie," I begged.

"I have one in Atlanta."

"I know, but your patients can get someone else."

"That's not the point, Becca. Good grief."

"We have crazy people here. I'll introduce you to some."

"Can we move on please?" Allie asked.

"My mother-in-law can be your first client," I offered.

She was silent for a minute. "That would mean I would have to have the birdhouse on display in the lobby." And she laughed like Woody Woodpecker.

"I could get you other clients, Allie. Dozens of them."

"Hmm."

Then I tossed the bomb. "Rachel needs you."

Three words with a lot of pull.

I'm thinking Allie is seriously considering the move because she let out three very big *hmms* after I said that and followed them with a lingering sigh.

Oh, Allie and I could have so much fun together!

"Why, you haven't changed a bit since high school—not one bit," Julie McGregor-Talbot says to me as we stare at each other in a booth at the Red Lobster, far enough from the kitchen so we don't hear the lobsters screaming.

"And neither has the Sphinx," I say, and laugh. "But, seriously, Julie, you look great."

"One word," she says, and looks around. "Botox," she whispers.

"Botox?"

"It's no biggie. We have ourselves a little party."

"Like Pampered Chef or Tupperware?" I fake a smile.

"A little Brie, a little prick."

"But does it last?" I ask.

"For about three months," she informs me. "Two-fifty a pop. But if you host your own party, it's free. Let me know if you're interested."

For a moment we don't talk. I think how strange it is that inserting hypodermic needles in your face is table conversation. I play with my salmon. My mind floats away, to Rachel.

"So what are you thinking about, Becca?"

"About my baby, I guess."

"My husband, Joey, wanted a baby."

"And you couldn't . . ."

"Sure we could. As far as I know, anyway." She blinks a few times.

"Then . . . why?" I ask.

"Why is it so hard for people to understand that I never wanted a baby? I mean, I don't have a maternal bone in my body. Besides, do you know what having a baby would do to this perfect figure?"

"Yes, I do know what having a baby can do to a figure." I pat my midsection.

"And Joey," she continues. "The man is hardly home. He's really into his job. What kind of a father would he have been?"

"We do what we do, and that's what we do." I wonder what I just said.

"But I'm not going to be worried to death about every little thing." Julie sips her iced tea. "Maybe I did miss out; I guess I'll never know. But, hey, I've made some fashion statements. Not bad for a girl who held up her underwear with safety pins because the elastic was so stretched out."

"As long as you keep busy and stay happy."

"Yeah . . . well. I may never be a Park Avenue princess, but I intend to die trying."

I don't know what to say to that. Actually, I do, but how?

"Anyway, I'm jazzed about the reunion next year," she says.

"I guess I'm looking forward to it too. I stopped by at the tenth reunion but didn't stay long."

"I'm sure you heard that Suzie Hughes was killed by a drunk driver," Julie tells me as she clarifies her lipstick.

"Yes, I did hear that." I remember that Suzie once said she wanted to spend a year in Paris. I wonder if she ever did.

"And Lloyd Crane has cancer."

"I didn't really know Lloyd well, but that's too bad."

"And you heard that Frank Stevenson's wife, Bunny, died two years ago from breast cancer."

"No, I didn't," I say sadly.

"She left behind two daughters, ages eleven and thirteen."

"How awful for those girls. You know, Frank and Allie were close."

"I know. Everyone always thought those two would marry. What's the deal there, Becca?"

"Life is not a movie script."

Julie goes on and on about the class divorces and who owns what company and all the little bits and pieces of scandal she's picked up from having lunch with her former classmates. But I'm still back on Frank Stevenson.

∽ ❧ ∾

Valerie called last night. She's called twice since she left. There was something different about her spirit. I wanted to tell her so, but I didn't want her to take it wrong. She did ask me a question that I'd never thought of before. She asked me why I always called her "Valerie" and never "Val," like most of her friends and our other siblings call her.

"Because you seem more like a Valerie to me."

She was quiet for a minute, and then she said with a sort of ache in her voice, "Would you mind trying to call me Val?"

"Of course not. I'll be happy to call you Val."

"And Becca," she added, "pray for Randy, will you? He's at a crossroads right now."

"I will," I said, thankful for the belated honesty.

She said good night.

"Good night, Val."

I sat for a long time in the dark after that; the rest of the family was already in bed. I thought about Randy that sushi night. I could see his eyes as I closed mine, and in those deep blue eyes of his, I saw a quiet desperation.

So I prayed for him. I prayed for a long, long time. I prayed until the baby cried around midnight, and then I prayed for Val while I was nursing Rachel.

"A wild surprise?" I ask Doug suspiciously as Tawny drops my suitcase near the front door on a warm May day.

"As wild as this accountant gets," he says.

The doorbell rings. Doug opens the door, knowing who is on the other side.

I am pleasantly surprised to see my dear friend. (Antoinette and her son are like family members now.)

"Antoinette!" I exclaim happily. "What are you doing here, madame?"

"It's mademoiselle, now," she clarifies shyly. "The divorce was final yesterday."

"I'm sorry." What else can I say?

She steps in the house and puts her sleeping baby down.

"You're getting buff there, girl." I squeeze her biceps.

"Dominique weighs sixteen pounds," she explains.

"He looks so sweet."

Doug shuts the door. "Antoinette has offered to baby-sit Rachel this weekend."

"That's very nice of you, Antoinette. But are you sure?"

"You have been such a good friend to me, Becca. I wanted to do something in return."

Time alone with my husband sounds wonderful.

Tawny hugs Antoinette. Carly joins in the sisterly hug.

"The whole weekend?" I ask.

"Why, of course." Doug fingers his freshly shaven face.

"So that's it; we just take up and go?" I ask.

"That's the general idea." He pulls me into his arms and kisses my forehead.

"Isn't this sort of spontaneous?"

"No," he answers. "This is *very* spontaneous."

"Mom, you have frozen breast milk in the fridge. I'll help Antoinette out," Tawny says.

"And I can help too," Carly chimes in.

*Ooh! I could eat anything I want without having to worry about colic.*

"So, what do you say?' Doug asks, looking confident.

"Kowabunga!"

"Cow-a-what-a?" Antoinette asks. "Is that a cowboy term?"

"It's a term Logan uses. Surfer slang," I explain.

"Surfer slang? But we don't have an ocean in Colorado, do we?" she asks innocently.

"No, Antoinette, we don't. But Logan wishes that we did." Doug grins.

# Chapter

# Thirty-Three

"I can't believe you rented this yellow Hummer." I lean back in my dream.

"I tried to find a yellow VW bug for sentimentality's sake, but they have one bad feature," Doug says.

"What's that?"

"Most of them don't run."

We laugh.

"Now, please tell me where we're going," I beg as we head down the highway.

"Not yet." Doug pulls my baseball cap down over my eyes.

I sink my body into leather and imagine owning the vehicle. "Perchance to dream," I murmur, and Doug understands my thoughts.

"You never know," he says. "One day we might have a Hummer like this. And maybe one day we'll drive around America, like we talked about. Rachel can come with us."

"Who knows?" I dream on.

"You could take pictures like you used to, Becca."

"Like I used to?"

"You know, pictures of squirrels: squirrels in trees, squirrels eating, squirrels on rooftops." He smiles, but his eyes never leave the road.

I pull off my red baseball cap and whack Doug playfully. Then I put it on backward.

"Well, I had hardly ever seen a squirrel," I say, amused with myself.

"I don't know why not. I lived in Denver, too, and I saw squirrels."

We laugh, and I love how we laugh.

"Douglas, darling, I love it when you make me laugh."

"Rebecca, darling, you have such a lovely laugh. You are a regular Tickle Me Elmo doll."

He tickles me, and the car veers slightly.

"Hey, watch the road, buddy."

I listen to the swishing of the cars as they pass and then get serious all of the sudden. "Doug, are we getting old?"

"Why do you ask?"

"Because we've lived through a lot of fads. Did you know that the Tickle Me Elmo doll's fifth anniversary was at least three years ago?"

"I absolutely did not." Doug adjusts his electric seat.

"Remember when Pound Puppies were the rage? That was practically twenty years ago."

"Pound Puppies? I don't think so." He looks at me sideways.

"Makes me feel old."

"Who defines age, Becca?"

"Social security."

"Besides social security?"

"Bodily decay."

"Nope." He shakes his head vehemently.

"The Census Bureau?"

"Step outside the box," he encourages. "Who defines us—besides God, of course?"

I smile.

"We do?"

"Good answer," he says.

# Tight Squeeze

❧❀❧

"I remember this place so well," I say as we hike the littered rock path up a mountain road near Glenwood Springs, 150 miles from home.

"I'm glad, because if you didn't, I'd be worried, since this is where we had so many of our high-school moments, and it's where I proposed!" Doug takes a sip from his water bottle.

I watch his face, windswept by the outdoors but still as handsome as a movie star to me.

It was a romantic proposal. He had hidden my diamond among the rocks. Cleverly, he asked, "Oh my, what's this?" I wept from elation and then yelled, "Yes, yes, yes!" before his trembling lips uttered the question.

We reach our destination and look down at the lake. I claim a spot and drop my backpack as afternoon sunshine covers the ground like a blanket.

"There's no one around. Can you believe it?"

"Another huge blessing," Doug says.

I rub my ankles, which are not used to long, steep hikes these days.

Tonight we will stay at the Holiday Inn, and tomorrow we will visit the Storm King Mountain memorial, honoring the fourteen firefighters killed in the 1994 wildfires. But in this romantic moment, there are only two people in this world, and those two people can only see each other.

We sit down, our fingers entwined like vines, our eyes meeting like magnets.

"I wrote some massively good love letters on this mountain," I say.

"To whom?" Doug asks as I brush my fingers across his cheek.

"Some skinny guy."

"I was sorta skinny back then, wasn't I?"

"Yeah. But let's not tell your mother." I laugh.

We are still out of breath.

"Funny. I don't remember us huffing and puffing this wildly before," I say.

"It's just the pant of mad love." Doug kisses me and says my lips are like rose petals.

"And yours are like candy," I say, then think how stupid that sounds. But Doug doesn't seem to care.

I am caught in his kisses, so caught that I do not bother with the unidentified bug on my knee. Finally, when the little bugger cannot be ignored, I slap him bloody.

"I have another surprise for you," Doug says.

"Bug spray?"

"No, not bug spray."

"Give it up, baby!" I demand.

He unzips his backpack and pulls out a Ziploc bag full of envelopes, yellowed, tattered, and torn. "I saved every single one of your love letters. Ever since the first you wrote me when you were sixteen."

"I didn't know that!" *I should have saved more of his.*

"Sometimes when you're away at your parents' house, I go through them."

"You never told me that, Doug."

"Sometimes I even cry."

"Why didn't you ever tell me that before?" I ask, turning my face, trying not to cry.

"I'm a guy. Guys are cautious with their secrets."

He pulls out the stack and reads the letters aloud, one by one. I am slightly embarrassed, slightly amazed that my young brain could have come up with such meaningful words.

When he reaches the end of the pile, I am a weeping willow— droopy, tearful, practically shedding leaves.

"This one is for last," he says, exhibiting a letter. "It is the most special because you gave it to me here on this mountain the day I proposed."

"I did?"

"You may have forgotten it."

"Never, Doug. Never. I remember every word."

"I don't know. It may surprise you." He drops it at my feet, then stands up and stretches. "I'm going for a little walk. Read that, and see if God doesn't know our hearts."

He walks away as I twirl a new woodland flower between my fingers.

I settle into the ground like a cozy chair, curious, maybe fearful too.

I pick up the purple envelope, which was once my favorite color. The letter inside is white, with flowers drawn in faded pen.

*Doug, my man,*

*Can you picture us in twenty years sitting on a mountain like this one? Maybe even this one? You with some wrinkles, me with one gray hair, or maybe two.*

*What will we be like when we are older? Will I still love the same things? Will you? Will we be wiser?*

*You asked if you would be enough always, and my answer is yes. I don't want diamonds, Doug. I don't want a fancy house with a swimming pool. I want you and a houseful of children. Five would be good, because it would be just right—half the size of my family growing up.*

*I want to hold you night and day; I want to dream the years away. I never want to stop dreaming.*

*Will you still chase me around when I turn forty? Tell me that you will. 'Cause I want to grow old with you, my man. I want to grow old with you.*

*Does that sound like a song? It is. And it's growing in my heart like flowers in spring.*

*Love, Becca, your forever girl*

I sit there for one awe-filled moment, bursting inside, from this deep and hidden place.

Doug comes up from behind and kisses the nape of my neck. "We still have it, don't we, girlfriend?" He pulls me up and into his chest and looks through me.

Suddenly I feel vulnerable; I can't take the heat. I push him playfully and run away. And then he chases me along the trail.

"I'm not forty yet!" I yell.

"It doesn't matter," he calls back.

"And I can run faster," I assure him.

"No you can't!" He catches up with me and kisses me as an unexpected soft rain falls and wets our faces with the tears already running down our cheeks.

*Dear Ducky:*

*I've never dreamed so much as in the past few months, and the thing about it is, it really isn't dreaming. It's living the dream, and maybe that's the dream after all.*

*The monsters have been caged. I'm referring to the joy stealers . . . those nasty hormones with alligator teeth and lion's claws that reap havoc on a woman's spirit. But they'll get out again when I give up breastfeeding, if I ever give up breastfeeding.*

*Antoinette is helping Tawny with her high-school French. They are like sisters, those two. And they had this bet that had something to do with American Idol. Anyway, Tawny lost, and escargot was the booby prize. (You should hear Antoinette pronounce booby prize—it's so cute.) Yes, my Tawny ate a plateful of slimy snails. Get this . . . she loved it: "like, it was totally an experience."*

*I asked her if she still thought that boiling a lobster is murder.*

*"Well, lobsters have crusts," she said, then shivered.*

*"What do you call a snail shell if it's not a crust?"*

*"Well, they don't raise them to kill them. They're just around."*

*I tried to reason with her. "You mean to tell me, Tawny, that you think the restaurant manager goes out in his front yard and picks up garden snails and takes them with him to work in a cooler? They farm them, Tawny."*

*"Gross. Mom, don't tell me how they do it. I love escargot. And caviar too. I was born to be rich."*

*"Then you had better get used to lobster."*

*End of conversation.*

*Isn't that too funny for words?*

# Chapter
# Thirty-Four

I have a letter received in this morning's mail that I want to open so badly, but it is not addressed to me. My moral fiber is strong; my spirit is weak.

I think at first that maybe the glue didn't stick, like sometimes happens, but that isn't the case. I blow on it, knowing what a ridiculous idea it is, but still hoping the envelope will just fall open; you know, like bank safes just fall open.

But still the letter lies perfectly sealed with official Courier ten-point lettering, awaiting the addressee who won't be home for hours, upon hours, upon hours.

Defeated, I finally hear Rachel, who has been crying in her crib for who knows how long, unbeknownst to my distracted brain. I feel like a terrible mommy when I see my baby's sweet face looking at me like I have betrayed her.

I further traumatize my child by feeding her a spoonful of dry baby cereal flakes because I forgot the water. She nearly chokes on it. And if that isn't enough, twenty minutes later I lock her inside the house.

Of course, I didn't lock her in and me out intentionally. I have this thoughtless habit of turning the lock on the door every time I touch the doorknob. I wanted the door open long enough to snatch something from the freezer in the garage, but not long enough for field mice to scurry in. Yep, that was the intention, all right.

But, unfortunately, doorjambs fail.

I run out the garage door and across Judy's perfect lawn and bang on her door.

"What is it, Becca?" She's behind the screen, holding a paint-brush.

"I locked Rachel in the house. What can I do?" I ask, because I can't think under pressure.

Judy says she knows just what to do. The next thing I know, we are headed down the sidewalk with her toolbox.

Long story short, Judy saved the day.

Rachel was reaching for Ben's ten-thousand-piece Where's Waldo? puzzle when I whisked her off the floor.

"Ooh, Ben would not have been happy," I say, relieved.

While Rachel plays in her crib, watching her Hebrew language video (she loves it), Judy and I have a cup of tea. I tell her all my troubles. She listens while I whine and bite the inside of my mouth to pieces.

"I'm bringing you over some macadamia nut cookies," she says.

That cheers me up some, especially since I'm back to my one-year-before-getting-pregnant weight and can eat them with no guilt. Gotta love breastfeeding.

I play with Rachel after that, but lackadaisically. She falls asleep again, probably because I'm so boring.

Now I am back to staring at the letter. I'm hoping we have a tornado, so the lip of the envelope will fly open and the results will fall out, landing on the floor in plain view.

I keep asking, *Why Hawaii? Why not here? What does Hawaii have that we don't have?*

Okay, I know the answer.

*What does the letter say?*

The first sentence will tell the story.

Are they happy or regretful?

If they are happy, I will be regretful; if they are regretful, I will be happy.

I know I made a wisecrack back in chapter 22 about how when Logan leaves for college that would solve the baby-space problem, but I was only joking. Mostly, anyway. I don't want my baby to leave.

As I hear the front door open, I am sitting at the breakfast nook, anguished, munching on my third Macadamia nut cookie, but not even tasting it.

My after-school children greet me and grab cookies without asking.

I do not scold them.

They fly away, all but Logan. I can barely stand to look at him, but I do. He already looks like a man, with his broad shoulders and handsome face, but he's still at the stage where he doesn't know it yet, despite the one hundred calls a day he receives from his giddy female admirers.

"Did the letter come for me, Mom?"

"The letter." We both know what "the letter" is. He only applied to one college. Why couldn't he be one of those typical high-school seniors who don't know what they want?

"Mom. Mom. Did the letter come?" he asks again, forcing me back into reality.

Fear strikes me dumb until I manage to ask, weakly, "Don't you want to wait for your father?"

"Uh . . . no," he says.

I extend the letter—his future—to him.

He rips it open.

*The University of Hawaii,* I say in my mind, the last of the vowels reaching high in sarcastic emphasis. *So what if it made the list of America's best colleges? What does that mean? Boulder made the list too . . . well, maybe.*

"Kowabunga! Hilo, here I come."

I smile for Logan's benefit, but he doesn't notice. He's doing this boogie dance he used to do in the end zone when he made a touchdown, until he got suspended for it. The coach called it "excessive celebration." So I went and saw the principal about it. I asked him, "Why shouldn't a boy be happy for making a touchdown? What was he supposed to do? Sit straight-faced with his hands under him like at a bus stop?"

I forget what he said, especially now.

That's what I'm doing now. Sitting straight-faced with my hands under me like at a bus stop.

"More poster paint?" I ask, feeling good about my parenting. (All summer I've been doing craftsy projects with my younger children.)

"Can we go out and play?" Carly looks bored in her paint-smeared T-shirt.

"Why?" I ask, surprised that my efforts do not seem to be appreciated.

"It's just . . ." Ben starts.

"What, Ben?"

"Well, this is fun and all, but . . ."

"Tell me." I try to rub the blue paint off his chin but smear it more.

"Well, we've kinda outgrown this stuff, Mom," Ben says tactfully.

"Back in kindergarten," Carly adds.

My expectations crumble. "That's fine. I just thought a Purim mask would be a lot of fun." I snap the air with my scissors and then lay them down, pouting in that disguised motherly way. "I thought you would enjoy dressing up as Queen Esther, Carly. And, Ben, you could wear your Haman mask. We could put on a play for the rest of the family." I fan myself and feel persecuted.

Ben is still reading me; Carly is just wiggly.

"Is that Haman?" I ask Ben, pointing to his mask, because the face looks too pleasant to be a villain intent on destroying the Jewish population.

"I know he doesn't look very mean."

"No, he doesn't," I say. "But it's really good, Ben."

"Mom, you do know Purim is in March?" he asks, like asking, "Why are we picking apples in February?"

"Yes, I do, but I didn't know you did."

Carly looks like a butterfly in a jar; Ben is standing as stiff as a solider.

"Carly, you were right to want to play outside. It's summertime, and you should be in the fresh air. Out, scouts."

Carly flutters outside, but Ben stays.

"Mom, are you sad that Logan is going away to college?"

He is such a perceptive child.

"I'm not going anywhere." His brown eyes turn serious with his words. "I'm staying in Denver, Mom. If that's any consolation."

"Consolation?" I'm impressed by his vocabulary.

"That was the word I missed in the spelling bee. That's how come I know it," Ben says as he smiles and walks away.

I glue a piece of yarn on my own Haman mask and boo it (it deserves booing, the pathetic project).

Tawny walks in. "What is that?"

"This is a bad reproduction of Haman." I put on the mask and then lay it down. "And this is a mess." I wave at the glue, yarn, glitter, paper plates, stapler, and construction paper.

"Purim? Isn't that in March?" Tawny asks, her hair in a low, neat braid.

"You know that too, huh?"

"Sure."

I stand there hot and absent-minded, feeling the onset of a sudden headache.

"Where's Rachel?" Tawny asks.

"Napping. She should be waking up any minute."

"I'll clean this up, Mom. And if Rachel wakes up, I'll take care of her. You go take a nap."

I pat Tawny's shoulder. "I could use one."

I suppose she's feeling sorry for me. I imagine I do look rather abandoned.

✧❀✧

Weeks after the Purim project, I take another nap. This time Curly watches Rachel in the room the sisters now share—and share happily, I might add. Carly is a little mother, never tiring of playing with her little sister or caring for her needs.

Rachel is now eight months old, and breastfeeding is history. She's eating fruits and vegetables and despising green beans and yellow squash in particular. Her crawl is a funny crawl, mostly backward or in circles. We've discovered that she has a temper, but most of the time, she is happy. Sometimes we spend entire evenings trying to get her to laugh her guttural laugh, which seems too big for her small body. Rachel's latest achievement is ripping up magazines, and we all think she's brilliant for it (except Tawny, whose magazines are the ones being ripped).

Ben decided he likes making masks. He has a collection by now. So far he's got all the disciples and several of the Old Testament prophets. At night sometimes he puts on plays, and we cheer his dramas. Sometimes I hear him muttering to himself, "Artist or actor. Artist or actor."

Oh, to be so talented.

Tawny spends a great deal of time with Keegan, but they are

"just friends" now. She says it is less confusing. She says she's getting closer to God. I notice her jeans aren't as tight these days and that she's eased up on her makeup and perfume. Thank you, Lord.

Logan . . . my baby. He is always on my mind.

Doug says I am distant these days, and it may be true. He's handling the impending separation differently than I am. He's spending more time with Logan. He took him camping last weekend, and they had a blast with the night-vision goggles.

I cry a lot.

*Will there ever be a year without tears?* I ask myself.

I talk to God, and in the middle of my sentence, I fall asleep.

When I awake, a familiar sight awaits me.

I walk over and smile at what I know is Ben's picture he has slipped under the bedroom door.

I pick it up and smile even wider. It is a picture of Logan surfing, and the side lettering says, "Kowabunga, dude!"

Another picture slips under the door. I pick it up and sigh appreciatively for Ben's benefit.

I hear him shuffle down the hall.

It is of Ben standing next to the tepee, a big smile on his pencil-drawn face.

*How do you know, Ben? How do you always know?*

# Chapter

# Thirty-Five

August, like lightning, comes too fast.

Mother and son, we stand together by the tepee, staring at the sun-baked earth. I am afraid to look up or cry. My emotions are ruling over me like a tyrant.

But I do look up. And my face melts when I gaze at my beautiful son Logan on his last day at home. Home as we now know it.

So many of our family moments have been shared under the mighty oak tree by the tepee. Not one unimportant—no, not one.

The tepee was originally Logan's idea. Back when he was nine, he wanted to be Lewis or Clark—one of the two anyway. He was convinced the Old West was the best, as he used to say continually, sometimes every hour. One time I dressed up as Sacagawea. One time we drew a map on tree bark. One time we made beef stew in a kettle and called it "buffalo stew."

Somewhere along the line, Logan decided he wanted to be a football player and then a basketball player too. And then about the ninth grade he wanted to be a surfer after meeting a missionary surfer dude from Australia. The surfer idea seemed to stick, like a surfer's sea-sprayed hair sticks.

I could try to shatter that dream, because Logan has never surfed in his life. Skateboarding and snowboarding do not make you a surfer. But tell that to a self-willed young man who is too much like his father and see what answer you get.

"I can do it!"

I seize my impulse to hold him too tight and too long. There is a thorn in my heart, the tip of which is poison; the poison is traveling through me. But I must not let it show. It must be half of a mother's job, not letting your feelings show.

My efforts to hold it all together fade to an interior daydream. I'm living inside myself. I am back in time, hearing my child's sweet voice.

*Mommy, why did God make weeds?*

*Weeds?*

*And where does the sky end? And where—*

*Whoa, Curiosity. One question at a time, please.*

"There are some really cool surfing spots not far from the university," Logan informs me. "This girl I know from school named Tracey has an older brother who is a youth pastor, and he lives on the Big Island. Tracey told him about me, and he's going to take me to this radical surf shop and help me pick out my first board."

"That's fantastic, Logan."

*I don't understand why he shot that bird with the slingshot, Mom. He was sitting there on a tree looking pretty, and Tommy just shot him for no reason.*

*You don't understand because it was wrong, Logan. Tommy should not have done that.*

"Tracey's brother also said the geology program is one of the best anywhere."

"That's nice, sweetheart. Honestly."

"I don't know much about the football team. Just that they're in the NCAA."

"Is that right, Logan? Is that right?"

*I'm never going leave you, Mom. I'm going to stay at home forever.*
*You will one day, Logan. I promise you.*
*I won't, Mom—not ever.*
He's forgotten. How could he have forgotten?
"Mom, you look upset."
"Do I?"
"Yes."
*Selfish. Selfish. Selfish.*
Logan holds my betraying hand, which is shaking like a salt-shaker.

"I just want to say, Mom, that I'm going to do something good here. I'm going to try something I haven't tried, in a place I've never been. I don't want you to be worried for me; I want you to be excited about it."

Concern marks his dark eyes.

*Shall I say what I think? Do I know what I think?*

"I guess what I'm trying to say is that I'm not going off to war or anything terrible like that . . ."

When he says that, he lets go, and I feel suddenly and completely awake.

"No, you're not, are you?" I say, the pitch of my voice shifting unnaturally.

He hugs me, as hard and as long as I wanted to hug him. And then he walks away, not looking back, because he's crying too.

In that moment I want to cry out in a loud voice, but not for Logan or for me. I want to cry out on behalf of all the mothers sending their sons to war. I am more sorry for them than myself—for now.

My own words come back to me. From nowhere, it seems.

*One day I want you to leave home, Logan. We are meant to move on. Children grow up and mothers let go. It's part of being a mother . . . letting go.*

The bewildered face of a young boy does not understand what I am saying.

*Life is about letting go. You'll find that out, Son. You'll find that out one day. But not for a very long time. A very, very long time.*

I laugh aloud and wipe my tears.

I am the one who has forgotten.

*Dear Ducky:*

*Guess who is moving to Denver in the spring? I'll give you a hint. Spelled backward her name is Eilla.*

*So my all-out campaign worked, or she was just tired of hearing it.*

*With respect to Eilla, I just happened to find out that Frank Stevenson has a flower shop in downtown Denver. I just happened to walk into said flower shop to buy Antoinette some flowers for no reason. And I just happened to mention that single Allie is moving to Denver and looks fantastic (she lost her ten pounds, by the way) and that she is going to be at the reunion in June.*

*Frank just happened to get this glint in his eyes and said that it was very hot in the room, even though it wasn't.*

*As I was leaving, I turned and asked Frank, casually, "You can still quote Robert Louis Stevenson, can't you?"*

*Judging from his expression, he knew exactly what I was saying.*

"Allie, you couldn't have moved here at a better time. I'm missing Logan so unbelievably bad. It's been almost nine months, but I still can't step in his room without bursting into tears. I even miss the silly things, like picking up his socks."

"You pick up Logan's socks?" Allie opens a kitchen box and takes out a picture frame.

"I know. I'm ruining him for his wife, right?"

Allie doesn't say. She looks tired.

"We should take a break from all this unpacking," I suggest.

"Okay," she says, and we plop on opposite brown leather couches, our bare feet sharing the glass coffee table.

I reflect for a moment as a cool breeze passes through the light and cheery room. "Who would have thought two years ago we would be where we are? I was in the bathtub that day, feeling like it was all over, and I hardly remember why."

"Hormones," Allie says with conviction.

"Oh yeah."

"So, was it worth it?" she asks, already knowing my answer.

"Yes, it was, Auntie Allie. I've been over here for four hours, and I feel like I've been away from Rachel for four days. I can't imagine my life without her. What about you?"

"I always thought that I wanted my own practice. I gave it my loving attention and expected it to flourish, and it did."

I gloss my lips with the fruit-flavoured ChapStick lying near.

"But I didn't flourish," Allie continues with a sad shake of her head. "I didn't really have time to go through my own stuff, to deal with my own loss."

I pick at my nail.

"I know what you went through now, Becca. Giving to everyone else is fine, but you have to take care of yourself too."

"I hope you're intent on doing that now," I say.

"I am." She looks reflectively out the window. "I'm in a position where I don't have to worry about money, so I'm going to take my time finding a job. Maybe take some trips. I've always wanted to do that."

"You should," I encourage her.

"Want to come with me . . . my treat?"

"I would love to Allie, honestly. But I've found that, for me—right now, anyway—taking care of myself is taking care of my family. I'm in this place, this place I've always wanted to be. Maybe later," I add.

"That's okay, really. Geraldine and I are going on an Alaskan cruise in July, and we're talking about going to Israel. I've always wanted to go to Israel."

"That's great, Allie."

"I know. I'm excited. Geraldine is such an important part of my life now. Of course, she'll never replace my mom. But we sure are having a good time."

"I'm sure you're important to her too."

Allie smiles.

"Hey, the reunion is coming up next month, and you've lost all your weight!"

"You too, Becca. You look better than you did before having Rachel."

"It's my spirit," I chirrup.

"It shows," she says.

"Are we anxious to see Frank?" I slip in the words, like a giraffe in a forest.

"Didn't I tell you? I know I must have," Allie asks, looking suddenly upset.

"What?"

"That he's going to Cuba on a mission trip."

"Cuba?"

"Yes, Cuba." She attempts a laugh. "I had dinner with Julie McGregor-Talbot last night. She showed me his picture. He looks much the same, actually better."

"I know he does," I tell her . . . and I smile.

# Chapter
# Thirty-Six

*I don't know any of these people. I mean, I really don't know any of these people*, I think as I stand awkwardly at the punch bowl with Allie at our long-awaited high-school reunion.

"Here comes your hair guy," Allie says.

"These stupid high heels Manhattan sold me . . ."

"What . . . do they hurt?" Allie asks.

"That too. But they're the pits to run in," I tease.

"Why, if it isn't the bubblegum duo: Allie Ray and Becca Carney," a round, bald man announces as he walks up, the woman on his arm looking none too happy.

"Why, Kevin Shriver," I say, and Allie echoes the name as he shakes both our hands with his big, clammy one.

"And this is my lovely wife, Tammy."

"Hello, Tammy."

"Hello," she murmurs, miserably.

It's easy to see she has a problem with me.

"These two were inseparable," the Kevin Shriver imposter tells his wife. His shirttail is already wrinkled and untucked, even though the night is young.

"Still are," Allie says.

I nod in agreement.

"Why, I just heard from a little fairy that you were my husband's crush," Tammy Shriver says to me in a snippety tone, followed by an elongated hissing sound heard only by dogs and the female species.

"Not exactly," I clarify. "You see, he didn't know I was alive."

"Good thing," she says and walks away. He follows and then glances back, shrugs, and gives a helpless look, giving the impression she runs the household.

"Did I ever really like him? I mean—at all?" I ask.

Before Allie can answer, a total stranger comes up and gives us that familiar, unfamiliar stare: *I know you, but I don't.*

"Algebra, third period," he mutters as he scoops punch from the silver bowl.

Allie and I look at each other. She doesn't know him either.

"Half of the girls don't look as good as I remember." He eyes us like a painting. "But you guys look the same."

"Bye." And just like that, he walks away.

I moan; Allie sighs.

"This is boring, isn't it?" Allie says, disappointed.

"I'm still trying to figure out the 'bubblegum duo' comment from Kevin Shriver. I never even chewed gum. I had braces."

"I don't have a clue either," Allie tells me.

Lots of people remember Doug, even though he wasn't in this class. "Yes, we're still married," I tell everyone who asks. I don't mention he hates reunions.

For a while we stand by the punch bowl in the gym and act as unofficial greeters. We listen to pieces of conversation, all the time smelling sweat from an earlier basketball game, which lends little class to the affair.

At our tenth reunion, we at least got to go to a park. We always were a lazy class. The pictures tell you that—only a few are pinned to the bulletin board that says *Then and Now*.

"Too bad they couldn't get a reunion committee together and organize a more classy event," Allie says.

"Oh well." I change the subject and relay the news that Alan something over there is a grandfather.

"No kidding." Allie's jaw drops.

"And over there in chiffon, isn't that Barbie Rafton?" Allie queries. I squint. "I think so, but it's hard to tell. You know, what with the anatomy rearranged."

"And over there, in the yellow flowing dress, isn't that the prom queen?"

"She still looks as good as she did at our tenth reunion. But you weren't there, were you, Allie? I wonder if she got her nostril fixed"

"What?" Allie asks.

"She only had one working nostril. Life can be pretty tough with one working nostril."

"Weird," she says.

"Not weird, Allie. U-n-u-s-u-a-l." I chomp unreservedly into a peanut-butter cookie just as Julie McGregor-Talbot snaps a picture. "Terrific! That will no doubt make the cover of the alumni news."

A blond in a "safe-bet" black dress waves at me from across the room.

"Isn't that what's-her-name?" Allie comments.

I nod. "Clarisa Skeets. We had lunch a couple of years ago. She apologized for hating me. I told her I didn't know she hated me."

"I did," says Allie.

"I got a free lunch out of the deal, anyway. She's a mortician, you know." I flash Allie my best sarcastic smile.

"No, I didn't know. You should have stayed in touch. She could have gotten you such a deal."

"I'm not looking for that kind of deal. Not yet, anyway," I say.

"So, how are the bubblegum girls?" our friend Celia asks, looking rosy in pink. "Having a fabulous time, I hope."

"Celia. Hi. Can you tell us something?" I ask in her ear as the band starts to play again.

"Sure."

"What's this with the 'bubblegum girls'? I don't get it."

"You know the incident in the gym with the bubblegum?" She grabs a mint and comments how at least they could have served appetizers.

"It was plaster," I explain.

"And I had nothing to do with it," Allie adds.

Celia excuses herself politely and runs across the shiny gym floor, on to the next person.

A constant stream of middle-aged faces passes by, and we exchange pleasantries. A hundred times I say I have five children, and Allie says that she is single. A hundred times we receive much the same reaction: surprise.

Melanie Sweeney lingers a few minutes talking about her mango-and-pistachio-colored living room with her old best friend, Rona, as Allie and I pretend to be interested.

When Rona leaves, Melanie says to us, "She is so channeling Nicky Hilton in that dress." Then she toddles away.

"She hasn't changed that much," Allie says wryly. "She always was into strange stuff."

"We're just adult versions of our former selves," I realize.

"It's a classic theme," Allie adds.

"So, I'm sorry about Frank." I know it has been the major topic on Allie's mind all evening, and she's trying not to show it.

"Hey, mission work in Cuba is not a bad thing. I'm proud of him," she says, averting her eyes.

"Here's my card," a guy says and then moves along.

"Networking, I suppose," Allie throws in.

I read his card and chuckle. "He's a *mechanic*, for goodness' sake."

The band takes a break, and I wish there was a La-Z-Boy nearby.

A guy in aviator glasses steps up to the microphone.

"Mitchell something," I remember. "He wanted to be an air force pilot but found out he got airsick."

"Why didn't he know that before?" Allie asks.

I wrinkle my nose. "How are you going to find out you're airsick until you're in the air, Allie? Think about it."

"So should we leave before they play some game recounting our most embarrassing moments or pull us onstage to do a Denver West High cheer?"

"The Cheesecake Factory would be great," Allie suggests.

"I think we've analyzed about everybody here. No serial killers—that's good."

"And now for a little game," Mitchell announces over the sound system as people moan at the inevitable. "Come on, people, we have some big prizes tonight. The first one is ten movie passes."

My cheap side kicks in. "Hold on, Allie. That's not too bad a prize."

"Who here tonight traveled from more than five hundred miles away?" Mitchell asks, surveying the crowd.

A few raise their hands.

"More than seven hundred miles?"

A hand drops.

"Eight hundred?"

Another hand drops.

"One thousand miles?"

Only two hands remain.

"One thousand two hundred miles and up?"

All hands drop.

"Allie did!" I yell.

Allie's body tenses, and she says "Becca" in this testy voice.

"From Atlanta," I claim. "How far, Allie?"

"Fourteen hundred something," she mumbles. "But, Becca, I've been here for nearly a month now. That doesn't count."

"Sure it does," I say. "Fourteen hundred miles," I yell and hold up Allie's arm.

Mitchell calls, "Come on up, Allie Ray."

"No, really," she murmurs, embarrassed, as some guy wearing his father's suit leads her to the podium.

Allie looks horrified on the stage. When she catches her breath, she starts explaining to the crowd that she is now living in Denver.

"Cuba. Cuba just walked in!" we hear from somewhere in the gym.

"Did I hear someone say Cuba?" Mitchell asks. "Come on up here, Cuba."

Frank Stevenson, looking classy in tailored pants and oxfords, makes his way through the crowd. The guy in the bad suit leads him to the podium next to Allie, and they stare speechless, in positive wonder.

Finally Frank says, "I'm not from Cuba; I was just visiting Cuba for a few weeks."

"Well, I *was* living in Atlanta, but I am officially moved here now," Allie explains again.

"Do any of you out there have any objection to these two old friends sharing the prize?"

"No!" the assembly explodes.

"Let them have it!" someone yells. "They look cute together!"

A big *yes!* resounds through the gym as Allie turns five shades redder than she already was.

"Here, Frank." Mitchell's voice booms into the audience. "I think you can manage to share them with Allie." He presents an envelope to Frank.

"Don't forget the alumni breakfast tomorrow," Mitchell continues. "I'll be back in a few. More games, more prizes. Stick around, people. We're giving away a weekend to Estes Park."

# Chapter

# Thirty-Seven

Dear Ducky:

Here's an end-of-the-year rundown.

What I've learned in the past few months is that the next best thing to youth serum is acceptance. We can't recapture our youth, and who wants to, anyway? I refuse to be one of those women who spend their lives worrying about every worry line. I'm not going to ignore the aging process, or even beat it—just recognize it and allow it. Besides, cunning beats youth and agility any day.

Life is good, and coffee is grand. Antoinette introduced me to a French press (not to be confused with a member of the media). It makes a powerful cup of coffee and eases my mind about burning the house down because I left a coffeemaker cord plugged in. I can deal with the sediment.

It's Christmas Eve, and the house is ready for celebration. Antoinette should be here any time. We had Rachel and Dominique's birthday party together last month at Chuck E. Cheese's. Our babies were both terrified of the rat at first, but he won them over with their first piece of candy. Now Rachel tries to say Chuck E. Cheese and mimic the rat dance.

Rachel calls me "Duck" because Doug calls me "Ducky." So now you know the origin of your name, little quacker.

With respect to birthdays, like Geraldine once said, time is like a rocket.

And speaking of Geraldine—which I have to or burst—Allie is picking her up from the airport later this afternoon, and she's going to stay through the new year. Allie wants her to meet her fiancé—yes, as in marriage. (As if we didn't know that she and Frank would make a love connection.)

Frank proposed to Allie in the grocery store with one of the twist ties from the produce section as a pretend ring. I know it doesn't sound romantic, but it was. You see, his fifth-grade proposal was in the grocery store with a twist tie. Only then he didn't know how to pick out a mango (apparently, there are fifty varieties in Cuba). That's where he hid the real ring, and I was hiding among the watermelons.

I will, of course, be Allie's matron of honor, and Geraldine and Valerie are going to be her bridesmaids. The wedding ceremony will take place at 2555 Mountain View Drive, with no animosity on my part.

The reception will be . . . drumroll . . . in the pristine wilderness, eight thousand feet up, via the Palm Springs aerial tram. We're going to wear jeans and have a caviar picnic.

It sure is something how a woman can get over her fear of high places when the occasion calls for it.

Frank told me he's going to quote a Robert Louis Stevenson poem at the reception. Happy thought: "The world is so full of a number of things, I'm sure we should all be as happy as kings." Yep, that's the whole poem. But he also is going to read a few of Allie's favorite poems her mother used to read to her as a child. That will mean a lot to her, I know.

She's excited about being a mother to Frank's teenage daughters. They are really sweet girls.

But I have to tell you the best thing: Val's news. Randy is back—

*physically, mentally, spiritually. Val also came to a correct conclusion, which is that she is not the center of the universe. We could analyze it all to death, but in the end, it doesn't matter. Carl Jung had his theories, but God puts it all in perspective.*

*Randy got over it, and Val forgave him. End of story . . . or hopefully the beginning.*

*Doug has shown no signs of the classic age disease. I try to keep life exciting for both of us. I buy him funny underwear. ("Captain Underpants," I call him; not that it has anything to do with anything.)*

*Judy gave me a cookbook for Christmas with simple recipes I can follow. I've been baking like crazy, and my family loves me, loves me, loves me. Judy gave me a poinsettia, too, but I already killed it.*

*Manhattan stills works at the shoe store. I've been giving her a great deal of business lately since my feet never shrunk back. Every time I go in there, she tries to talk me into impractical footwear, and I have to remind her that I am the customer.*

*Vanessa sold the pet shop, and she and Carol opened a business doing kid parties together. The jumping bubble thing is really fun. I know, because I help out sometimes.*

*Maggie is working part-time in corporate law and seems happier, and Marguerite Zwicker has a younger man: a seventy-seven-year-old boyfriend. (Alda Meyers told me that at Wendy's.)*

*Yes, Wendy's is still my habit. Until Carly graduates, I suppose it will continue to be my habit. With Logan gone, I'd like to cry every time I bite into a crunchy salad thing.*

*Logan is coming home tomorrow! Logan is coming home tomorrow! That is going to be my best Christmas present, no matter what I get.*

*I'm afraid he's still stuck on Hawaii, and now the kid can surf too. I've tried every mother's trick, including a Colorado cowboy care package with stuff to remind him of home: candy rocks and Buffalo Bill's everything . . . along with a picture of an adorable senior named Heidi Rafton, who goes to our church and is going to be attending Colorado U.*

*Doug keeps telling me to "cowboy up," which, loosely translated, Ducky, means, "Get tough . . . deal with it . . . don't be a wimp." You could write a book on what it means, and probably someone has.*

*Anyway, I have a better idea: spending our twenty-first anniversary in Hawaii . . . and our twenty-second and twenty-third . . .*

*Irene came by yesterday with Christmas presents on her way to somewhere warmer. She brought Doug season tickets to the Broncos and me something I wanted for once: an icemaker.*

*She is pleased that I'm baking for her son. What she actually said is that I "have promise," but hey, I'll take that; it's a start.*

*I'll end with Rachel, because that little lamb is such a joy, joy, joy down in my heart to stay. Imagine that I could ever have doubted it. That's like doubting that stars are bright or the sun is warm or flowers are beautiful.*

*I don't worry so much about doing things right these days. I figure all those gems I worked so hard to earn on my heavenly crown are going to be laid down anyway.*

*I had an odd thought the other day.*

*"How unusual," Allie said, smiling, and I said, "Grrr."*

*"What if when we reach heaven I'm the only one who doesn't want to lay down my crown? I'll be saying, 'But God, it's so pretty; can't I wear it for just one day?'"*

*"No flesh will glory," Allie quotes.*

*Wow. What a thought.*

*"You mean I'm not even going to care if Judy's crown is so heavily embedded it has to be towed by a heavenly AAA truck?"*

*She nodded. "That's exactly what I mean. We won't care who was who and who did what."*

*It blows me out of the universe thinking about it.*

*"Till my trophies at last I lay down . . ."*

*Hold on, there is some commotion going on.*

*Antoinette is here. Tawny just ran in the bedroom screaming, "Escargot! Escargot!" Like I would yell, "Giant Chocolate Brownie Ice Cream Sandwich!" (We fell in love again.)*

*So I guess I better get out of my fancy bathtub. I shouldn't be writing in my fancy bathtub anyway. It's rather a precarious position, writing in my fancy bathtub.*

*What fancy bathtub? I'm glad you asked, Ducky.*

*My birthday present from Doug was a Jacuzzi whirlpool bath, complete with a Do Not Disturb sign for the bathroom door.*

*Allie had a TV installed so I can watch I Love Lucy while submerged. She got me the entire collection on DVD.*

*My best present, however, came from Val. It's sort of embarrassing, but I love it. It's a heated toilet seat she ordered from Japan. Believe it or not, I could live without my icemaker before I could live without that seat now.*

*And speaking of sitting down, because I was bawling every time I sat on the old couch in the family room (Logan, you know), we bought a new one. It's burgundy leather and came with a repair kit we've only had to use twice.*

*I love couch-potato moments. Sometimes Don puts on a play, sometimes Carly plays her flute, sometimes Tawny shows us a new cheer. Rachel is a blast to watch—period. Sometimes I make everyone watch I Love Lucy with me, and when they don't laugh, I throw pillows.*

*I love smashing shoulder to shoulder on the couch with my family—lungs restricted, circulation cut off, practically suffocating.*

*Who would have guessed it?*

*Seriously, I love the tight squeeze. It feels like freedom.*

*I take my lessons from one of the wisest philosophers of all times: the Velveteen Rabbit. He said being real means being loved and being able to love.*

*Accuse me of being simplistic, but that just about says it all.*

# Debbie DiGiovanni

After months of getting up in the morning before work to write (coffee swishing dangerously), Debbie DiGiovanni quit her job as a legal assistant to pursue her dream. Her first novel, *Concessions* (River Oak), was recently published, and now Debbie can't imagine herself ever doing anything else.

Debbie was born in Tokyo, Japan, to missionary parents but has spent most of her life in Southern California. Ten years ago she and her family moved to Montana, where her husband is now a youth director. When Debbie is not hiking in the rural beauty that is her backyard, she frequents bookshops, reads, sings, enjoys her animals, and spends time with her family and friends. But God remains the center of her universe.

www.DebbieDiGiovanni.com

THE M♥therhood CLUB™

*Making a Difference One Kiss at a Time*

mc

...born from a simple idea: *honor Mom for doing
the most important job in the world.*

*Titles included in* THE M♥therhood CLUB™:

**Prayer Guide:** *The Busy Mom's Guide to Prayer*
—Lisa Whelchel

**Parenting:** *Mom-CEO*
—Teresa Bell Kindred

*There's a Perfect Little Angel in Every Child*
—Gigi Schweikert

**Inspiration:** *The Miracle in a Mother's Hug*
—Helen Burns

**Gift:** *Holding the World by the Hand*
—Gigi Schweikert

**Fiction:** *Tight Squeeze*
—Debbie DiGiovanni

**Devotional:** *"I'm a Good Mother"*
—Gigi Schweikert

*"At The Motherhood
Club, you'll find books
to meet all your
mothering needs."*
—Lisa Whelchel
*(From The Facts of Life)*

motherhoodclub.com
*Available where good books are sold.*

# Enjoyment Guarantee

If you are not totally satisfied with this book, simply return it to us along with your receipt, a statement of what you didn't like about the book, and your name and address within 60 days of purchase to Howard Publishing, 3117 North 7th Street, West Monroe, LA 71291-2227, and we will gladly reimburse you for the cost of the book.